## Praise for Susan Mallery
### and her fan-favorite, bestselling novels

"Susan Mallery is one of my favorites."
>—#1 *New York Times* bestselling author
>Debbie Macomber

"Funny, tender, moving, and shot through with enough emotional drama to resonate with anyone who's survived a family wedding, [*Daughters of the Bride*] is pure delight and a rewarding read for romance and women's fiction fans alike."
>—*Library Journal*, starred review

"As heartwarming as a hot chocolate by the fireside, this romance delivers a happily-ever-after that will delight you down to your toes."
>—*BookBub* on *Marry Me at Christmas*

"Romance novels don't get much better than Mallery's expert blend of emotional nuance, humor and superb storytelling."
>—*Booklist*

"Susan Mallery's gift for writing humor and tenderness makes all her books true gems."
>—*RT Book Reviews*

"The characters will have you crying, laughing, and falling in love... Another brilliantly well-written story."
>—*San Francisco Book Review* on
>*The Friends We Keep*

"Heartwarming... Deft characterization and an absorbing story line will keep readers coming back."
>—*Publishers Weekly* on *When We Met*

"Romance superstar Mallery's [*The Girls of Mischief Bay*] is both heart-wrenching and warmhearted... A discerning, affecting look at three women facing surprising change and the powerful and uplifting impact of friends."
>—*Kirkus Reviews*

For a complete list of titles available from
Susan Mallery, please visit www.SusanMallery.com.

# SUSAN MALLERY

*you
say it
first*

HQN™

HQN™

Recycling programs for this product may not exist in your area.

ISBN-13: 978-0-373-79933-6

You Say It First

Copyright © 2017 by Susan Mallery, Inc.

*you*
*say it*
*first*

# CHAPTER ONE

"DON'T TAKE THIS WRONG, but I really need you to take off your shirt."

Pallas Saunders winced as she said the words—this was so not how she usually conducted an interview. But desperate times and all that.

Nick Mitchell raised his eyebrows. "Excuse me?"

A valid semiquestion and certainly better than simply bolting, which, hey, he could have done.

"It's an emergency," she said, waving her hand in what she hoped was a *can we please move this along* gesture.

"I'm going to need more than that."

"Fine." She drew in a breath, then began talking. Fast. "I have a wedding in less than an hour and I'm one Roman soldier short. J.T. ran off to LA because his agent called about an audition. Note to self. Do *not* hire actors during pilot season. Anyway, I need a Roman soldier. You're about the same height as the other guys and you're here because you need a job, so take your shirt off, please. If you look halfway decent, I'll sponge tan you and you'll carry a very skinny girl in on a palanquin."

"On what?"

"One of those sedan chair things. I swear, she

probably doesn't even weigh a hundred pounds. I don't think she's eaten in three months. You look strong. You'll do great. Please? There's a check at the end."

Not a very big one, but money was money. And Nick Mitchell had answered her ad for a part-time carpenter, so he must be at least a little desperate for money. A feeling Pallas could so relate to.

"You want me to carry a girl in on a palanquin for her wedding?"

Why were the pretty ones always dumb, she wondered with a sigh. Because Nick certainly qualified as pretty. Tall with dark hair and eyes. His shoulders were broad and from what she could see, he looked to be in shape, so what was the big deal?

"The name of my business is Weddings in a Box." She gestured to the walls around them. "This is box-like. People come here to get married. I do theme weddings. The couple today want a Roman wedding. You'd be stunned at how popular they are. The Roman wedding includes the palanquin for the bride. Please, I beg you. Take off your shirt."

"You're weird," Nick muttered as he unbuttoned his shirt and tossed it onto her desk.

*Hallelujah*, she thought, walking around to view him from the back. As she'd hoped, he looked good—with broad shoulders and plenty of muscle. No massive tattoos, no ugly scars. Not that she objected to tattoos, but so few of them were Roman wedding appropriate and she really didn't have time to do her thing with concealer. As it was, Nick would fit in with the other guys perfectly.

"You're hired, but we have to hurry."

She grabbed him by the hand and dragged him down the hall toward the male cast dressing room. Because themed weddings required a cast of, if not thousands, then at least three or four. Roman weddings had the palanquin carrying crew and all the servers were dressed in togas. Not original, but the clients were happy and that was what mattered.

She pulled Nick into the large, plain room with racks of costumes at one end and a counter with lit mirrors above at the other. Three guys in various states of undress were already there. Two were stepping into white togas while the third was studying himself in the mirror.

Alan glanced up from his self-appraisal and smiled. "Hello, stranger."

"Not for long," Pallas muttered. "Please help Nick get ready for the wedding. Nick, Alan. Alan, Nick." She glanced at her watch and shrieked. "We have less than an hour, people." She turned to Nick. "Ever done fake tanning?"

"Do I look like I do fake tanning?"

Until that second, the man in front of her had been little more than a capable shoulder upon which she could rest one quarter of a bride. Now she actually *looked* at him. At the dark eyes watching her with a combination of disbelief and wariness. The firm set of his oddly attractive mouth. He had big hands, she noted absently, then did her best not to laugh.

Big hands? Seriously? Because she had time for *that* in her life?

She walked over to the counter and opened a

drawer. Inside were gloves sealed in plastic. Gloves coated with fake tanning product she could buy in bulk for a very happy price.

"I'm about to rock your world," she told him cheerfully. "Let's go."

NICK MITCHELL FELT as if he'd stepped into an alternate universe. One where the crazy people ruled and the rest of the citizens were left to stumble along, trying to keep up.

Before he knew what was happening, the woman who was supposed to be interviewing him for a carpentry job was rubbing some weird-ass glove thing up and down his back.

"Even strokes," she said as she worked. "It takes five minutes to dry, then you check for streaks. Do your arms and chest, then your legs. Front and back, please."

She slipped off the gloves and held them out to him. "Can you do this?"

Her expression was two parts earnest and one part frustrated—as if the world conspired to make her day more difficult.

He thought about repeating that he was just there for the carpentry job, but realized she already knew that. Okay then—fake-tanned Roman soldier it was. If nothing else, he would have a good story to tell his brothers.

He put on the gloves and began rubbing on the fake tan goop. It was less gross than he'd thought. Pallas showed him his toga costume and asked the other guys to get him in place.

"I have to go get changed," she said as she hurried to the door. "If you need anything, ask Alan. He knows all."

Alan winked at her. "That's true." Once the door was closed, Alan turned back to him. "And your story is?"

Nick took off the gloves, wiped his hands on a towel sitting on the counter, then stepped out of his jeans. "I'm a carpenter. I answered an ad." He put the gloves on again, bent over and rubbed up and down his legs.

"I see. Want some help with that?"

Nick didn't bother looking up. "I'm good."

"Well, I'm Alan, as you heard. Those two are Joseph and Jonathan. I call them the J's. They're high school students earning money on a Saturday. They play football."

One of the teens looked up. "It's basketball, Alan. We keep telling you."

"Whatever. It's sports and they're all the same." Alan turned back to Nick. "I've been on Broadway. That's how I met Gerald. He was my mentor, and then he retired and moved here. I came for the winter weather and stayed. After Gerald died, I moved to LA, but when I'm here, I do this because it's fun."

As he spoke, Nick realized that the other man was a lot older than he'd first thought. At least in his late forties.

"People really have Roman weddings?" he asked.

"You have no idea. There are cowboy weddings, too, but I don't do those." He shuddered. "Horses are the worst! And they smell. I do like a good princess wedding though. I'm a very handsome courtier, if I do say so myself. But today we're Romans. All hail Caesar."

Ten minutes later, Nick stared at himself in the mirror. He was wearing an honest-to-God toga. Or at least a costume. The short white skirt came to midthigh. The top tied over one shoulder and Alan had given him a circlet of grape leaves to stick on his head. Now, as he laced up sandals, he thought maybe he wouldn't be telling his brothers what he'd done, after all. They would never let him live it down.

"It's very simple," Alan told him when he was dressed. "The bride sits on the palanquin. We lift it up, carry her in. She gets off and we carry it out. The J's and I also serve at the reception, but I doubt Pallas expects that of you. So you're free to go."

Nick didn't bother pointing out that he'd yet to have his interview. To be honest, he was having his doubts about the job. He'd wanted something to fill his day while he figured out what he was going to do about his commission. While this place offered plenty of distraction, it wasn't exactly what he was looking for.

Pallas returned. She'd replaced her jeans and T-shirt with a simple dark green dress that brought out her hazel eyes. Her long brown hair was still in its fancy braid and he didn't think she was wearing any makeup. Of course she wasn't the bride—she was here to make the bride's dreams come true.

She walked up to him and nodded in approval. "You look great. Thank you for doing this. I would be in so much trouble if you hadn't agreed to help out. Did Alan tell you what was going to happen?"

"We carry in the bride, then quietly leave."

"Right. Oh, we still have to do our interview. I have no excuse for scheduling it so close to a wedding except to say I must have gotten the days wrong. There's just so much to do."

Emotions filled her eyes. He read worry, panic and more than a little determination. An interesting combination.

She squared her shoulders. "One crisis at a time, as Gerald always said. We are ready for the wedding. Gentlemen, if you'll take your positions, please."

She led the way downstairs. Nick wasn't sure what to expect, but quicker than he'd anticipated, they were in a room with a frazzled-looking bride, several bridesmaids dressed in what he would guess were Roman-inspired gowns and an honest-to-God palanquin.

He moved closer to the sedan chair and studied the carving on the sides. They were hand done, then attached to what he guessed was a lightweight metal frame.

Pallas got everyone in position. The bride took her seat. Alan took the front right position, which Nick would guess meant he was in charge.

"On three, gentlemen. We lift slowly, in unison and with our knees." Alan smiled at the bride. "Not that we have to worry about you, darling. You're no bigger than a minute and so lovely in your gown. It's designer, isn't it? Lucky, lucky you."

The bride visibly relaxed. "Thank you. I love my dress."

"It loves you back. Shall we? On three."

Nick waited for the count, then raised the bride. The crossbar had a padded, curved notch for his shoulder. He found he only had to use his hand to steady it, not support it. As Pallas had promised, the bride was light and the weight easy to bear.

He went with the others down the hall. A photographer snapped pictures. Huge double doors opened for them and they walked into a massive room with at least a twenty-foot ceiling.

Guests lined up on either side of the large aisle and a groom in a fancier version of a toga waited up at the carved altar. Despite the fact that it was the middle of the afternoon, flickering torches provided light.

They reached the end of the aisle. Alan directed them to lower the bride. When she was with her Roman groom, they carried the palanquin back out. Alan ushered them to a huge outdoor courtyard set up for the reception. The palanquin was set down in a corner.

"People love climbing all over it for pictures," Alan told Nick. "All right, you're free to go." He pointed to a door. "Go through there. You'll find a staircase that will take you up to the second floor. The dressing room is at the end, on the right."

"Thanks."

Nick followed his directions. When he went inside, he saw the staircase. Before he reached it, however, he spotted a partially open door.

"No way," he murmured as he moved closer.

He opened the door wider, swore under his breath and stepped inside.

Several large carved wooden panels hung from tracks where they could slide into place. He stepped to the side and visually followed the track. He would guess it led to the big ballroom he'd just been in.

These panels—easily ten feet tall and twice as wide—were exquisite works of art. The carvings depicted what he would guess was early palace life. There were several tableaux of a royal court and a few outdoor country scenes. Sure, the arrangements were cheesy, but the carving was incredible. Each of the characters in the first relief seemed ready to come to life. He traced the etched lines that created dimension in a few elegant strokes only to feel rough edges. He looked more closely and saw the panels were dinged, dry and in need of some serious TLC. Was this the job Pallas wanted a carpenter for?

He went back out the way he'd come, circling around the now-empty courtyard. He crept into the back of the ballroom and saw the carved Roman panels in place on the walls. They were as brilliant as the other ones and even from a distance, cried out to be restored.

And here he'd thought Pallas was looking for someone to repair windows or build cabinets. To work on something like this... Had Atsuko known about the panels? Was that why she'd suggested Nick apply for the job? Because while he'd grown up working with glass, in the past decade he'd fallen for wood.

Glass was cold and mercurial, but wood was alive. Wood had a soul.

He retreated back the way he'd come and headed up the stairs. The whole carry-a-bride-after-being-fake-tanned thing had put him off the part-time job, but now that he'd seen the panels, he knew he didn't have a choice. He had to restore them and make sure they were in good enough shape to last for future generations.

Dramatic much, he thought to himself as he entered the dressing room. Except the panels were worth the drama and oddness that was Pallas's wedding business. They deserved the very best of him and he was determined that they would get it. As much as he might want to deny it, he was, down to his bones, an artist. His father's blood ran through him and with it came the need to create. Or in this case, restore.

PALLAS RARELY SCHEDULED more than one wedding on a weekend. It was simply too difficult to set up everything and then break it down in time. The only exception was when a wedding party wanted a Friday event—then she could handle a second one on Sunday. Still, even with that option, and the slightly lower cost for choosing "off hours," most brides and grooms wanted the traditional Saturday night party. Which meant she had most Sundays off.

Bright and early Monday morning she made her way to Weddings in a Box and walked the property. The main building was three-sided, in a U shape with a courtyard in the middle. At the west end was the small lobby with a fairly traditional facade done with a slight Italian villa flair. The north side was finished with stone and resembled a medieval castle. The south side was covered with wooden siding—giving it a ranch-like, Old West, rustic feel.

One building, three options that could easily be fluffed to fit nearly a dozen wedding themes. Quirky, yes, but she loved every fake brick and nonworking window.

She checked for damage to the building and fence—because there was that one time a groomsman had run his car into the gate—and lost or abandoned property. Celebrations went late, liquor ran freely and more than one shoe, bra or pair of panties had been found on the lawn.

What was it about weddings and irresponsible sex? Sure, the bride and groom were likely to get some but that was tradition. Everyone else should wait until they got home—only they rarely did. Fortunately today all she found was a streamer and a few flower petals. No need for protective gloves to pick up those.

She made her way inside and headed for the business office on the second floor. She'd only moved into what she still thought of as Gerald's office a few weeks before. For the first month after his death—after learning that he'd left her his business—she'd been in shock. For the next two months, she'd been unwilling to make any changes. Last month she'd realized that running from her desk to his fifty times a day was just plain dumb. Gerald wouldn't have given her Weddings in a Box if he didn't want her to keep it going. So she'd moved into his office.

Instead of feeling sad, she'd realized that being where she always pictured him had made her feel closer to him. He'd been like a second father to her, and while she missed him every day, she knew he would be happy with what she was getting done.

Now she checked her calendar while carefully avoiding the pile of bills in her in-box. Weddings in a Box might be a happy, interesting place, but it was also hanging on by a financial thread. One that was constantly in danger of snapping. Theme weddings didn't come cheap, but neither did the venue and the special touches.

Tomorrow, she promised herself. She would be brave tomorrow. She checked her email and saw that two more brides had sent back signed contracts. That was good news. She would review them before—

"Good morning."

She looked up and saw a man in the doorway to her office. Not just any man—Nick Mitchell.

Several emotions collided. Gratitude for how he'd rescued her on Saturday, slight embarrassment at how she'd stripped him down and fake-tanned him, major embarrassment after she'd figured out who he was and disappointment that she was still going to have to keep looking for a part-time carpenter. Oh, and confusion as to why he was here.

She rose, ignoring the fact that he was the best-looking man she'd had in her office in oh, forever, and smiled. "Hi. How can I help you?"

He leaned against the door frame. "I thought we could have that interview now."

Because she'd accidentally scheduled the last one right before a wedding. Only there was no way he would want to work for her now, was there? "I really appreciate how you helped me out on Saturday."

"You're welcome. It's not every day a guy gets to be a Roman soldier."

"Unless you work here, then it happens way too often." She hesitated. "I'm sorry about how everything played out."

"I'm not. It was an experience I can talk about for a long time."

"I'm relieved you're not mad. Alan said you were a nice guy. He's generally a good judge of character."

"Glad to hear it."

"You're not threatened by Alan?" Because a lot of straight guys were.

"Not even close." He flashed her a grin. "I work with a chainsaw. It takes a lot to threaten me."

"That certainly puts things in perspective." She shifted her weight from foot to foot and decided to just say it. "I don't mean to be rude, but there's no point in us having an interview. When I set up our appointment I hadn't done more than pencil in a name on my calendar. I looked you up yesterday."

One eyebrow rose. "Google or Bing?"

She smiled. "Both, and they said the same thing." Her smile faded as she remembered everything she'd read. Nick Mitchell wasn't anything close to an out-of-work carpenter. He was a world-renowned artist who had won awards. Yes, he worked with wood, but on a completely different level. It would be like asking a successful race car driver to teach someone to drive.

"I don't know what my friend Atsuko was thinking when she gave me your name. You're some famous artist guy and I'm a small-business owner who needs some repairs done. On the cheap." She tried not to wince over the last word because someone like Nick Mitchell wouldn't understand what it was like to scramble for every penny to keep her business open.

"But I appreciate you coming by," she added. "And you being a good sport about the whole fake tanning thing."

"It was fun. I enjoyed myself. The tanning was… interesting."

"Not an experience to be repeated?"

"Um, no."

She stood by her desk, waiting for him to leave, but he didn't seem in a hurry to go.

"What did you want done?" he asked.

Why did he care? "Nick, I'm serious. I was going to pay a few dollars above minimum wage. That's all I can afford."

"Is it the wood panels?"

"Yes, but—"

He nodded toward the hallway. "Let's go see them."

She was more than a little confused, but okay. They went down the stairs and through the large, empty ballroom toward the storage areas on the side. She pulled open the big doors and flipped on the lights, then waited while Nick examined the panels hanging in place.

The rectangles of wood were huge—tall and wide, completely carved on one side. As she watched, Nick moved to the first one and placed his hands on the wood. He half closed his eyes as he traced the carvings with his fingers. Pallas had the oddest sense of watching something intensely personal, which was uncomfortable and more than a little fanciful.

"What do you know about these?" he asked, still studying them.

"Not much. They were here long before I started working for Gerald. To be honest, I never thought much about them except as decorative backdrops. When he died and left me the business, I did an inventory of everything. That was the first time I'd really looked at the panels. I realized they were in rough shape."

"They are. They're old, and the dry air is both preserving them and causing them to split. You can see the workmanship. Someone took a long time to create these. Someone with talent."

"I wish I knew more about them," she admitted. She should have asked Gerald about them, but it had never come up. She'd never realized what his plans were. In her mind, she'd been an employee and he'd been a great friend. The inheritance, an unexpected and unbelievably generous gift, had caught her off guard.

"My brothers work in glass," he said without looking at her. "They talk about the beauty, the cleanness of it. The purity. Glass can be anything. It doesn't exist until we bring it to life. But wood is alive. Wood has a soul—it tells the artist what it's supposed to be. You can ignore what it says, but if you do, the carving will never turn out right."

He turned to her, his dark gaze intense. "I want to work on these."

She stared at him. "What? No, that's ridiculous. You've been in *People* magazine."

He chuckled. "Why does that matter?"

"It just does." She was going to ignore the fact that he'd been in their Sexiest Man Alive issue and that the picture had been impressive. "I'm going to find some carpenter to—"

"No. Not a carpenter. These are incredible, Pallas. They deserve to be revered. I'll do it for whatever you were planning to pay. I want the job."

"Why?"

He turned back to the panels and placed his hands on them. "They told me they trusted me." He dropped his arms to his sides and faced her. "Don't worry. I'm not going off the deep end. This kind of work is rare. I'll enjoy it. I'm between projects right now, so I have the time."

He paused as if considering how much to tell her. "I'm up for a commission in Dubai. I'll know in the next couple of months if I'm going to get it. I doubt there's much question, but until I hear, I don't want to commit to anything big."

"Dubai?"

"A hotel wants to hire me to create a piece for its lobby. I would be there about two years."

"That's a long time."

"I know, but it would be an interesting experience. These will keep me busy until then." He smiled. "I promise to take good care of your panels."

"I don't doubt your ability," she admitted. "Or your commitment. But I'm serious about what I could pay."

"It's not about the money."

Right. Because a guy like Nick didn't necessarily work for the money, she reminded herself. Wouldn't that be nice?

"Take advantage of me," he urged. "You'll like it."

She knew exactly how he meant the comment but for one brief second, she pretended he was coming on to her. In a boy-girl kind of way. Because it had been forever since anyone had bothered.

She knew the reasons for that were complicated. She was perfectly normal looking with an average body and no habits that were outside of social norms. In theory she should be able to find some nice guy to date and take to bed. But while there had been the occasional man in her life, there hadn't been anyone close to "the one." Or even "the right now."

Part of it was where she lived. Happily Inc was a relatively small town and in her part of it, there weren't that many single guys. The ones she knew happened to be relatives, so ick. There was also the fact that she had a way of holding herself back, emotionally. She knew why—what she didn't know was how to change. Which meant being propositioned was rare and something to be treasured. Not that Nick had. He'd been talking about—

"Pallas?"

"Huh?" Oh, right. He wanted an answer. "If you're willing to accept my sad little hourly paycheck, then I'm happy to offer it," she told him.

"It's a deal." He held out his hand.

She shook it, ignoring how *large* it was and the brief heat she felt. Nick was so far out of her league as to be an extraterrestrial. Still, he was nice to look at. She would enjoy the show while it lasted.

"You can work whatever hours you want," she told him. "As long as you're not interfering with a wedding. I'll give you a time sheet for you to keep track of your hours. You'll get paid twice a month. Do you need tools or supplies or anything?"

"I'll bring my own."

"Good." Because she wouldn't know where to start. "Then I guess I'll see you around."

"You can count on it."

*If only that were true*, she thought humorously. She wondered how wrong it would be to ask him to work shirtless. Because he'd made a fine Roman soldier.

Maybe one of her brides would want a Garden of Eden wedding where the attendants would be naked. Nick could be an extra. A fantasy to brighten her day, she thought as she returned to her office. One she would be sure to remember.

# CHAPTER TWO

NICK HANDED HIS brother a beer. The evening was clear and promised to be cold, but for now it was warm enough. They sat on Mathias's back patio, overlooking the sixteenth hole of the golf course to the right. To the left was, well, definitely an open, grassy area. It wasn't the landscape that required an explanation so much as the residents.

"You'll get used to it," Mathias offered as Nick stared at the shapes moving in the near twilight. "They head in for the night."

"To what? A barn?"

"I've never asked," Mathias admitted. "Something. My guess is they get out of the open to avoid predators."

Nick didn't bother pointing out there weren't any predators—at least not that he knew about. Instinct was instinct and he'd long since learned there was no arguing with nature.

A couple miles southwest of town, just beyond the golf course, were hundreds of acres of grassland. If you kept going, you got to the city dump—a high-tech, ecofriendly kind of place where everything that could be recycled or reclaimed was. But the most interesting part wasn't the fact that Happily Inc had one of the lowest trash-to-resident ratios in the country, it was the animals that made the grasslands between the dump and the golf course their home.

So far Nick had seen zebras, gazelles and something that looked a lot like a water buffalo. All grazing animals. In the past few days, he would swear he'd seen a giraffe strolling around, but that could have been a trick of the light.

"It's odd," he muttered, then took a drink of his beer.

"We grew up in Fool's Gold," Mathias pointed out. "We don't get to say any other town is odd."

That was probably true, Nick told himself. And a reason why he was already comfortable in Happily Inc. Once you'd lived in a weird place, it was hard to settle for normal.

But there were differences. Fool's Gold was in the foothills of the Sierra Nevada. Happily Inc was on the edge of the desert. There were mountains in both towns, but the ones here seemed newer, with sharper peaks and more edges. As interesting to his artist's eyes were the changes in colors. Dawns were a mix of oxblood and carnelian with umber and sepia for shading.

He'd been in town for three weeks. Mathias owned a ridiculously large house on the edge of the golf course and had offered him a place to stay until he figured out what he wanted to do.

"Why'd you move here?" Nick asked. "Why not Sedona or some artists' village in Tennessee?"

"Atsuko was already selling our work," Mathias said, mentioning the gallery owner in town. "She wanted us to meet, and when she heard we were leaving Fool's Gold, she suggested we stop by and visit her. One thing led to another and here we are."

His brothers had a sweet setup, Nick thought. Atsuko had contacts all over the world. With her acting as broker, they didn't have to bother with the business side of what they did. Instead they could focus on their art. Their studio was large and open. They had each other for company and yet plenty of space.

While Mathias lived here, by the golf course and the zebras, Ronan had a house up in the mountains. Built mostly of stone and native materials, the structure blended perfectly with the surroundings. There was even a large studio out back, when Ronan didn't want to make the drive into town.

When Nick had figured out it was time for him to get somewhere else, he'd considered a lot of options, but Happily Inc had been the obvious choice. Especially with the Dubai commission looming.

Twilight turned to night. There were a million stars out here. Nick studied the sky and wondered if they were far enough south for it to be different from what he was used to. Probably not.

"Any regrets about leaving?" Nick asked.

"No."

Because of their father, Nick thought grimly. Ceallach had made an impression on all of them. Some good and a lot bad.

There were five Mitchell sons. The oldest two hadn't been blessed—or was it cursed?—with any form of Ceallach's talent. They had been mostly ignored by their father, while the younger three had gotten the brunt of his attention.

"Ronan okay?" he asked. Their youngest brother had had the most to deal with.

"We don't talk about it."

"Still?"

"Always."

Which had to be a bear. Mathias and Ronan had always been tight. Probably because they were twins—or they used to be.

Neither of them would want to talk about that so he changed the subject. "How was your date Saturday night?"

Mathias looked at him over his beer bottle. "It wasn't a date."

"You didn't take a woman to dinner, and then have sex with her?"

"Yeah, sure, I did that."

"How is it not a date?"

"I'll never see her again."

"I guess that does change the definition."

Since moving to Happily Inc, Mathias had started taking up with the various bridesmaids that came into town. He hooked up with them for a night or two, then they were gone.

Nick enjoyed women as much as the next guy, but he'd never been that into volume, or variety. He liked the idea of having someone in his life—as long as he could keep things under control. He wanted enough passion for things to be interesting, but not so much that he was consumed. Sometimes that balance was difficult to find so he erred on the side of not doing.

"Just be careful," Nick warned. "You don't want some woman coming back in six months and saying she's madly in love with you."

"Not gonna happen."

Nick hoped he was right.

"Atsuko says you're going to be working for one of the wedding venues," Mathias said.

"Yup. Weddings in a Box."

His brother frowned. "Doing what? Folding napkins?"

"I've never folded napkins. It could be interesting."

Mathias stared at him. "Do I have to worry about you?"

"I don't know. Do you?"

His brother's stare turned into a glare. Nick laughed. "I'm going to be restoring two sets of wooden panels. They're old and in bad shape. The work is brilliant. I need to do some research to see if I can figure out who made them."

"You should ask Atsuko. She knows things and has a lot of connections in the art world."

"That's a good idea. I'll take some pictures and see if she can show them around."

He'd only known the gallery owner a few weeks but he was already impressed. The fifty-something woman had buyers everywhere. She drove a hard bargain, got an excellent price, then handled shipping. He'd sold more through Atsuko in the past three weeks than in the past three years.

His father's philosophy had always been to let the

art buyer come to him. Nick was beginning to believe that was a very shortsighted way of doing business.

"Heard anything on the Dubai commission?" Mathias asked.

"No. It's going to be a couple of months until they decide. Then I'll have to figure out what I want to do. Two years is a long time."

"Is this where I point out you don't have the job yet?"

Nick grinned. "Hey, it's me. Who else would they give it to?"

"Someone with talent."

"You're jealous."

"Not of you, big brother."

Nick laughed and turned his attention back to the night. "Any bats around here?"

"Scared?"

"Intrigued. I keep getting flashes of a piece that has a lot of bats in it."

Mathias shook his head. "There's something wrong with you."

"Probably."

"Bats. Fruit or vampire?"

"Fruit. I think. I should do some research."

"On bats." Mathias took a drink of beer. "Do you think Mom dropped you on your head when you were little?"

Nick laughed. "Not as often as she did you."

WHILE PALLAS ENJOYED lunch out with friends as much as the next woman, lunch with her mother was a completely different animal. First there were the logistics involved. They didn't trade off picking restaurants. Instead the command performance always occurred in the bank's executive dining room. A fancy title for a slightly nicer than average display of tables and chairs in a square, windowless room. There wasn't a kitchen, so food was brought in. Still, there was an assigned server and white tablecloths were the norm. All of which meant changing from her usual jeans and T-shirt into a dress.

As she drove across the river to the north side of town, Pallas told herself she would be fine. She'd been dealing with her mother for twenty-eight years. She knew how to get through the conversations with a minimum of pain and judgment. She just had to smile and nod and say what was expected. No big deal.

Except it always was a big deal—one way or another.

All her life Pallas had wanted desperately to please her mother, which shouldn't have been a problem. Libby Saunders loved rules. The most sensible plan would have been for Pallas to follow said rules and voilà—motherly love. Only it hadn't worked out that way. Not even once.

Perhaps it had something to do with the old saying about the road to hell and good intentions. Or the fact that Pallas had felt torn between wanting to make her mother happy and wanting to make herself happy. Whatever the reason, her childhood had been an ongoing battle—one she'd never won. Not for a lack of trying.

Cade, her twin brother, had been much smarter.

He'd simply withdrawn from the field of conflict and
had gone his own way. Emotionally *and* physically.
Pallas still remembered their shared fifth birthday.
Libby had asked her children if they wanted to work
in the bank when they grew up. Pallas had immediately said she did, even though she had no understanding of what "working in the bank" meant. All
she knew was that her mom went there every day
and it was important and that working in the bank
would make her mom love her enough that she didn't
feel scared inside.

Cade had smiled that happy smile of his and said,
"No. I'm going to grow up to be a cowboy."

Libby had been unamused, but Cade stood firm.
He loved horses, not stuffy banks. He'd never once
wavered. At eighteen, Pallas had dutifully gone off
to college to major in finance and Cade had taken
off to learn his trade at a famous breeding farm in
Kentucky. Five years later, he'd moved on to Texas.

They stayed in touch, and from everything he'd
told her, he was blissfully happy. Life away from
Libby and the bank was, apparently, very good. Pallas wouldn't know. She was still trying to prove herself to the stern matriarch of the family.

Pallas parked in the customer parking lot, careful to take a spot at the far end so as not to inconvenience anyone, then walked into the bank.

Her great-great-grandfather had established California First Savings and Loan in 1891. It wasn't the
first S and L in the state by a long shot, or even the
second, but it was still standing and she figured that
had to be a point of pride. A lot of people thought

that if she came from a banking family, she must be rich. Alas, no. While her grandfather had been the only one to inherit, he'd produced seven daughters, all of whom had children. Not only was Pallas's sliver incredibly tiny, she wouldn't inherit anything until she was thirty-nine. Because if nothing else, Grandpa Frank had a sense of humor.

So making her own way in the world wasn't an option and she had the student loans to prove it. She also had Gerald's business, which wasn't exactly the shining example of flush.

It was early April. Except for one oddly vacant date in June, she had a wedding booked every weekend from now until late September. If all went well, she would be able to pay her bills, make a few repairs and continue to take a small salary herself. Assuming she kept the business. Because as much as she loved Gerald and appreciated his completely unexpected gift, she'd never planned on making Weddings in a Box her life's work. She'd always thought she would go to work with her mother at the bank.

Pallas walked into the old, Spanish-style building. The combination of high ceilings and dark wood made her feel as if she were stepping back to a more elegant time. A floor-to-ceiling mural depicting the desert at sunrise dominated the east wall. It had been an old WPA project paid for by the government during the Great Depression in the last century. For reasons not clear to Pallas, her mother had always hated the mural, but there was nothing to be done. It was as much a part of the bank as the marble floors and old-fashioned teller windows.

She passed through the lobby and headed toward the executive suites. Despite her brisk steps, she felt a growing need to bolt for the door. Her stomach clenched and her chest tightened. When Pallas was ten feet from the door to her mother's office, Libby stepped out into the hall and gave her a tight smile.

Pallas instantly felt as if she were eight years old and had broken a treasured plate. Or tracked mud on the floor. Or been responsible for one of a million transgressions that had marked her childhood.

"Hello, Pallas."

"Mom."

Libby offered her cheek for the expected brief kiss. The Saunders clan weren't much for hugging.

Pallas had inherited her brown hair and average height from her mother. She knew she had her father's hazel eyes, but other than that, Libby's genes dominated. Their smiles were the same, as was the way they walked. As a teenager, Pallas had hated looking so much like her mother. Eventually she'd surrendered to the fact and had tried to appreciate that despite the passing years, Libby never seemed to age. At least that was something to look forward to.

As always, her mother wore a dark suit and a white blouse—appropriate attire for her senior vice president position. Her hair was pulled back into a tight bun at the nape of her neck. Her makeup was light and tasteful, her jewelry elegant and simple. Pearl studs and, despite being a widow for eighteen years, a gold wedding band.

"Thank you for being able to make lunch," Libby said as she led the way to the small dining room.

Pallas didn't know what to say to that. "My pleasure" wasn't exactly the truth and "You're welcome" seemed oddly snarky. She settled on a noncommittal throat noise.

As per usual, the table was set with china and crystal. Two large delivery bags sat on the sideboard. As a kid, Pallas had been so impressed to learn that any restaurant in town would happily bring in food for lunch. Now she wondered why Libby couldn't simply go get a sandwich or bring her lunch from home like the rest of America.

She also noted the lack of server, which was not a good sign. Not that she needed anyone plating her food—it was more that Libby didn't want anyone else overhearing their conversation. Pallas spent a couple of seconds trying to figure out what she'd done wrong this time, before giving up. No way could she guess. Besides, Libby would tell her over and over again, when she was ready.

"Would you like to dish us up?" Libby asked, taking her seat.

"Sure."

Pallas brought the bags to the table and opened them.

Inside the first were green salads, broiled chicken and a side of vegetables. The second bag contained bottled iced tea and one roll, along with a single, tiny square of butter. The latter were for her, Pallas thought, not sure if she should be amused or not. Libby wouldn't eat carbs at lunch.

Pallas put the food onto plates, and then collected ice from the small refrigerator in the corner. Her mother poured the iced tea and they sat across from each other.

Pallas told herself that there was no need to feel defiant, yet she took two spoonfuls of salad dressing to her mother's delicate drizzle. What was it about being around Libby that made her feel like a cranky preadolescent?

"I'm so pleased you've finally finished your degree," her mother said with a smile. "I'm sorry it took you so long, but that's water under the bridge."

Pallas put her fork down and told herself to just breathe. Time would pass and she would get to leave. Or she could throw something or scream. That would work, too.

While Libby had paid for Pallas's college in Southern California, there had been several stipulations. First, that Pallas maintain a B+ GPA. Second, that Pallas earn her own spending money. Pallas had gotten a job working at nearby Disneyland. She'd loved it so much, she'd taken on extra hours, and in her third semester, her GPA had fallen to a B-. Within hours of finding out, Libby had sent an email explaining she would no longer be paying for college, her dorm room or anything else. Pallas was completely on her own. Permanently.

With less than thirty dollars to her name, Pallas had been forced to return to Happily Inc and move in with a girlfriend while she figured out what to do. She'd eventually gone to work for Gerald at Weddings in a Box and had put herself through community college, then a state school. It had taken eight and a half years, but she'd done it. She was now the proud owner of a degree in finance.

Her mother looked at her. "I assume you've learned your lesson."

"I don't even know what that means, Mom."

"That you won't be foolish again."

Pallas wanted to point out she'd simply gotten a C in geology. That she hadn't been arrested, done drugs or even dated inappropriately. But there was no point. Libby wouldn't care. The rules had been broken and there were always consequences. For everything.

"I'm pretty sure everyone but you is foolish every now and then," she said instead. "Regardless, yes, I have my degree."

"Excellent." Her mother smiled. "Then it's time. Pallas, I'm delighted to offer you a position here at the bank. You can start in two weeks."

There it was. The one thing she'd wanted since she was a little girl. The chance to work here—with her mother.

Pallas waited for the wave of excitement or even a sense of satisfaction. *Finally.* Finally she would gain respectability. Stability. She would be part of the family legacy. She was thrilled. Really.

Or not. Because in truth what she felt was…nothing.

Her mother frowned. "What's the problem? I thought you would be overjoyed."

"I am. I appreciate the offer…"

"Do not say *but* to me, Pallas. I mean it. I've been waiting for this for almost a decade. If you hadn't screwed around at college, you wouldn't have wasted the last eight years of your life."

"It was one C, Mom. Because I was working extra hours."

"At Disneyland," her mother said between clenched teeth.

"I loved my job there and I learned a lot. For the record, I don't consider my life a waste, but thanks for the vote of confidence."

Libby's expression turned impatient. "Then what is your problem? You should be jumping at this opportunity."

"I can't leave Weddings in a Box in the next two weeks. I have weddings booked through September. I have employees who are depending on their paychecks."

"Dear God, you can't be serious. Are any of your employees full-time? Isn't there someone else who can handle the weddings? It's people getting married. How hard can it be?"

It was one thing for Pallas to wonder about making Weddings in a Box a success, but it was another to hear her mother denigrate the business. Her hackles went up and she went from mildly irritated to seriously annoyed.

"I owe Gerald," she said, doing her best to keep her voice low and calm. "He left me his life's work and I am going to do my best to honor his gift."

"The man is dead. He doesn't care one way or another."

"That's harsh, even for you."

"It's practical." Libby's brown eyes snapped with

anger. "I absolutely can't believe this. What is it about you, Pallas? You simply will not do what is expected. You've always been this way. Defiant. Stubborn. You get it from your grandfather."

Something Pallas had heard her whole life. She found it difficult not to roll her eyes. Plus, she really loved Grandpa Frank, so where was the bad?

"So how long do you plan to keep that ridiculous business open?" her mother asked.

"You may not like what I'm doing, Mom, but that doesn't give you the right to mock Weddings in a Box. It's a legitimate firm that makes people happy. Even you should see the value in that."

Libby pressed her lips together. "All right. How long do you plan to work there?"

"I'm not sure. As I said, I have weddings booked through September. I was thinking I would sell it then." Maybe to Alan, not that he'd ever expressed any interest in owning the company.

"That's a long way from now. I can't promise there will be an opening then. Or ever." Her mother's stern expression returned. "This may be a one-shot deal, Pallas. Are you willing to give up everything you've worked for because of a worthless inheritance?"

And there it was—the Libby-like ultimatum. She shouldn't be surprised. Or hurt. And yet...

"It's not worthless to me." Pallas still remembered how stunned she'd been to find out her boss had left her Weddings in a Box. She'd known they were friends and that he cared about her but to leave her the business—just like that—had been incredible.

"There will be consequences for this decision," her mother warned.

"There always are."

She looked at her plate and realized there was no way she was going to be able to eat anything.

"If there's nothing else, I'm going to go," Pallas said as she tossed her napkin on the table. "I'm sorry I've upset you."

"You're mistaken. I'm not upset. I'm disappointed. There's a difference."

A familiar one, Pallas thought grimly. Because she'd always been the disappointing child.

"Goodbye, Mom."

Libby only sighed.

As Pallas walked back to her car she wondered why it was always like this between her mother and herself. No matter the circumstances, they clashed. Libby ended up disappointed and Pallas was left questioning the fact that she continually had to earn her mother's love. Nothing was freely given. It wasn't that way for Cade or any of her cousins, but it had always been like that for her. She had no idea why, and was equally clueless on how to get things to change.

# CHAPTER THREE

PALLAS WENT THROUGH a fast-food drive-through window on her way back to work. By the time she arrived, she'd finished her double cheeseburger and only had a few fries left. She tossed them in a belated attempt to be virtuous, then took the stairs to her office at a jog. As if that would burn off any excess calories.

"Mothers," she muttered as she changed from her dress into jeans and a T-shirt. "What was God thinking?"

She tied her tennis shoes, then drew in a breath. She was restored to her regular self. The day would go on as if the unfortunate lunch incident hadn't occurred. Pallas genuinely didn't know what to do about Libby's job offer. She'd earned her degree in finance because it was expected and required to go into the family business. Shouldn't she be thrilled at the thought of working at the bank? It had always been her dream. Weddings in a Box was hardly making her a fortune. The sensible decision would be to sell it and start living a normal life. Only she just couldn't seem to do it.

"I'll decide in September," she said aloud. "When the season is over. I'll know what to do." Assuming there would still be a job waiting with her mother. There was no way to know.

She went downstairs. The ballroom needed a good vacuuming and doing that would probably count as exercise. She would—

She turned the corner and screamed when she saw a man in the hallway.

The intruder turned and morphed into Nick. Pallas pressed a hand to her chest.

"What are you doing here?"

"I work here and have a key."

Both were true, she told her rapidly thudding heart. "I forgot."

"Which part?"

"Apparently all of it."

He flashed her a smile. "Second thoughts on hiring me?"

"Gifted artist willing to restore my sad wooden panels for almost nothing above minimum wage? No second thoughts, although I do worry about *your* mental state. Not that I'm complaining about it. As long as you fall in the nonthreatening spectrum of crazy, I'm good with it."

He chuckled. "I told you. I'm between projects and I'm excited to work on the panels. They need some serious love."

She knew what he meant but had to admit the phrase "serious love" had her thinking of something other than wood restoration. She'd been without that particular brand of maleness for a long time now. Her lifestyle didn't exactly lend itself to dating. For one thing, she worked weekends. For another, when guys found out she was "in the wedding business" they tended to get nervous.

To distract herself, she thought about how lucky she was that Nick was interested in helping her. What with him being talented and famous. Not that she knew more than the basic information. It wasn't as if she'd actually seen his work in person. There had been lots of pictures online, but that was different than seeing the real thing. Maybe she should go to Atsuko's gallery and poke around. Or not. Staring at what he'd created, complete with five- or six-figure price tags, would probably give her a heart attack.

"I came by to figure out what tools to bring with me when I get started tomorrow," he added.

"You're going to have to take them down, aren't you?" She eyed the massive panels. "How is that going to work? And where will you put them?"

"I thought I'd move all the princess wedding props to the Roman wedding prop room and take over that space. My brothers and Alan will help me get the panels down and onto supports."

"You've thought this through."

"It seemed best to have a plan." He hesitated. "You okay?"

"What do you mean?"

"I don't know. You seem upset or something."

Ack! Having lunch with her mother was starting to leave actual marks. "It's nothing. Family drama."

Nick stayed right there in the hallway, as if waiting for her to say more. She told herself to keep quiet, but then belatedly remembered she generally caved under pressure.

"How much do you know about the history of Happily Inc?" she asked as she leaned against the wall.

"I don't know. It was founded and people moved here?"

She laughed. "Probably. I'm talking more recent history. Say the 1960s."

"Before my time. Yours, too."

"But not my grandfather's." She drew in a breath. "In the 1960s Happily Inc was struggling. My grandfather on my mother's side owned a local bank. If the town failed, no one would pay back their loans and he would lose piles and piles of money."

"Bad for anyone," Nick acknowledged.

"Exactly. Being the kind of man who wasn't going to let that happen, Grandpa Frank invented a story about a stagecoach full of brides-to-be heading for the gold rush in northern California."

Nick frowned. "I know this one. The stagecoach broke down right here and it took several weeks for the repair parts to arrive. By then, all the brides had fallen in love with local guys and the stagecoach continued its journey empty. That's where the town gets its name."

Her grandfather would be so proud, she thought humorously. "That *is* the legend."

"It's not true?"

"It's a total crock, made up by Grandpa Frank. The thing was, he not only knew how to make up a good story, he knew how to sell it, and to whom. It played very well in Hollywood. Several movie stars were so intrigued, they held their weddings in Hap-

pily Inc. The media followed and now we have this."
She waved her arm to indicate the building. "An entire town devoted to the destination wedding."

"Built on a lie. Pretty slick."

"He's an impressive guy."

"Still around?"

"Grandpa Frank will outlive us all."

"I hope I get to meet him."

"I'd be surprised if you didn't."

He nodded slowly. "There's a family bank and
you work here. That's interesting."

"You mean what's a nice girl like me doing in a
place like this?"

"Something like that."

She told him the abridged version of her failure at
college and having to finish putting herself through
school before she could be considered for the family firm.

"Working full-time, it took a little longer, but I
got there. I have officially matriculated."

"Damn, you're impressive."

She blinked. That wasn't exactly the reaction she
was expecting. "I did what a million other people
do every day."

"You did great. So what's got your mom all in a
snit? You got a C. The world shouldn't end."

"She has a lot of rules."

His gaze shifted to something beyond her. "Some
parents are like that. They want things done their
way."

"Tell me about it." Pallas thought of all her at-
tempts to be her own person while still having her

mother's approval. For some reason she couldn't seem to learn that those two things were mutually exclusive.

"I was supposed to go work in the bank as soon as I got my degree. Which I did last January. Then Gerald died and left me the business. I've been running it ever since. Now my mom has offered me a job and I don't know what to do."

"Why do you want to go work in a bank?"

"I always have. It's a family thing. I've planned on working at the bank since I was a little girl."

"But?"

She sighed. "Gerald loved this business. He was like a second father to me. I don't want to let him down."

"Plus you love it, too."

She was less sure about that. She liked it and the work was always interesting, but was it her passion? "I'm confused."

"What did you tell your mom?"

"That I have weddings booked through September. I'll decide after that. It's one of the reasons I want the panels fixed. They're a big part of the business and if they're in good shape, that should help attract a buyer." She shook her head. "Wow, that was a serious amount of information you probably didn't want. That'll teach you to ask me anything."

"I like knowing more about you." He tilted his head toward the hallway. "Come on. I want to show you something."

They went into the storage area where the panels

were hung. He flipped on the overhead lights and motioned for her to step close.

"Give me your hand," he commanded.

The eight-year-old inside of her silently murmured "but then I'll only have one," which totally explained why she really wasn't ready to work anywhere serious like a bank.

She did as he'd asked. Nick pressed her hand to the panel and placed his on top of hers. The combination of cool, smooth wood and warm male skin was unexpected. And kind of nice. Especially when she felt a little tingle start low in her belly. It had been a long time between tingles.

"Can you feel it?"

She had no idea what he was talking about. Him or the wood? Because if he meant the tingles, that was a big ole yes.

Before she could fake an answer, he moved her hand across the relief. "The work is exquisite. So detailed, so rich. The birds look ready to fly off and the plants should still be growing. This isn't just a panel or even art. It's life. Whoever did this was a master artist. They're something you should treasure. But if things ever really get bad, you can sell them, Pallas. For a lot of money."

That got her attention even more than the tingles. "Like how much?"

"Hundreds of thousands."

"Of dollars? Are you kidding me? For these?"

"Not really an art major, huh?"

She shook her head. "Okay, then. I have more respect for them now. Not that I can pay you any more than I offered."

"I believe you. Don't worry about it. Just know that they're here if you need them." He flashed her a grin. "Like money in the bank."

ALAN GLARED AT the panel. "I prefer skinny brides who haven't eaten in three weeks. That sucker was heavy."

It had taken Nick, his two brothers, Joseph, Jonathan and Alan to wrestle a single panel onto the supports Nick had put in place. Everyone else had already left but Alan lingered to complain.

"Is it inappropriate for me to say man up?" Nick asked.

Alan chuckled. "No. But next time I'm going to be busy and unable to help."

"Fair enough. At least we know they're solid wood."

"Was there any doubt?"

"Not really."

Nick walked around the single panel, studying it from all angles. He would take pictures and start his research when he got back to his brother's place. For now he simply wanted to take in the piece, to get to know it so he could figure out where to begin.

"Have you done this sort of thing before?" Alan asked. "Restoration work?"

"No, but I understand the process."

"No wonder Pallas got you for cheap. You're not going to ruin it, are you?"

Nick looked at the other man. "I give you my

word. I know what I'm doing. I've worked with wood for a decade now. I'm not going to screw these up."

Alan didn't look convinced. "I guess I don't have a choice. Pallas trusts you." His tone indicated that might not be a good thing.

For reasons he didn't fully understand, Nick wanted to win the other man over. Maybe because he was someone Pallas trusted.

"Thanks for your help with the heavy lifting."

"You're welcome. At least I don't have to go to the gym today." Alan walked around the panel. "I should check on some of the costumes. They're getting a little ratty. I don't suppose you know how to sew?"

"Not my thing."

"Too bad. It's not mine, either. Pallas has a friend, Violet, who repairs the costumes when they need it. I know it would be better to simply replace them, but there's the cash flow issue. Keeping this old place going isn't cheap."

Nick would imagine there was a lot of outflow—moneywise. "Moving the panels in place would take time. I wonder why she doesn't replace them with lightweight frames with paper panels that could be changed out for different types of weddings? That would lessen the manpower needed."

"An interesting idea. You should share it with Pallas."

"I just might. How long have you known her?"

"Years. Nine or ten. Ever since she came to work for Gerald." He smiled. "She was so earnest. He liked that about her. She also worked hard and enjoyed what she did. That can be hard to find."

"Do you live in Happily Inc?"

Alan wrinkled his nose. "God, no. I did for a while, when I moved here." His expression turned mischievous. "I'll save you the trouble of the subtle questioning. Yes, I came here for Gerald. He was my mentor and then my lover. We were together five years, and when it ended, we stayed friends. I miss him."

"I'm sorry."

"Me, too. Dying sucks, or so I've been told. Now I live in LA and come out on the occasional weekend to help out Pallas."

Nick put the pieces together. "She's like family."

"She is. Gerald and I had Pallas in common, as well. We needed her and she needed us." He sighed dramatically. "I've only met her brother once and he seemed decent enough, but her mother… Have you met Libby?"

"Not yet."

"Brace yourself. On the surface she's oh-so proper, but underneath, she's a total bitch. At least to her daughter. I mean seriously, what's up with all the rules? I keep telling Pallas to stand up to her. That once she does, all will be well, but she doesn't believe me. Not a surprise. It's easy to tell someone else what to do and more difficult when you're the one who has to do it."

"Families are complicated," Nick said, thinking of his own troubled relationship with his famous father.

"They are. What I can't figure out is why Libby resents Pallas so much."

"You think that's why she's always on her?"

"It's the only explanation. That or Libby hates her own daughter and trust me, no one wants to go there. My guess is there's some deep dark secret in Libby's past. Maybe *her* mother resented her and she's just passing it on. We'll probably never know. Gerald and I would run interference when we could."

"I'm sure it helped."

"I hope so." He glanced at Nick. "So what's your story?"

"I'm waiting to hear on a commission in Dubai. If I get it, I'll work there for two years."

"I wonder if I'd like Dubai." He considered the thought for a moment. "If you move there, I'll come visit and decide for myself."

Nick had no idea what to say to that. "Ah, sure. Great."

Alan winked. "If you could see your face. All right, my little woodcarver friend. I'll leave you to it. And if you see Libby approaching, throw water. I'm fairly confident she'll melt."

WEDNESDAY PALLAS LEFT work early as she did every week. It was her night to get together with her friends. In a town that catered to weddings, no one had weekends off. With the exception of high school football games and Sunday morning church services, almost nothing social happened Thursday through Sunday. Everyone was too busy supporting the weddings that kept the town coffers full.

She drove north to the Rio de los Sueños and across the Transfer Bridge. Not only was the rhythm of the town affected by the dominant industry, but so were most of the local businesses and even street names. She lived in a neighborhood referred to as The Arcs. To the west was Honor Arc, to the east, Love Arc. There were streets named Serenity Boulevard and Hope Chest Drive. And if anyone found that really, really annoying, she could cheerfully inform them it was her grandfather's fault.

She was still smiling when she turned onto her street. She lived in a small Spanish-style bungalow. When she'd first come back to Happily Inc after her college failure, she'd had to find a permanent place to live. Moving home with Mom had been out of the question. Along with a job offer, Gerald had told her about the bungalow and she'd become both his employee and his tenant. When he'd died last January, in addition to the business, he'd left her the small property.

His generosity still astounded her and she felt guilty for not appreciating him more when he'd been alive. All her life she'd been taught that love and one's place in the family had to be earned. But not with Gerald. He'd loved her and had expected nothing in return.

Pallas parked in her narrow driveway. She looked at the sky and whispered a brief prayer of thanks for the man who had believed in her, then got out of her car and headed for the front door.

Twenty minutes later she had the French doors open to her walled garden. She'd already cut up the rotisserie chickens she'd bought at the grocery store for her curried chicken salad sweetened with mango chutney. She'd bought mini quiches to bake and a veggie plate with ranch dressing. Her friends expected good company, not home cooking.

When the salad was finished, she put it in the refrigerator, and then began cutting up grapes and kiwi for her chardonnay-based sangria. She set up her large drink dispenser that had a drop-in ice container to keep the liquid cold without diluting it. She put out glasses and plates on the small island in her kitchen, then stuck her phone on the docking station that was attached to the speakers in her living room. Seconds later, music began to play.

She glanced at the clock and saw she still had a few minutes before everyone started to arrive. She changed into white jeans and a lime-green cotton shirt, then slipped on espadrilles. As she returned to the living room, she heard someone walking up her front path.

Her girlfriend squad had six members. Carol, Violet, Natalie, Silver and Wynn. She'd known Silver and Wynn all her life. Wynn was a couple of years older, but Silver and Pallas had been friends all through school.

Carol and Violet were sisters. They'd moved to Happily Inc about three years ago. Natalie was the newest member—she'd been in town a little over a year. Pallas had first met Natalie when she'd been a bride. One horrific wedding disaster later, Natalie was single again and working for Atsuko at the gallery—a few weeks after that, Wynn had brought her to a girlfriend dinner and the rest was history.

Pallas opened the front door and smiled when she saw Carol about to knock.

"Hi, you," she said, and hugged her friend.

"Hello, yourself." Carol held out a container full of cookies. "I semibaked. They're refrigerator sugar cookies, so technically an oven was involved. And I iced them."

"You're practically a Food Network star."

"Tell me about it," Carol said as she entered the small house. "I keep saying no to my own show, but they won't stop bugging me. It's getting embarrassing."

Carol was tall, about five foot ten, with short red hair. She was strong and sensible. Her idea of glamor was jeans and a blouse rather than her usual uniform of khaki cargo pants and a T-shirt. She didn't wear much makeup or bother with jewelry. Pallas frequently wondered how much of that was Carol's personality and how much of it was necessitated by her career.

Carol worked for the animal preserve outside of town. She was in charge of the various animals—taking care of them, making sure they had what they needed. When she'd been two, her parents had moved to South Africa to live on a preserve. After their parents' divorce, she and Violet had split their time between the preserve and New York City.

Pallas led the way into the kitchen. She put the cookies on the counter and got the oven started, then poured sangria for them both. They walked out onto the back patio.

Pallas frequently thought the garden was the best part of the bungalow. It was walled, with a trellis, and covered with climbing and creeping plants. She didn't have to do much other than make sure the drip watering system was working and trim off a stray shoot or two. In return she had purple and pink flowers nearly all year long. There was a small gas fireplace when the evenings got chilly and enough privacy that she could dance around naked if she wanted, without anyone ever seeing.

Not that she did. She'd never been the dance-around-naked type.

"How are things?" Carol asked when they were seated on the covered patio.

"Good. Busy. Wedding season is ramping up. You know how we all get. What's going on with you? Did your giraffe arrive?"

Because last week Carol had been excited about the arrival of a new-to-the-animal-park giraffe.

"Millie's here and she's settling in." Carol didn't sound all that happy.

"What?" Pallas asked.

"I can't figure out if she's having trouble adjusting or if she's not feeling well. She seems off."

"No giraffe laughter?"

Carol smiled. "There is that. She's eating, but not as much as she should. I know it's hard for the animals to adjust to a new location. They don't understand what's happening and why everything familiar to them is gone. I wish I could talk to her."

Before Pallas could comment, she heard a voice from inside the house. She stood and turned to see Violet and Natalie walking in together.

Violet looked a lot like her sister—tall and red-headed—but the similarities ended there. While

Carol dressed for comfort, Violet was all about style. She was an expert with a sewing machine and could transform the plain into the extraordinary. She believed in accessories, being girlie and making a statement. Her hair was long and curly, her makeup impressive.

Natalie was a petite brunette with big brown eyes. She also had her own style, but while Violet was cutting-edge chic, Natalie was more bohemian with an Earth Mother chaser. Her glasses were bright red, her maxi dress a patchwork of color. She wore a necklace made of metal shapes that were probably rescued from the local recycling center and each of her brightly painted toes sported a different geometric design.

Pallas got everyone drinks. Natalie had brought brownies, which meant they would have plenty of sugar to finish their meal. Always a good thing. She'd barely finished filling glasses when the final two arrived.

Wynn was a curvy woman with long black hair. Her mixed-race heritage had gifted her with killer cheekbones and a dark olive complexion. She was a couple of years older than the rest of them, with a ten-year-old son. Silver was tall and true to her name, a platinum blonde. Her wild streak was reflected in both her tattoos and her career choice. Silver owned a fifth wheel trailer she'd converted into a traveling bar called AlcoHaul. The party on wheels was popular with brides, not only because Silver was good at her job but because she got into whatever theme the bride had requested—dressing in costume, tailoring the drinks menu and frequently dazzling with the perfect signature cocktail.

Mini cheesecakes were added to the dessert collection. Everyone got a glass of sangria before heading out to the patio. When they were seated, Violet turned to Pallas.

"I have a lot of ideas for the black-and-white wedding. Easy ways we can transform the courtyard without spending a lot. I've been working on modifications for the servers' outfits, too."

Pallas groaned. "Why did I agree to her idea? It's already going to be a nightmare."

"It's going to be great," Violet told her. "Different is fun."

"Different is more work."

Silver raised her eyebrows. "There's that go-to spirit we all love."

"Sorry." Pallas sipped her drink. "I'm grateful for the work. It's just…she wants everything black-and-white, including the horses pulling the carriage. We have a limited horse selection. When I explained that, she asked if they could be painted."

Wynn laughed. "I hope you told her no."

"I did."

The black-and-white wedding was an unfortunate offshoot of the regular princess wedding that Weddings in a Box offered. At first Pallas had thought that adding the black-and-white part would be no big deal, but she was starting to have her doubts. The wedding menu of services existed for a reason. There were certain things that were available and that was it. Going too far, going "out of the box" made events too different. Although even as she thought the words, a part of her whispered she was sounding way too much like her mother. And that was so not a place she wanted to go.

"She's having to make do with the horses we have," Pallas continued. "The linens were easy, as were the flowers."

"Black roses?" Silver asked drily.

"White flowers with black vases."

"Are you going to make a black cocktail?" Carol asked Silver. "There are a lot of white drinks, but black ones?"

"I have some ideas. We've been emailing." Silver grinned. "You owe me, Pallas. I've steered her away from some of her more outrageous ideas."

"Then I owe you forever."

Violet pulled a small cloth bag out of her quilted jacket pocket.

Carol sighed. "Seriously? Again?"

"They're beautiful," her sister told her. "And it's interesting."

"Only to you."

Pallas secretly agreed with Carol. She loved Violet and appreciated the other woman's ideas and help with the costumes, but Violet was obsessed— with buttons. Not just any buttons. Antique ones. The older and more ornate, the better. Even more scary—she actually made money selling them to designers around the world. Violet was known to be a great button dealer—if that was the description for what she did. She had contacts everywhere. Mostly elderly women who went into family attics and flea markets where they bought buttons on her behalf.

Violet opened the bag and turned it upside down. Eight glittering buttons rolled onto her palm. They were deep blue and edged in gold.

Wynn leaned closer. "Oh my God! Are those sapphires?"

"Uh-huh, surrounded by eighteen karat gold." She smiled impishly at her sister. "See. My buttons are fun."

"If you say so."

Pallas chuckled. "I'm going to put the quiches in the oven. I'll be right back."

She headed for her kitchen. Natalie came with her. "Can I help?"

"You can keep me company."

"I'm good at that."

Pallas set the small quiches on a cookie sheet, then set the tray in the oven. She leaned back against the counter.

"Can I ask you a question?"

Natalie nodded. "Of course. What?"

Pallas hesitated. "Nick Mitchell is working for me. He's restoring those wood panels we use for backdrops. They're in pretty bad shape." She raised a shoulder. "I looked him up online and he's this gifted, successful artist. I'm not sure why he's helping me out. I'm not paying much and this is way beneath his abilities."

Natalie grinned. "You do realize you didn't actually ask a question."

"I'm not sure what it would be. I guess I want to know if I should be worried or something."

"You shouldn't. I don't know Nick very well, but I've known his brothers a couple of years now and they're both good guys. Crazy artists, but decent men. As for Nick being better than the project—if he doesn't think so, I would say go with it. I've seen Mathias spend two days on a vase that will sell for fifty dollars because he needs to get it exactly how he wants it, and don't get me started on Ronan. Talk about a guy who needs to chill out. They take pride in their work, and when something captures their attention, they're all in."

"I guess that makes sense."

As they walked back out to the patio, Pallas told herself she would do as Natalie suggested—in other words, shut up and be grateful. She smiled to herself. She was very lucky when it came to her friends. They were there for her and kept her grounded. As she took in the walled garden, the pretty house, and thought about her business, she once again thanked Gerald for giving her a wonderful life.

# CHAPTER FOUR

NICK SANDED THE sliver of wood so the point was sharper, then used tweezers to carefully put it into place. This time the fit was perfect. The restoration of the panels was painstaking work, but worth it, he thought. Something this beautiful deserved to be made whole again.

"Do you have a second?"

He looked up and saw Pallas in the doorway. Not a surprise—this was her business and from what he could tell, she was in the office every day. However, right now something was very different and every cell in his body noticed.

Instead of her usual work uniform of jeans and T-shirt, she had on a long dress. But not just any dress. It was low-cut, with a tight, black leather corset over a white short-sleeved puffy blouse and full, black-and-white vertical strip skirt that fell to the floor.

She had curves he hadn't noticed before—the kind of curves that got a man to thinking about touching and tasting. While he'd known that Pallas was female and someone whose company he enjoyed, he hadn't exactly seen her *that way* before. That he did now was unsettling. Worse was the possibility that now there was no way to *unsee* her.

She held out the skirt with both hands. "I have a princess wedding with a black-and-white theme. My friend Violet wants to make these changes to the server costumes." Her voice sounded doubtful. "We've used this basic style forever, but she added the corset and the overlay on the skirt."

She spun around for him to see the back, then bent over to look at the—well, he didn't know or care what. Not with her breasts practically spilling out. Was it him or was it hot in here?

"I can't figure out if it's sexy or slutty. I thought I could get a man's opinion."

He had to clear his throat before he could speak. "It looks good."

"Really? Do you think it will be a distraction?"

"Probably, but is that bad?"

"As long as the bride isn't pissed." She smiled. "I guess we'll risk it. I'll tell her we're a go with the slutty dresses."

"Sexy, not slutty."

"I can only hope."

She released the skirt and crossed her arms under her breasts. The full curves seemed to swell toward him, which made it difficult to think about anything but walking over and pulling her close. What he would do after that wasn't totally clear. Mostly because there were so many possibilities—there was no way to pick just one.

"I always worry when we go outside the box."

Her words were so at odds for what he was thinking that it took him a second to respond. "What do you mean?"

"There's a menu the brides get to pick from. All the things we offer. This time it's different."

"How? Don't you usually coordinate colors with the wedding party?"

"Yes, but not this much. She wants weird things. Matching horses and other things. There are packages. I understand them. But when people want to…"

"Color outside the lines?" he offered.

"Something like that. I get nervous. I'm not like you."

"In what way?"

"You're an artist. You're trained to see possibilities. The unexpected. I'm too sensible for that. I always colored inside the lines. I like the lines." She winced. "Oh, no. I was going to say 'I like the rules' but I won't. I refuse to turn into my mother."

An interesting assessment but one that made sense based on what Alan had told him about her. "You're saying you're not spontaneous or fanciful, but you throw weddings for a living. By definition, you're fulfilling people's dreams. That's a little outside the box."

"Maybe. I just worry that when we try different things, something will go wrong. A wedding is a big deal. I want everything to be perfect."

"You can't control every aspect of what's happening."

She smiled. "I can sure try."

"Sometimes the mess-ups are the best part. It's where the magic happens."

"I'm too pragmatic to believe in magic."

"Now you do sound like your mother."

Pallas's mouth dropped open. "You can't say that. You've never met her."

"You told me all I need to know."

She drew in a deep breath, which was a hell of distraction.

"I want to say you're wrong, but you're not. It's funny, I was just thinking about this last night. I'm Libby's daughter and sometimes she's the voice in my head. I'd love for that to change, but I don't know how. It wouldn't be so bad if it was a good voice, but mostly what I hear from it is disappointment."

"Tell the voice to shut up."

She smiled. "Good advice. I'll try it next time." She tilted her head. "It's funny how we're all so different. I have a twin brother—Cade. He and I are so completely different. He never wanted to go into the family business. I know he loves our mother but he never worried about making her happy. He always did his own thing."

"You envy that."

"I do. I hate disappointing her but I can't seem to fall into line. It's not a comfortable place to be. I envy Cade's ability to simply be his own person." She wrinkled her nose. "You know, now that I think about it, a lot of my friends are creative. Violet made this. Silver has her business and it has a creative side." She wrinkled her nose. "Natalie's a super gifted artist."

"Natalie Kaleta? Our Natalie?" The part-time office manager-slash-artist from Willow Gallery?

She nodded. "Have you seen her work?"

He thought about the large pieces Natalie did—paintings, but using paper and found objects instead of paint. They were bright and textured and offered an optimistic view of the world.

"She's very talented," he said.

"Right? I'm surrounded by you artistic types. Maybe I should let that rub off on me instead of paying attention to my mother."

"Does Weddings in a Box help?"

"Mostly. I like what I do. I like the variety."

"As long as they stick to the menu."

She grinned. "Yes, the menu is our friend." The smile faded. "There are challenges. I'm not in the best financial shape, but I'm working on it."

"Do you pass on costs to the wedding parties? If they want something off the menu do they have to pay for it?"

"Sure. They buy a package. Anything extra is on them."

"Then why not offer crazy things? Make them pay for it. With the right markup, you'll increase your profits."

She shifted from foot to foot. "In theory," she began.

"But?" he asked, doing his best not to smile, because he got it. On the one hand, Pallas knew exactly what to do to make her business more solvent. On the other, the thought of making changes made her uncomfortable.

"Some of the things the brides want are unreasonable."

He raised his eyebrows and waited.

She sighed. "This black-and-white princess wedding. She wanted zebras."

Nick thought about the grazing animals by his brother's house. "The ones from the animal sanctuary?"

"That's them. Zebras. Can you believe it?"

"You told her no."

"Of course. I looked into it and I just can't. According to the Library of Congress zebras can't be domesticated. They're unpredictable and are known to attack people. To be domesticated, animals must meet certain criteria. They have to have a good disposition and shouldn't panic under pressure."

"Has the Library of Congress ever met a cat?"

She laughed. "I didn't ask. My point is zebras aren't going to work at a wedding."

"Sure they are. Just put them in a pen somewhere and have someone watch over them. The bride pays, you make money. It's a win-win."

"It must be nice to simply be able to do as you please."

"It is," he told her. "You should try it."

She stared at him. "Why are you here?" She smiled. "I mean why are you in Happily Inc and not wherever you're from? I'm not asking the existential question."

"Good because I'm not all that deep." He considered how to answer, then decided to tell her the truth. "I'm from a small town at the foothills of the Sierra Nevada. It's called Fool's Gold. I moved here to get away from my father."

Her eyes widened. "That's honest."

"I already know your family secrets. You might as well know mine."

"I appreciate the fairness of that." She nodded. "I know your dad is a famous glass artist, right? Ceallach Mitchell."

"Impressive."

"I told you, I Googled you before the second interview. That's how I knew you were so successful."

"Not that successful. Not when compared to him."

"Is that the problem?"

"His fame? No. It's him. He's a driven man who likes to control everyone around him. Especially his sons." Not the ones who weren't artists, Nick thought, but he wasn't about to go there. "When I was twenty-two, we did an exhibition together. It was a year of hell. He told me what to do and how to do it. It wasn't how I wanted to live my life."

"The result wasn't worth it?"

"Not even close. Opening night, there was a lot of press, a lot of attention. He loves that—I don't." He turned his mind away from those times and the memories that still lingered. "I learned that there is such a thing as too much passion when it comes to my work."

The past seemed closer than it had in a while. Probably because he didn't usually think about it. "When my brothers and I were kids, my dad drank a lot and he had a temper. He would go on a rampage and destroy a year's worth of work in an afternoon."

She winced. "That must have been terrifying."

"It was. After he and I had worked together and

had the show, my girlfriend broke up with me. I found myself throwing pieces against the wall."

"You didn't want to be like him."

"Exactly."

"So too much passion is a problem in both art and life?"

"Yes," he said firmly. "Passion consumes."

"Isn't it supposed to?" Her voice sounded wistful.

"Being consumed isn't always a good thing. People talk about being motivated, about having fire in their belly. Fire can also destroy. After the show and the breakup, I backed away from my art for five years before starting back in a different medium."

She reached out and touched the panel. "Wood," she said softly. "Because it's alive."

"You remembered."

She nodded. "Is that why you're not married? Passion consumes?"

"Uh-huh. I've seen the price people pay. My mom lives her life for my dad. My dad lives his life for his art. She swears it's fine, but I don't believe her. I don't want to destroy anyone or be destroyed."

"What brought you back to being creative?"

"I was drowning without it. I may not always like being an artist, but it's who I am. I worked in secret. When my father found out, he hounded me to switch back to glass, to work with him. That's when I left."

"Wow. All I have in my past is a con man for a grandfather. You're lucky."

He laughed. "Is that what we're calling it?"

"Why not? You are talented and famous and really

good-looking." She stopped talking as color stained her cheeks. "What I mean is…" She looked away.

"Go on."

She shook her head. "Nope. I'm going to wait for the earth to open up and swallow me. If that doesn't happen, I'll just slink away."

Nick took a step toward her. He had to admit he liked Pallas. She was honest and funny and earnest and easy to talk to. There was also how she looked in that dress. He had a bad feeling he would never quite see her the same way again.

"Don't slink," he told her as he moved a little closer. "There's no need to slink."

She stared up at him. "Not that you're not good-looking, but it's embarrassing to say."

"Why? I liked it. I think you're hot, too. Especially in the slutty dress."

She put her hands on her hips. "You said it wasn't slutty."

"I lied."

He bent his head and lightly brushed his mouth against hers. He felt her quick intake of breath and wondered if she would pull back.

She didn't. They both stayed exactly where they were, only their lips touching.

He wanted to pull her close and feel her against him. He wanted to deepen the kiss and taste her. But he didn't. Not just yet. He straightened.

She stared at him. "That was confusing."

"Then I'm doing it wrong."

She smiled. "No, I mean I thought you said passion consumes."

"Not sex. That kind of passion is just fine."

"Of course it is. How very convenient."

"I'm a lucky guy."

She laughed. "I have no idea what to say to that, so I'm going to take my slutty dress self back to my office."

"Feel free to model for me anytime."

She opened her mouth, closed it, shook her head, then turned and walked away. Nick watched her go. Next time, he promised himself. Next time he was going to kiss her in a way that neither of them would forget.

BY THE FOLLOWING Monday Pallas still hadn't been able to put the kiss behind her. Annoying but true. While she knew in her heart that Nick had only been teasing her, she found it more difficult to put the brief contact in perspective. Mostly because men didn't randomly kiss her very often. Or ever.

Something she could remedy if she started dating. She didn't bother adding "again" because that would imply there had been dating before, and there hadn't been. Not in a while now. Maybe when she got her future settled, she would think about finding a guy to go out with.

Her brain immediately supplied a very nice visual of a shirtless Nick, which she promptly told herself to ignore. And speaking of ignoring, while she was at it, she really should forget about the kiss. It had been nice and she'd enjoyed the accompanying tingles, and yes, Nick was definitely swoonworthy, but she had to be real. He was not for her. He was a big-time artist guy on his way to Dubai. She was a small-town girl who ran a destination wedding business. They had nothing in common.

As she walked down the sidewalk, she told herself that they had kissing in common and maybe that could be enough. She'd never had a sex-based affair before. She might like it. Which meant what? That if Nick offered, she would say yes?

She considered the question as she entered The Boardroom Pub, then felt her toes curl ever so slightly as she scanned the crowd already there and saw the man in question sitting at a middle table next to one of his brothers.

For a split second, she didn't know what to do. Keep looking in his general direction? Run? Look away? Before she could decide, he glanced up, saw her and waved her over. She hesitated a single heartbeat before she found herself moving in his direction.

As she approached the round table, both Nick and his brother rose.

"Hi," Nick said with a grin. "I didn't know you came here."

"I try to make it a couple of times a month. Especially on Monday, when we have tournament night. When did you start showing up?"

"This is my first time." He turned to his brother. "This is my brother Mathias. Mathias, Pallas." He winked at her. "Nobody likes him, so don't expect very much."

Mathias laughed. "Thanks, bro. Very smooth. Nick has always been a giver." He smiled at her.

"I've seen you around town, but I don't think we've been introduced. Nice to meet you at last."

"Thanks. You, too." She shook hands, then sat at the table. "I'm friends with Natalie," she told them. "I was hoping she would join me tonight, but she's working late. Should I blame either of you?"

Nick held up both hands. "That's on Atsuko, not us. We're just the artists. Those two deal with the high finance."

One of the servers came by to take orders. The guys ordered beers while Pallas asked for herbal tea. Game challenge nights could go long. Not only did she need to stay sharp, she had to drive home.

The Boardroom was a pub on the south bank of the river. The decor was board game based. Two walls were open shelves filled with hundreds of different games. Patrons were encouraged to play any they liked, as long as they put them back.

Every Monday was a challenge night. People could play in teams or individually. The games started easy, and then got harder as the night progressed. Sometimes there were themes. Word games or Monopoly night. Once they'd had a Clue tournament. Trivia evenings were always popular, as were the nights devoted to games intended for players under the age of five. Pallas always enjoyed watching adults swear when they lost at Candy Land or Chutes and Ladders. Tonight would be a regular tournament, with simpler games early in the evening and the more difficult ones later.

"Too bad," Pallas said. "Natalie's good at board

games. She always helps with the table's average score."

Nick leaned back in his chair. "You take this seriously."

"Sure. Otherwise, why play?" She glanced around, hoping to see one of her friends. She smiled when she saw Silver walk in, then felt the smile fade as she realized what would happen when Nick met her friend. The same thing that happened when any man met Silver.

It wasn't the other woman's fault, she told herself, as her tall, leggy, blonde friend approached. Silver was one of those sexy women men naturally gravitated toward. There was a sensuality about her—one those of the male persuasion seemed to find difficult to ignore.

"I was hoping you'd be here," Silver said as she walked over. She spotted Nick and Mathias and wrinkled her nose. "Oh, is this a date or something?"

"Not at all," Pallas said quickly. "Nick's restoring the panels at Weddings in a Box and Mathias is his brother. Would you like to join us?" She looked at Nick. "Unless you were saving the seat for Ronan?"

"He's not a board game kind of guy," Nick said easily as he came to his feet. Mathias did the same and they shook hands with Silver. "Nice to meet you."

"You, too." Silver sank into her chair. "Is Jasper here?"

"I haven't seen him," Pallas said. "And I've been looking."

The two brothers glanced at each other.

"Who's Jasper?" Mathias asked.

Silver waved over the server. "He's an amazing player. He always wins. If it's a team event, his team wins. He knows everything."

"He lives outside of town," Pallas added. "He's a thriller writer."

Nick stared at her. "Jasper *Dembenski*? Are you kidding? His books are great. I can't put them down. He lives here?"

Silver grinned. "Uh-oh. A groupie. You leave Jasper alone. He's asked me to be on his team twice and I don't want you messing that up. If you fawn on him, you'll scare him off."

"I'm not fawning."

"You're practically swooning."

Nick's expression turned wounded. "I'm impressed by his talent. That's all." He leaned toward Pallas. "I need you to defend my honor here."

"I think you're on your own on that one."

Mathias chuckled. Nick groaned and the server returned with their drinks.

Like Pallas, Silver had ordered hot tea. As she poured a cup, she glanced at Mathias. "Nick repairs wooden panels, so what do you do?"

"I make kitchenware out of glass."

Silver brightened. "The ones Atsuko sells? Those plates and glasses?"

Mathias nodded.

"I have several of your pieces. I'm working on collecting a set. The ocean-colored ones. They're beautiful."

"Thanks."

Pallas listened to the conversation. So far neither man showed any signs of falling for Silver's considerable charms. Were they immune? She hadn't realized that was possible. On the bright side, maybe it meant a shot at more of Nick's kisses, and wouldn't that be nice?

"I wish I had some talent like that," Silver said. "To be able to create something out of just an idea."

"Me, too." Pallas shook her head. "I can draw stick figures, but that's about it."

"You create weddings," her friend pointed out. "I'm just a bartender."

"You're not," Pallas reminded her. She turned to Nick. "Silver owns a tavern."

Silver rolled her eyes. "I own a fifth wheel that's been converted into a bar. I take it to weddings and other events in town. I like it. I get to meet a lot of interesting people."

"Sounds like fun," Mathias said.

"It is. And honest work, even if it's not classy enough for some people."

The brothers exchanged a look of confusion. Pallas recognized the potential danger and quickly changed the subject.

"Nick and Mathias are from a small town north of here. What was it called?"

"Fool's Gold," Nick said.

"The town has California's longest serving mayor," Mathias added. "Mayor Marsha Tilson. She's a strange old lady who knows things she shouldn't. We can't figure out if she has friends at the NSA or God on speed dial."

"Equally scary options," Pallas murmured, glancing at Silver.

Her friend raised her eyebrows as if asking what was wrong. They both knew the answer. Silver had been about to go off on Drew—Pallas's cousin and heir apparent to run the family bank. Back in high school, Drew and Silver had been an item. More than that—they'd been in love. But after graduating, Drew had broken up with her, saying he needed someone who ran in his social circle.

Pallas had never been sure of the exact phrasing but the message had been clear. He'd dumped Silver and had taken up with a sorority girl at his college. Ten years later, there was still bad blood between them.

The servers started passing out games. Pallas laughed when she saw the first one. "Hungry Hungry Hippos is one of my favorites," she said happily. "I love this one."

"Is it actually a board game?" Nick asked.

"If there's a board somewhere, it counts," Silver told him. "Watch out for her," she said, pointing at Pallas. "She's cutthroat when it comes to collecting marbles. There is no mercy in that one."

Pallas stuck out her tongue, then turned the board so she had her favorite blue hippo in front of her. She stretched her arms, flexed her fingers a few times, then waited for the signal to begin.

Nick looked at his brother. "I think we're in trouble."

"Me, too."

"How do you feel about playing a courtier?"

Nick looked up from the panel he'd been sanding. Alan stood in the doorway to the workroom.

"Welcome back," Nick said. "When did you get into town?"

"This morning. I'm here for the wedding tomorrow. So, are you up for it?"

"What do I have to do? More bride carrying?"

"No. This is a princess wedding. The bride rides in a coach. It's glass, but not pumpkin shaped. We are a nonspecific princess kind of place. It's very democratic."

Nick tried to make sense of the information. "So this is the black-and-white wedding?" Somehow he'd thought it wasn't for a few weeks. Had Pallas had time to get all the server costumes modified?

Alan shook his head. "Silly man. That's a *regular* princess wedding. This is a *Regency* princess wedding. They're totally different."

"They don't sound that different."

"The Regency era is a specific period in history. Do you remember *Pride and Prejudice*? There have been maybe fifty different movie versions. Elizabeth Bennet and Mr. Darcy?"

Nick thought a girlfriend or two may have made him watch something about that couple. "Maybe."

Alan sighed. "Despite your lack of knowledge, the Regency wedding requires specific dress and music and food. The princess wedding is much more 'I am a princess and I wear a poufy dress.'"

Nick shrugged. "Whatever."

Alan stepped closer. "Fine. Let me put it in terms

your artist brain can understand. Turquoise and co-
balt are hardly the same color yet they can both be
called blue. It's like that."

"Why didn't you say so in the first place? That
makes sense. So what do you want from me?"

"To wear stockings and knee breeches and a
floppy hat."

Nick put down his sandpaper. "You're kidding."

Alan smiled. "Do I look like I'm kidding? The J's
have a tournament. Football, I think."

"Basketball," Nick corrected, wondering how
awful the costume was going to be. He wasn't totally sure what knee breeches were but sure didn't
like the sound of them. Would they be better or worse
than a toga?

Of course if the J's were busy, then Pallas was
probably shorthanded.

"I'm in," he said. "Tell me when and where."

"That's what I was hoping to hear. Tomorrow. Be
here at two." The older man hesitated. "You like her."

Nick thought about their brief kiss and how much
fun they'd had at The Boardroom a few nights before. Her competitive streak had been unexpected,
but enjoyable.

"We're friends," he said as casually as he could.
"You've known her awhile. What's her story?"

Alan folded his arms across his chest. "You mean
where was she born and did she ever want a pony
when she was little?"

Not at all what he'd been asking. "No."

"I thought not. Let me be clear. While I appreciate you helping with the weddings and restoring the panels, I'm team Pallas, all the way."

"She doesn't need protecting from me."

"Neither of us know if that's true or not, do we?"

Nick realized Alan had a point. "I would never hurt her on purpose."

"Sometimes people don't even have to try. It just happens."

"Point taken. So there's no guy?"

"You're persistent." Alan smiled. "Have you met Libby yet?"

"No."

"Libby explains a lot. She taught her daughter that love had to be earned. All love. It was never freely given. Which means that sometimes love is more trouble than it's worth."

Interesting, Nick thought, but it didn't answer his question. "Is there a guy?" he asked again.

Alan smiled. "Nuance isn't your thing, is it?" He started for the door. "If you want to know anything else, ask the lady yourself."

# CHAPTER FIVE

NICK REFUSED TO look at himself in the mirror. He figured if he didn't see the whole image, he wouldn't get a picture stuck in his brain. It might be the coward's way out, but he was comfortable with that.

Alan hadn't been kidding about the Regency costume. He was wearing some kind of pants that ended just below his knee, along with long socks that looked suspiciously like stockings. He had on weird, fancy black shoes, a white fluffy shirt and an embroidered cropped coat. To be honest, the whole thing freaked him out.

He stepped into the hallway and headed downstairs. He found Pallas in the main ballroom, doing a last-minute check for the ceremony. Rows of chairs had been set up, with a long center aisle. There were flowers and candles. Sunlight streamed in through the stained glass windows.

She smiled when she saw him. "Don't you look handsome."

"I look like the male version of an umbrella drink," he grumbled. "You have to swear not to tell either of my brothers. Or take pictures. I'll never live it down."

Her hazel eyes danced with amusement. "Feeling a threat to our masculinity, are we?"

"You have no idea." He took in her simple, dark blue dress. It followed the lines of her body, without being too tight. The floor-length fabric moved with her. The sleeves were long, the neckline scooped, but modest. "You look nice." He nodded slowly. "Era appropriate without calling attention to yourself."

"That's what I'm going for," she admitted. "Today is all about the bride. And the wedding, but mostly the bride." Her mouth twitched. "Lucky for you, Atsuko isn't performing the ceremony."

He swore. "She does that?"

"Fairly often. She gets into character and has great costumes. But the bride brought in her own officiant. You get to be anonymous, and I am Lady Pallas, of no particular importance."

He studied her. "Pallas is an unusual name."

The humor returned. "It is. From the Greek. Pallas is the daughter of Titan. Some accounts say she was a childhood playmate of the goddess Athene, who later accidentally killed her. Rumor has it Athene felt really, really bad so she had a statue created of her. That's where we get the Palladium from. It stood in the temple of Vesta."

"I haven't met your mother, but I have a hard time believing she would have chosen Pallas. Was it a family name on your dad's side?"

"Oh, no. I was supposed to be called Alice. But Grandpa Frank took it upon himself to fill out the birth certificates for my brother and me. David became Cade and Alice became Pallas. According to several aunts who were there, my mother was furious when she found out, but she felt that changing the names to something else would cause a scandal, so here we are."

"Interesting. So you defied her from birth."

Pallas laughed. "Not me, exactly, but I'm happy to take credit." She pulled up her sleeve and glanced at her watch. "We are close to start time. Alan will show you what to do. Basically you're there to help carry the bride's train."

"I thought that's what the flower girls did."

"No, they scatter rose petals in front of the bride. You're doing the work. I promise the train is much lighter than carrying the actual bride."

The bride hadn't been that heavy, so he wasn't concerned. "I'll go find Alan. He'll enjoy telling me what to do."

"He always does."

Pallas hurried off. Nick watched her go before he turned toward the stairs. He hoped she didn't take her mother up on her offer of a bank job. He couldn't imagine Pallas sitting behind a desk. She was in her element at Weddings in a Box. Where else could she play dress-up and create memories?

He found Alan in the men's dressing room with two other guys he didn't recognize, all dressed in costume.

"There you are. My favorite courtier." Alan waved him close. "You're very handsome. The ladies will swoon. Now let's talk logistics. The wedding party is huge."

He paused for dramatic effect. "There are fifteen bridesmaids and fifteen groomsmen, along with three flower girls. The parents have all remarried, so we have two moms, two stepmoms, two dads and so on. You three will go downstairs and stand by the doorway, so guests can see you. Some will want to take your pictures. Smile for the camera, gentlemen."

Nick held in a groan. He'd wanted not to have his outfit memorialized in any way. Hopefully none of the guests knew his brothers or figured out what he did in his day job.

"I'll be in the bride's room, making sure everyone is calm. When the bride is ready, we'll meet her in the hallway," Alan continued. "We will walk behind her, carrying her train. When she reaches the groom, we walk back down the aisle."

He pointed at Nick. "You're free to go after that. I'm part of the scenery and these two will be serving. Everyone clear?"

Nick nodded and joined the other two guys out by the entrance to the ballroom. The reception would be held outside. One of the advantages of the desert was that rain rarely got in the way of outdoor plans. With the afternoon temperatures barely hitting eighty, the weather couldn't be more perfect.

Nick smiled at the guests and posed for a few pictures. When it was time, he and the other guys went to join Alan behind the bride. The older man was in his element, guiding the bridesmaids into place and offering words of encouragement.

Alan was a natural at this, Nick thought. He wondered why Gerald had left his business to Pallas instead of his former lover. Had they had a falling-out? Or was there another reason?

"Take that side," Alan said, pointing to the edge of

the train. "We will lift as one. Our beautiful Tiffany will set the pace. Come on, darling. I can't wait to see the look on your soon-to-be husband's face when he sees you. What a prize. He's a lucky, lucky man."

Tiffany flashed him a grateful smile before starting for the wide, tall open doorway. As they walked into the ballroom, he saw the panels were in place and the candles had been lit. There was a fairy-tale-like quality to the space. While this wasn't his style, he could see the appeal.

As they moved down the center aisle, he glanced at the panels. They were magnificent and added lots of ambience, but he couldn't help thinking they were outdated. Maintaining them was going to be an on-going project. He would have to talk to Pallas about switching to lightweight frames with custom paper inserts instead. They wouldn't cost much and she would be able to personalize the services even more.

They reached the end of the aisle. He waited for the signal from Alan, then lowered the train to the floor before turning and walking out with the other guys. When they reached the foyer, Alan and the other two courtiers headed for the catering area while Nick went to change back into street clothes.

By the time he was downstairs again, the ceremony was well under way. He circled around to the courtyard and saw the tables had been set for the reception. There was a dance floor, several ice sculptures and at the far end, a fifth wheel trailer.

He walked toward it, taking in the faux shutters and the silk plants that made it look a lot more like a tavern than a trailer. Fake wooden fencing hid the tires. There were wooden benches out front and several barrels, along with twinkle lights and what looked like a couple of Maypoles. He spotted Silver. She had on a dress much like Pallas's, only hers was deep violet. She waved when she saw him.

"I heard you helped with the train," she said. "I'm sorry I missed you in costume."

He shuddered. "Let's not talk about it. I'm trying to pretend it never happened." He motioned to the decor. "You've done a great job."

"I can fake just about any wedding Pallas can offer," she said. "It only takes a few items to create an illusion." She pointed to the blackboard up on the wall. "Signature drinks are described there. Some couples only want that plus beer and wine while others go all out with an open bar."

"What's happening with this one?"

"Open bar all the way. Don't think about being on the road tonight."

"I'll stay in." He looked around. "I like this. How you all create a special world. The bride and groom are going to have unique memories."

"That's one way to look at it."

"Not your style?" he asked.

"No way. I don't see myself getting married, but if I ever did, I would so elope."

"Vegas?"

She wrinkled her nose. "I'm more an island paradise kind of girl."

He briefly wondered what Pallas would want for a wedding. Something formal or would she, too, want to—

*Back the truck up*, he thought, stunned by the ques-

tion. He barely knew the woman. Why would he care
what her wedding dreams were? The most he was interested in was to take their kissing to the next logi-
cal level—or ten. That was as much as he did. Ever.

"You okay?" Silver asked.

"Yeah. Fine. I just remembered I have to be somewhere. I'll see you."

He took off as quickly as he could without breaking into an actual run.

It was those ridiculous stockings, he told himself. They'd messed with his head. He was going to
spend the rest of the afternoon with a piece of wood
and his chainsaw. Because that was what men did.

DESPITE HER DEGREE in finance, Pallas didn't enjoy the
number side of her business. Going over the bank
statements always depressed her. At the end of the
month, bills due came perilously close to cash in.
No matter how she tweaked and massaged, there
just wasn't much left over.

She supposed that was better than having nothing left over, or worse, a negative balance, but still.
She wanted to make Weddings in a Box a success.
To do that, she would have to invest in the company,
and without money, that was going to be a challenge.

She studied the list of services offered. Raising
prices was always an option. She just wasn't sure
it was a good one. After all, she had competition.
Not only in town, but in other destination spots. She
didn't want to price herself out of the market.

She told herself she was still incredibly lucky.
Thanks to Gerald, she now owned her own home.

She had Weddings in a Box and plenty of determination and energy. She would figure out how to grow things and—

Or she could sell.

She tried to push away the thought but it refused to budge. Probably because selling was a legitimate option. Her mother certainly expected her to. Maybe someone else would do a better job. Maybe someone else would have better ideas or hey, an influx of cash.

Talk about a depressing thought. She saved her latest data, then closed her accounting program. She didn't want to sell. But if she didn't, she couldn't go work in the bank and hadn't that always been her dream?

She supposed the truth was, after so many years, she wasn't exactly wild about the bank job anymore. Maybe she'd never been—maybe it had all been about belonging. Which was way too much to contemplate after looking at her bank statements.

She went downstairs, locked the front door behind her and started toward the river. It was nearly noon. She would take a walk, get some lunch and clear her head. If that didn't work, there was always ice cream.

She crossed the pedestrian bridge but instead of turning toward her favorite Thai take-out place, she turned left and found herself in front of Willow Gallery.

She'd been there a handful of times, mostly for various social events or fund-raisers. She wasn't exactly gallery clientele. Her home decor consisted of framed posters and garage sale finds. But she had to admit, the art in the windows was stunning.

On the left was a painting of a flower. It was

huge—maybe four feet by four feet—done in every shade of yellow imaginable. From what she could tell, the painting was heavily textured, as if the artist had used a palette knife to apply the paint instead of a brush. And she might be totally wrong about that, she thought with a grin. What she knew about how to create a painting could fit on the head of a pin with room for directions to heaven.

Tucked in a corner was a smaller piece—also floral. But this one was created with torn bits of paper and featured more of a field of reds and oranges rather than any single bloom. Pallas smiled as she recognized Natalie's work.

In the other window was a large vase of tulips, although to call it that was like saying Mount Everest was a big pile of rock.

The flowers, each created individually, hung down over the mouth of the vase in a cascade of reds and oranges and pinks. The stems were perfect, as were the leaves, and the petals were just imperfect enough to be real. There had to be dozens of them, forming the arrangement. The vase was simple and elegant, a swirl of gold and white and silver, and the entire piece from vase to stem to petal, was created from glass.

She didn't know how it was possible. The flowers looked as if they would flutter in the lightest breeze. She supposed that was the genius of the work.

She walked into the gallery. There were more glass pieces on display, along with several wood carvings. She studied a large one of a nearly life-size ballet dancer up en pointe. Her arms were so graceful, her hands and fingers perfect in every detail.

"That's one of Nick Mitchell's creations," Atsuko said as she came out of her office. "He's my latest find. The one I shared with you. Hello, Pallas. I don't usually see you in here."

"I know. I'm checking things out."

They hugged. Atsuko was a slim, fifty-something woman with short dark hair and beautiful features. She dressed like a fashion executive, had elegant jewelry and favored thigh-high boots—even in summer.

"Nick's great," Pallas admitted. "He's helping restore the panels at Weddings in a Box." She raised one shoulder. "He swears it's an interesting project while he's waiting to hear on the commission in Dubai."

"I'm sure it is. Nick enjoys the unusual." Atsuko motioned to the various items on display. "Have a look around. Oh, Natalie is probably going to want to take her lunch soon, if you two girls would like to hang out."

"Thanks. I'll go find her."

Atsuko smiled and retreated to her office. Pallas moved closer to the dancer and desperately wanted to touch the smooth surface. Instead she tucked her hands behind her back, terrified that a "you break it you bought it" policy would mortgage her future for the next fifty years.

She walked around the girl and admired the lines of her body. Everything about her spoke to movement—from the turn of her raised foot to the forward thrust of her chin. Pallas could see the shadow of her ribs, the muscles in her calves. She had trouble imagining how Nick had seen this beauty inside of a block of wood. What must it be like to be so talented?

She moved to the next display. A small sign informed her that the stunning glass tulips sculpture in the window had been created by Ronan Mitchell. She found samples of Mathias's more "real world" work in the rear of the gallery—plates and pitchers, vases and mugs, all in the various color schemes he favored. She smiled when she spotted the lower shelf with the cheerful sign proclaiming "Fails."

There were mugs with crooked handles and plates with uneven color, all deeply discounted. Pallas liked that Mathias had a sense of humor about his less than perfect work and was sure people appreciated the chance to buy something by him, quirky or not.

She walked through the door marked Employees Only and found Natalie in her small office. Her friend looked up.

"Hey, you're an unexpected treat. What brings you here?"

"I couldn't face my own bookkeeping, so I took a walk." She didn't mention that she'd been secretly interested in looking at one of Nick's creations in person. "Atsuko said you're about to go to lunch. Want some company?"

"I'd love some." Natalie typed on her computer for a second, then pulled open a desk drawer and drew out her colorful woven purse. "Thai?"

"I won't say no."

As they left the gallery, a car drove by with the windows covered with Just Married graffiti.

"Looks like the lovebirds are heading home," Natalie said. "Or to their real honeymoon."

Pallas nodded. Couples frequently spent a night

or two in town after their wedding before heading to more exotic destinations.

"I'm not sure I'd enjoy being a maid at one of the hotels here," she admitted. "You know everyone's been having sex."

"I'm sure they wear gloves." Natalie chuckled as she spoke. "I know I would."

"Me, too. Although sex would be nice."

"Dry spell?"

"I think I've moved past a spell and into a season. Or epoch."

Natalie laughed. "If it's any comfort, I'm right there with you. I *remember* it being good, so that's something."

Pallas thought about her brief kiss with Nick. He was amazingly talented with wood—she wondered if that skill translated into other areas of his life.

"I wish I could get into the idea of hooking up with a groomsman," she admitted. "I just can't seem to summon any interest in a brief encounter."

"Not the one-night stand type? Me, either. I want to know the guy before I meet his penis. I guess we're old-fashioned."

"Or not yet desperate enough."

They went into the restaurant and claimed a table. Pallas ate there enough that she didn't have to look at a menu. Natalie glanced at it before putting it down.

"How was the princess wedding?" Natalie asked. "I saw some pictures and it looked beautiful."

"Everything went smoothly, which is my main goal. No one had a meltdown that I saw. A total win."

Natalie studied her. "But?"

Too many people were reading her emotions these days, she thought. She either had to have fewer problems or work on her poker face. "Just stuff. My mom and the bank. Do I keep the business or sell it?"

Natalie's eyes widened. "You'd sell Weddings in a Box? But why? It's such a great business and you love it. Pallas, no. Don't conform. Seriously, anyone can work in a bank, but how many people can do what you do? It would be like Ronan taking a job in window repair and installation. Sure he could do it, but what a waste of talent."

Pallas laughed. "Thank you for that, but I'm hardly in Ronan's league."

"Close enough. I don't know the whole story with you and your mom, but honestly, Pallas, don't give in to her unless it's everything you want."

"I worry that I'm not doing well enough."

"By whose standards?"

That was an interesting question. Libby was all about success, but only on her terms. "I want to be able to grow the business," Pallas said. "Right now that's not possible."

"All the more reason to keep it. You've only been running things for a few months. It's going to take time to make changes. Give yourself more time. I know it's your life and you have to decide, just please, please think long and hard before you consider selling. I think you'd realize too late that it was a mistake."

She dug in her bag and pulled out a flat, plastic box. When she set it on the table, Pallas couldn't help smiling. She knew what was going to happen next.

Natalie opened the box and took out a purple square of paper. She waved it at Pallas. "This is what working at the bank looks like. It's perfectly fine and very respectable." She took out several more sheets.

She began to fold the paper, her fingers moving more quickly than Pallas's eyes could follow. In what felt like seconds, there was a small, purple origami owl sitting on the table.

"You're wise," Natalie told her. "Listen to yourself and believe." She held up both hands, palms facing Pallas. "This is me officially stepping back. I've been bossy enough today."

"You haven't been bossy at all. I appreciate your advice and I trust it." She touched the small owl. "How do you do that?"

"Years of practice." Her smile faded. "Please, don't let Libby win. She has her own agenda and I'm not convinced any part of that is your happiness. Gerald left you Weddings in a Box for a reason."

Pallas grinned. "This is you stepping back?"

Natalie groaned. "Sorry. I'm really, really done now. I swear."

"Want to take a bet on that?"

PALLAS LEANED AGAINST the tree and told herself a second brownie wouldn't hurt. It wouldn't help, but she wasn't going to go there. It was a brownie kind of day.

She'd brought in leftovers from the most recent girlfriend dinner and had made coffee, then asked Nick if he was interested in a picnic break in the courtyard. He'd joined her outside. As she stretched out her legs, he lay on his back, on the grass, staring through the tree leaves to the sky.

"You're thinking about something," he said. "I can hear your brain working."

She smiled. "I'm contemplating a second brownie."

He rolled toward her. "That's not good. When women start talking about a second anything with chocolate, there's a problem."

"You think you're so smart."

"Tell me I'm wrong."

"You're not wrong, not exactly. There isn't a problem, I'm just thinking."

He shifted onto his back. "Which is where I came in. Start at the beginning and remember I'm a guy with all the emotional intelligence of a plant."

She laughed, then grabbed a second brownie. "I went to the gallery yesterday."

"Okay."

"I saw the ballet dancer you carved or made or however you want to describe it."

She wasn't sure, but she thought he might have tensed. "And?"

"She's beautiful. Amazing. I kept waiting for her to come to life."

He glanced at her, his expression wary. "But?"

"There's no but. She's incredible. You're so talented." She took a bite and chewed. "The price tag was three hundred thousand dollars."

Nick returned his attention to the sky. "Atsuko sets the prices."

With his input, she thought. There was no way

he would agree to just any price. "Will you get that for the piece?"

"Maybe."

Which she took to mean yes.

"You're not going to start in about me working on the panels, are you?" he asked. "I like the work. It's important."

"I think *important* is stretching it, but no, I'm not going to start in on you. I appreciate the restoration." She loved the panels and wanted them to last a long time. "It's just… My business is so small by comparison to what you do, or the bank or a zillion other companies or people doing things in the world."

"You make memories happen. That's important. Probably more important. No one dies thinking 'gee, I'm really glad I bought that piece of art.'"

"You don't know that."

"I'm pretty sure."

"I wish I could do better with Weddings in a Box," she admitted. "We're doing okay. I'm paying the bills and I get a salary, but there's not much left over. If I want to grow, I need to change that, only I don't know where to start. Worse, I have a degree in finance. I should be all over the money."

"You could sell the panels. Atsuko could find you the right dealer."

"No, I can't do that. They're a part of the business." A part of Gerald.

He shifted so he was lying on his side, facing her. "Okay, so the panels stay. Let's talk about that fancy finance degree. You know that if you want to make more money, you need to cut costs or charge more."

"I'm not sure how I would cut costs. To provide the weddings people want, I have to offer certain services. There's no way to trim there. My overhead is fixed. As for charging more, I have thought about it. I'm just afraid of losing the business."

"Then offer what they can't get anywhere else, but make them pay for it."

"You mean different kinds of weddings?"

"Sure." He sat up. "Take the panels. They're beautiful, but they only work in a limited way. What if you had simple frames the same size made out of a lightweight material? With today's printing capacity, you could easily fill them with whatever your client can imagine. Weddings on the moon or in a volcano. The panels would provide the backdrop and set the tone. You'd provide everything else and the client would pay for it. People will cough up extra to have something exclusive. Trust me. I'm an expert on that."

She thought about his idea. "You're saying instead of a menu, I would offer a unique wedding to anyone who asked?"

"Exactly."

"I'd be reinventing the wheel every time."

"Not completely. The basics of a wedding are the same. Ceremony-reception. You're simply changing the delivery system."

He had a point. Food was food. The same with the drinks. The server costumes could be more challenging, but maybe if she got some kind of simple uniform that could be covered with a theme-specific apron or tunic or something.

"I'll have to think about it," she said. "I understand what you're saying. If people will pay for unique weddings, I could grow the business and they would pay for the expansion. Plus it would be kind of fun to have a different challenge every now and then. Not that I don't love a Roman wedding."

"Who doesn't?" He stretched out on the grass.

"I have a couple coming in tomorrow. Maybe I'll offer them a moon wedding."

"I could see it. I'll bet you could rent space suit Halloween costumes for the staff."

She stared at him. "Why didn't I think of that?"

"Space suits aren't everyone's go-to idea."

"Not that. Renting Halloween costumes. They're not being used except one night a year. If I could find a couple of really great places that have a big selection, I could contract with them. That would give my brides a catalog of ideas to consider."

She would have to do some investigating, but there had to be several large costume firms in Los Angeles. She could set up appointments and go talk to the owners.

Before she could thank Nick for the brainstorming session, a young couple walked into the courtyard. He was of medium height with dark blond hair, while she was petite and Asian. Pallas scrambled to her feet as she wondered if she'd forgotten an appointment. The only one she could remember was for later in the week.

"Hello," she said with a smile. "Can I help you?"

The woman, in her midtwenties with sleek black hair and luminous skin, nodded. "I'm Nova and this is my fiancé, Joel. We were supposed to see you on Thursday, but we came by hoping you could see us early."

Pallas had a moment of chagrin. She wasn't prepared for an impromptu meeting, nor was she dressed the least bit professionally. But if her potential clients didn't care, then she would go with it, too.

"Of course. I'm Pallas. Nice to meet you."

They shook hands. Nick stood and she introduced him, as well. Nova glanced around at the courtyard.

"This is really lovely. Is this where you have the receptions?"

"Usually. We don't get much rain out here." Pallas pointed to the west. "The sun sets over there so we're in shade here by six, even in the summer, and I have fans I put out if need be. There's a large ballroom that can accommodate either the ceremony or the reception, depending on how you want things to flow. Tell me about your wedding."

The couple looked at each other. As Joel reached for Nova's hand, Pallas felt the back of her neck prickle. She was getting a strange vibe from the young couple. Not a we're-getting-married-but-we're-not-excited-about-it, but definitely something. She'd learned that when her gut started talking, she should listen. If nothing else, she increased the non-refundable part of the deposit.

"Joel and I develop video games," Nova said, her voice soft. "Our most successful game is Concord Awaken."

"I love that game," Nick said. "CA. We always joke about the initials being the same as the state of

California." He looked at Pallas. "CA is based on a—" His expression turned sheepish. "Never mind. You don't want to know and they're already experts."

Nova smiled. "I like your enthusiasm. That's going to be helpful." She looked at Pallas. "We want a wedding based on our game world. The colors, the decorations, all of it. I know it's a lot to ask, but it's what we need to do. We can pay for the custom elements. We're very successful."

Nothing about this felt right. Nova sounded more desperate than happy. What on earth was going on?

"Your wedding is going to be wonderful and unique," Pallas told them, even as she took a tiny step back. "However, I'm not sure this is the right venue for a gamer wedding. We do more traditional work here. Princess weddings and Roman weddings. Nothing high-tech."

Nova nodded, even as her eyes filled with tears. "We've heard that a lot. We know what we're asking is unusual. We'd do it ourselves, only we don't have the experience or much time. It's just..." She brushed away tears on her cheek. "It's my dad. He has cancer and he's dying. He wants to see me happily married and we want that, too. It's just him and me."

Joel moved close and put his arm around her. He kissed the top of her head. "It's okay, babe. We'll find someone, I promise."

Pallas flinched as if she'd been kicked in the gut. She felt Nova's pain as if it were her own. She wanted to help, but how? A video game wedding? She didn't know anything about the world or what they would expect, let alone how to make it happen.

"It wouldn't be that difficult," Nick said quickly. "Come on. I'll show you."

Before Pallas knew what was happening, Nick had led them into the main ballroom.

"It would all be about smoke and mirrors," he said, gesturing to the walls. "Panels or giant posters of the landscape of CA. The colors would be easy—they're totally defined. Maybe some black light to make things interesting. The game has a killer soundtrack. We'd base the music on that. Food could be fun. I might be able to do something with papier-mâché for decorations and ambience."

Nova's expression turned hopeful. She looked at Pallas. "Could you do it?"

"I don't know. I'd have to think about it. I only have one open weekend in the middle of June. That barely gives us six weeks." They were asking for the moon. Actually they were asking for a whole other planet and she honestly didn't know if she could give it to them. Still… It did sound fun.

"I already have my dress," Nova told her. "Please. My father and I are depending on you."

Pallas drew in a breath and admitted, if only to herself, there was no way she could refuse the project. At least not without more information. "Let me work the numbers and talk to my vendors and get back to you."

Nova and Joel exchanged a look. "We need to know in forty-eight hours," Joel said. "Time really is precious to us."

"I understand."

Pallas got their contact information. Nova wanted to write her a check, but Pallas refused.

"I'll need plenty, if we come to terms." She smiled. "I'll take your money then."

The couple left. Once they were gone, she glared at Nick. "Did you do this on purpose? Was I just set up?"

"No way. It wasn't me, but it's totally cool. You have to take the wedding, Pallas. Not only can you make a dying man's wish come true, you'll get the chance to see what you're capable of. You can use this as a test to decide on how you want to run the business."

"Maybe. I'll have to talk to everyone first and find out if they can get everything done in time. To be honest, I don't even know where to start."

"I'm in," Nick told her. "Everyone else will be, too."

*Easy for him to say*, she thought as excitement battled with terror. If this didn't work out, he could simply create another three-hundred-thousand-dollar piece of art and call it a win. She could screw up a wedding, damage the last memories of a dying man and ruin her reputation all in the same day. But hey—no pressure.

## CHAPTER SIX

FOR HER EMERGENCY meeting with her vendors—aka her friends—Pallas had set up a couple of big tables in the ballroom. They would have more space there.

She hadn't slept at all the night before. Not only had her mind been filled with all the possibilities, she'd spent hours wrestling with self-doubt.

Could she pull off the wedding Nova and Joel wanted? What if she failed? Did she really want to step so far out of her comfort zone? What if she failed? Could everyone come through with what was necessary to make the wedding spectacular? What if she failed?

Somewhere close to dawn, she'd given up on sleep and had started making a master to-do list. With only six weeks between now and the wedding, not to mention all the ground breaking required, there was plenty to write down and plenty to worry about. By the time her afternoon meeting rolled around, she'd kind of worked herself into a frenzy.

Wynn and Violet arrived first.

"This is going to be fun," Violet said, sounding excited. "A new kind of wedding. You didn't say much in your text, but I am totally up for a challenge."

"I hope so. It's going to be that."

Silver arrived next, with Nick on her heels. Pallas introduced her "artist in residence" to Violet and Wynn, then they all sat down at the first table and Pallas explained what she was hoping to accomplish.

"At this point, I want to know if we think we can pull this off," she said. "I told Nova I'd get back to her by tomorrow, but I know time is tight so I'd really like to call her tonight with a yes or no."

"Yes," Violet said. "I'm in."

"You don't even know what it is."

"I don't care. I'm in. So what's the wedding theme?"

Pallas set a box on the table and opened it. "Nova overnighted these to me." She passed out copies of the game. "It's called Concord Awaken. Nova and Joel created the game and they want their wedding set in that world."

"A video game?" Silver sounded doubtful. "How is that possible?"

"The best games all create a world," Wynn told her. "They can be very detailed with complex story lines. Some are just shoot to kill, but a lot get into the world's past. There are characters we care about. As you work through various levels, you learn more about what's happening. Sometimes information about the backstory can help save you."

Everyone stared at her. She shrugged. "Let's all remember I'm the mother of a ten-year-old boy, people. I live this stuff." She glanced at the label. "Oh, good. It's not rated mature. I'll have Hunter play it tonight." She smiled. "I'll revel in being the cool mom for a couple of hours."

"I've played the game," Nick said. "It's set on another planet but has a dystopian quality to it."

Silver raised her eyebrows. "Seriously?"

"I was embarrassed for him, too," Pallas said, her voice teasing.

Nick leaned toward her. "Do you want to hear this or not?"

He was so close. She'd been so focused on her worry and panic that she hadn't noticed he'd taken a seat next to her. Now she was aware of him in the next chair, his body perilously near her own. She could almost feel the heat of him, and his eyes... The way they focused on hers. She wanted to get lost in his gaze, or maybe just his arms. She wondered if she could get him to kiss her again.

"Pallas?"

"Huh?" She blinked and realized everyone was looking at her. Hoping she wasn't blushing she said, as casually as she could, "Um, sorry. Go ahead."

He gave her a quizzical look before turning to her friends. "As I was saying, Concord Awaken takes place on a distant planet. Sunlight is precious and only lasts for a few hours. Shapeshifters, called The Yellow, are deadly and can be anything. They're the bad guys. The population is divided into three segments. All are fighters. At one time they lived on separate continents but there was a violent earthquake and the land masses collided. Now they have to work together to defeat their common enemy."

Pallas listened as attentively as everyone else.

Nick reached for the box and pulled out several

rolled posters. He spread them out on the table and pointed at the various images. "The three populations are The Steadfast, The Pureheart and The Cunning. We never have a picture of The Yellow because they're always changing. The world itself exists in shades of purple, teal and black."

"Oooh, I could do a lot with that," Violet said happily. She tucked a strand of red hair behind her ears. "I'll have to go through my button collection, but I'm sure I have some amazing things. Do we know what the dresses look like? Not that I'd do anything to the wedding gown, but the bridesmaids' dresses could be transformed to fit the game theme."

Pallas looked through the box and pulled out a folder. She opened it and saw pictures of a bridal gown and bridesmaid dresses. She fanned out the pictures on the table.

"The bridesmaid dresses are already the colors of CA," Pallas noted. "But you could jazz them up."

Violet nodded. She traced the lace on the wedding gown. The dress itself was a fairly traditional— ivory lace with netting, a mermaid style—fitted to midthigh. The rest of the skirt flared out to form a train. While there was extra fabric in the front of the skirt, it fell straight to the floor. A good choice for Nova, Pallas thought. That way the style wouldn't overwhelm her petite frame.

Nick picked up the wedding gown picture. "I could paint this."

The four women gasped.

"What?" he asked.

"It's a wedding gown," Silver breathed. "I'm the least traditional of anyone here, but even I know you don't mess with that."

"I agree." Pallas looked at the picture of the designer gown. "Still… You're thinking fabric paints on the lace?"

"Something like that. Maybe black light paint, as well. Let me think on it."

"You'll have to talk to Nova first. She may not want her dress painted on."

Nick's mouth twitched. "Untwist your panties. I'd have to talk to her to get her to send it to me. Don't worry. I'll get her approval first."

"Perfect." Pallas turned to Wynn. "What are your thoughts on the graphics? Could you do posters or something?"

"I could, but I'd prefer to put them in a frame. Or several. Giant frames."

Nick began to sketch on piece of paper. "Like this? I've been thinking about different ways to frame huge graphics."

"Exactly like that," Wynn told him.

Pallas told herself it was wrong to get excited about the thought of someone else paying for the frames Nick had mentioned. "Can you work up a bid?"

"Sure." Wynn took notes. "I also want to think about invitations. I'll bet I could do something on a thumb drive pretty easily. And something fun for the nontechy bunch. I'll put a few different ideas in my bid."

"I'll do the same," Violet said. "She'll want accessories and we have to spice up those bridesmaid dresses. Especially if Nick's going to paint the wedding gown."

"I want to see if I can do something in papier-mâché," Nick added. "From the world. Things to be scattered around. I'll get you a bid, too."

Silver sighed. "I feel useless. I can do whatever she wants at the regular price." She looked at the posters. "Okay, a couple hundred for me to buy accessories to match the colors. Catering should be about the same as usual, too. Unless she wants specific plates and serving dishes. The same for the linen rentals." She paused. "Should you talk to Natalie? What if she came up with a great origami mobile or several for the reception? With all this information, she could make it amazing. Or maybe favors for the table or something."

"I hadn't thought of that," Pallas admitted. "I'll speak with her." She glanced at her lists. "I think that was everything I had. If you could all get me your information by noon tomorrow, I'll take it to our bride."

Violet grinned. "Are we doing it?"

"If Nova agrees to the bids," Pallas began, then paused. Was she up for this? She thought about Nova and her dying father. Saying no would just be mean-spirited. And maybe Nick was right. She could use this experience to see what she could do, creatively. Maybe her weddings didn't have to be so regimented.

"I'm going to tell her yes," she said firmly.

Everyone seemed excited. They took a copy of the game with them and headed out. Nick lingered.

"You okay?" he asked when they were alone.

"I'm not sure. It's exciting and scary. I wouldn't want to mess this up."

"You're good at planning weddings."

"Not alien planet ones."

"We talked about this yesterday. The premise is always the same. A couple in love wants to get married. The theme of the wedding might be unique, but everything else is simply a variation on the same theme."

He made it sound so easy, she thought wistfully. It must be nice to always be confident like that. She'd been the kid who wasn't completely sure of her place pretty much anywhere. Except here, she reminded herself. She'd always belonged at Weddings in a Box.

"I don't want to let Nova or her father down. And Joel."

"Hey, he's just the groom. It's her day, right?"

She smiled. "It shouldn't be, but sometimes that's how it works out."

Was it just her or had he moved closer? He seemed to be staring really intently into her eyes. That was good, right? It meant he liked her. She wanted Nick to like her. Before she could figure out a way to say that, assuming it wouldn't come out sounding too dorky, he leaned in and kissed her.

The soft, warm pressure of his mouth on hers was exactly what she needed in order to forget the swirling thoughts in her mind. The second their lips touched, she could only feel, which was a very good thing. His arms came around to hold her and she found herself leaning into him.

He was strong and steady, his body hard with plenty of muscle. He smelled good, too. Like soap and man and a hint of wood. When she rested her hands on his shoulders, she felt the solidness of him—as if he were someone she could depend on.

He moved his mouth against hers. She felt the first tiny sparks popping in the middle of her chest. As he increased the pressure on her lips, the sparks began to fan out through her body. When he touched his tongue to her bottom lip, she parted for him.

He kissed her deeply, moving slowly, as if he had all the time in the world. She relaxed into their kiss, even as tension filled her body. No, not tension. Desire. Wanting. All those delicious things she hadn't felt in so long.

Their tongues stroked and circled. She leaned in more so that they were touching everywhere. She thought briefly about the table next to them. While it wasn't exactly fluffy, it was a horizontal surface and maybe they could—

He drew back and pressed his forehead to hers. "You're a bigger temptation than I'd realized."

The sweet words were almost enough to make up for the lack of kissing. He thought she was a temptation? Seriously? Her? Did he want to be tempted some more?

He kissed her lightly once more on the mouth before stepping away. "You have bids to arrange and I have to figure out how to work with papier-mâché."

And with that, he was gone. Pallas pressed her oddly trembling fingers to her mouth. She didn't know exactly what was happening with Nick, but she found she liked it a lot.

"IMPRESSIVE, NICK," Ronan said as he spun molten glass to create the flat shape he needed.

"It's harder than it looks," Nick grumbled. He spread another strip of gooey newspaper over the inflated balloon. It *was* harder than it looked, he thought. The YouTube video had made things look so simple. A little secret sauce, a few strips of newspaper and voilà—a masterpiece. Only he wasn't having much luck with his first attempt.

For one thing, the balloon wasn't an easy form to work with. It wasn't completely spherical and once his fingers were wet, the balloon got both slippery and sticky—a combination he would have said was impossible. For another, he didn't like how the form was turning out.

Nick shifted the balloon in his hand, bumped against a jar of sharp pencils and popped the balloon. The paper he'd already applied sank into a soggy mess that draped across his hand.

Mathias strolled over. "You might need a different form."

"Bite me."

His brother ignored that. "What are you going for?"

"I'm not sure. I'll know it when I see it." He nodded at the video game sitting on the bench next to him. "Ever play this?"

"I'm not into games." He held it up. "Ronan, you ever play Concord Awaken?"

"Sure. It's a decent game."

"Decent?" Nick tossed the dripping paper into the trash. "With enthusiasm like that, you're going to get a call from their advertising agency to be a spokesmodel."

He walked to the sink and washed up, then returned to Mathias and explained about the CA world.

"I didn't have anything specific in mind," he admitted. "The colors are purple, teal and black. I guess I was planning to do balloon-shaped orbs." He grimaced. "Not exactly original."

"What's on the planet? Anything interesting? Two-headed frogs? Dragons?"

"No. It's not a fantasy based game. There's the usual stuff. Houses, roads, people. They're fighting a war, so some weapons. I doubt the bride and groom want those at the wedding."

Nick crossed to his drafting table. He had the east side of the huge studio—slightly less than a quarter of the space, but plenty for him. His brothers shared the rest of the open room. There was a large furnace used to generate the heat needed to melt glass. It was a big operation with two ovens, three workstations, shelves, raw material and a venting system that rivaled any at the Center for Disease Control. Ronan also had a studio up at his house but he generally came into town when he was working.

Both Ronan and Mathias exclusively used glass.

Nick was the only outlier, switching to wood and now dabbling with papier-mâché.

"There is a flower," he said more to himself than his brother. "It only blooms when the sun is out, which is a handful of hours a day. The leaves cure nearly any injury and the nectar is food."

"Don't you need a bee to make nectar into food? Isn't that honey?"

Nick sat in front of his table and started sketching the flowers. "Your knowledge of botany is impressive, but I'm pretty sure you can eat nectar straight from the flower." He drew the stem and added leaves. "Besides, it's a game. It can be anything we want it to be."

He stared at the drawing. "I swear I could carve forms faster than using a balloon. There's a place in Mexico making animals out of papier-mâché. How do they do it?" He grabbed his laptop and booted it.

Ronan strolled over. "You forgot the orbs on the flowers."

"Orbs?" Mathias asked with a wink. "Is this a female plant?"

Ronan ignore him. "The power orbs. They provide light." He added a couple of circles at the base of the flower. "No way to show light with papier-mâché. You should use glass."

"That's not going to happen," Nick muttered. He hadn't worked with glass in years. Ronan was right about the orbs, though. They grew at the base of the plant. Still, if he could come up with a form...

He logged online and then searched YouTube videos until he found the one he wanted and began to watch. After he'd been through it several times, he figured out the molds he needed to make. He decided three different flowers could be grouped together in several ways. The trick was the mold. He could easily create a clay version of the flowers, if that could be the basis of the mold.

Fifteen minutes later he was on the phone with a guy in Sacramento. Yes, he could make a mold from a clay rendering. Yes, it could be done in a couple of days. He hung up as Atsuko walked into the studio.

She walked over to him. "You're looking happy about something."

"Molds for the alien wedding."

She pressed her lips together. "Decorative molds?"

"So I can make papier-mâché flowers."

"Why not use the molds to make plastic flowers? Or go to an arts-and-crafts store and buy silk flowers?"

He winced and pressed his hand to his chest. "You wound me. These are special alien flowers."

"Of course they are." She shook her head and murmured something about boys being boys. "Have you thought about working with metal?"

"Sheet metal?"

"Rods, sheet metal, whatever. It's different than wood or glass, but you might like it. Someone I know is selling all his equipment. I'm going to buy it. You can play around and see if it suits."

Metal. He'd never considered the medium. "I'm game for experimenting."

"I thought you might be. You know how to weld?"

He started to point out that working with glass meant working with fire all the time, then reminded himself that welding was completely different. "I took a couple of classes in high school."

"You might want to brush up on your skills." She leaned against his drafting table. "When will you hear on the Dubai commission?"

"In a couple of months." He glanced at the drawing of the flower and added a couple of orbs to the base. "I still don't know if I want to take it or not."

She raised her eyebrows. "Cart, meet horse."

He grinned. "You think I might not get it? Seriously? I'm a Mitchell. Who could be better?"

"There's nothing wrong with your ego."

The sound of glass shattering interrupted them. They both turned to look at the hot glass on the concrete floor. Atsuko shook her head. "What was I thinking, inviting you three here? I could have nice, quiet painters. But no."

"You love us," Mathias called as she turned to leave. "We're your favorites."

She waved in his general direction, then left. Nick turned his attention back to the drawing. He sketched a second flower, then a third. He wasn't worried about Atsuko actually being upset about the broken glass. She wasn't the type—after all, she'd offered him access to a welding torch.

He stood. "Anyone know where I can get a lot of clay? I need to sculpt the flowers and get them to the mold guy."

Mathias's mouth twitched. "I'm sure he's a perfectly nice man. Can he have a different name?"

"Check the supply room." Ronan jerked his head in that direction. "I sometimes use clay to work out a piece. There's about fifty pounds of it. Just tell Natalie to order more."

*Better and better*, Nick thought as he headed for the storeroom. He would create the alien flowers in clay. While the mold was being made, he could figure out how he wanted to use the world's colors. However he designed the color scheme, he would have to make sure it worked with Nova's dress.

Funny how he'd expected his time in Happily Inc to be nothing more than ordinary while he waited to hear on his commission. From the first second Pallas had asked him to take off his shirt and fill in as a Roman soldier, it had been anything but.

PALLAS HAD NEVER attended a video game night, so wasn't sure what to expect or even serve. She'd borrowed a couple of TVs from friends so three groups could play at a time, then had put out the word to all interested parties. The open invitation meant she had no idea how many people would be stopping by. Nick was coming, of course, along with Wynn and her son. A few of her friends from The Boardroom had said they would come over. Nick had warned her the party could last well into the night, so she had to be prepared to serve breakfast, as well.

She debated various foods, then decided anything offered would have to be easily picked up and eaten and not be sticky. She ordered mini wraps from the grocery store deli, along with caprese salad she could put in individual bowls. There were cookies, but she'd avoided chips. Too greasy for the controllers.

She was ready by five, with everyone due to arrive between five thirty and six. She put out bottles of water and cans of soda. There wouldn't be a specialty sangria tonight—she needed everyone to be alert. Her plan was to observe, rather than play. She wanted to take notes on the various levels and look for ideas for the wedding.

She'd already spoken to Nova twice. The bride-to-be was excited and so grateful. The latter made Pallas happy she'd accepted the job. So did the huge retainer check. Nova had meant what she said about there being no limit on spending. If the wedding went well, it would go a long way toward filling the business's sad, empty checking account.

Pallas also appreciated the chance to figure out if this was a direction she wanted to go. She'd spent so much of her life trying to please her mother—and failing badly at every attempt—that she wasn't sure about her own hopes and dreams. Was she more comfortable just doing the same type of wedding over and over, or did she want to expand into the great unknown? Did she want to keep Weddings in a Box at all or sell? She had a feeling that by the time Nova walked down the aisle, Pallas would have most of her answers.

Wynn and her son, Hunter, were the first to arrive. The ten-year-old went directly to the first TV, grabbed a controller and started to play.

"You forgot to say hello," Wynn said, her voice filled with affection and exasperation.

"Hi, Pallas," the boy said without glancing away from the screen. "Thank you for having me over tonight."

Pallas hugged her friend. "See? He has potential."

"I keep telling myself that." Wynn set a plate of brownies on the kitchen table. "Easily grabbed dessert that shouldn't be sticky. I believe that's what you requested."

"It is. Thanks for coming by. Are you going to play?"

Wynn grimaced. "I can get my video game butt kicked at home. I don't need more witnesses. I can't figure out if I'm just too old to get it or if I don't have the right gene pool. What about you?"

"I'm observing and collecting ideas."

"Good. I'll keep you company."

More friends arrived. By six, her small living room was full. People found places to sit on the floor. All three TVs were on and blasting out the music along with fiery kill shots. A few people were going to have to wait to play, but Pallas figured that couldn't be helped. Eventually a player would run out of lives or turns or whatever it was and have to give up his or her seat.

Nick was next to Hunter. They were both staring intensely at the screen. She couldn't tell if they were working together or trying to destroy each other, then decided it didn't matter. As long as everyone was having fun.

"Someone told me there was a party here."

Pallas turned and saw her grandfather walking into her house.

"Grandpa Frank." She hugged him. "What are you doing here?"

He smiled at her. "Like I said—I heard there was a party."

"We're playing video games."

While her grandfather was a great old guy with a zest for life, he was pushing ninety.

He winked at her. "Prepare to be amazed."

"I always am."

He walked into the living room and stared at the crowd. "Where's the line to get a turn?"

Silver held up a small dry-erase board. "I'm taking names." She smiled at Grandpa Frank. "I'll move you to the top of the list because you're so handsome."

"You've always been my favorite of Pallas's friends," he told her.

"I know."

Grandpa Frank turned back to Pallas. "Is there anything to eat at this shindig?"

"In the kitchen."

There were only a couple of people getting food there and it was quieter away from the game. Grandpa Frank took a paper plate, then started to fill it. Despite his years, he stood with perfect posture. His hair was white, his skin tanned. He looked much younger than his actual age, which Pallas guessed had a lot to do with the ever-present twinkle in his eye.

"I heard this was for a wedding you're throwing," he said as he took a couple of Wynn's brownies.

Word certainly traveled in their small town, she

thought. "It is. Nova and her fiancé developed the game. They want to use the world as a backdrop. It's going to be original—that's for sure."

He took a bite of a small wrap and chewed. "You always did have a knack for finding your way, Pallas. You make me proud. You and your brother, both, striking out on your own."

"Thank you," she said, a little surprised at the compliment. She'd never seen herself as someone who found her way. Most of the time she felt as if she were fumbling and failing. It was nice to know things looked different from his point of view.

"You have a lot of your father in you," he continued. "You're ambitious, willing to do the work. Libby is a company girl, but you'll never be that."

Pallas's eyes widened in surprise. Her father? How could she be like him? She barely remembered him. He'd died when she was ten, but for her it seemed like he'd never been around at all. She had vague memories, but nothing that wasn't mentally blurry.

"I don't remember Dad being a rebel," she admitted.

"He was, in his way. He was also determined." Grandpa Frank hesitated. "I'd like to think you get your character from me." He winked.

"Grandpa Frank!" Silver yelled from the living room. "You're up."

Her grandfather handed her his plate. "Someone wiped out early. This is my lucky day."

Pallas laughed. "I had no idea you were so ruthless."

"You gotta be tough to make it," he told her. "Tough and willing to take chances. That's the secret, Pallas. You remember that."

## CHAPTER SEVEN

PALLAS WOKE EARLY the morning after the party. She'd called it a night a little after midnight, despite the fact that the games were still going strong. She'd had no idea that there were so many die-hard Concord Awaken fans in Happily Inc.

She'd put out the rest of the food, mugs for coffee and had told everyone to help themselves. She'd left extra towels, soap and toothbrushes in the guest bath, then had retreated to her bedroom. Now she showered quickly and got dressed.

Only one TV was still on in the living room and it was obviously on hold or whatever it was called when a game was paused. The picture was frozen, with a purple-clad warrior in midshot. Hunter was curled up asleep in one of her upholstered chairs. Grandpa Frank was stretched out on the sofa, with Silver draped across the other upholstered chair. Judging by the sound of water running in her guest bath, she had one more overnight guest. Good thing she'd planned ahead and had bought plenty of eggs for breakfast.

She retreated to her kitchen and collected the ingredients for a simple baked frittata. She preheated the oven, then sprayed the large casserole dish and began cracking eggs into a bowl. Yesterday she'd already prepped the veggies she would need. She added them, along with milk and cheese, then poured everything into the casserole dish. Just then Nick walked into the kitchen.

She had to admit, the man looked really good rumpled. He'd washed his face, but hadn't shaved, so there was dark stubble along his jaw. His hair was mussed, his shirt wrinkled. He looked tired, but was smiling. It was an impossible combination of sexy and vulnerable.

"Morning," he said, his voice low and gravelly. "You're up early."

"I could say the same about you, only I'm not sure you've been to sleep at all."

He raised one shoulder. "Hunter conked out first, around three, but Grandpa Frank and Silver hung in until nearly five."

"Wow, you've had a whole hour of sleep. This is probably not the day to work with a chainsaw."

He moved close and put his hands on her hips, then drew her against him. "I was thinking the same thing," he murmured right before he leaned over and kissed her.

His mouth was warm and gentle against hers. He tasted of minty toothpaste. She relaxed into him, liking the heat of his body and the way she could tell he was still a little sleepy. His hands roamed up and down her back, making her wish he would touch her everywhere. When he brushed against her lower lip, she parted for him, giving herself up to the desire just waiting to explode.

Even as their tongues brushed, she arched into him, pressing her belly against his growing erection. Her breasts ached and between her legs she felt the first rush of need.

Maybe it was the fact that they were both not awake enough to have defenses in place. Maybe it was the man himself, but for a heartbeat or two, she thought about pointing out that the counter was probably the perfect height for a quick rendezvous.

Only she wasn't someone who ever offered that kind of thing. At least not for a first time. There was also the fact that there were three people, including a ten-year-old and her grandfather, not twenty feet away.

As if reading her mind, Nick drew back. His expression was serious, his eyes dark. He rubbed his thumb against her lower lip. "I'll admit to fantasizing about spending the night, but somehow never imagined this particular scenario."

"Me, either."

He kissed her lightly. "Rain check?"

"Absolutely."

"Good." He stepped back. "Now how can I help?"

"Are you awake enough to fry bacon?"

"I am."

She pointed to the refrigerator. "It's in there. I'll get out the frying pan."

Nick collected the package and opened it. Pallas got him set up at the stove, put the casserole in the oven, then started cutting up fruit.

She had to admit she felt good. Better than good, maybe. She had a lot of ideas for Nova's wedding, a house full of people she cared about, and she was still tingling from the toe-curling kisses of a man she liked a lot. All in all, it was a very nice way to start her day.

NICK STOOD NEXT to Ronan and studied the drawing on the wall. It was to scale and in color, showing the installation as it would be when it was finished.

The underwater scene would be ten feet high and thirty feet long, and filled with the familiar—sea grass, fish, rocks, along with a mystical mermaid swaying in the ever-present tide.

Every element, every glowing color, each shape, was made of glass. There was movement in the forms, a sense of life. As if just standing there you could hear the rush of the ocean all around. Nick honest to God had no idea how his brother did it. A project like this was at least a year's commitment. While he had help from Mathias and the apprentices who came to the studio to learn from him, he did most of the work himself. He preferred it that way.

Ronan pointed to the sand on the ocean floor. "I haven't figured that out yet. Real sand is the obvious solution but it doesn't look right. It's too flat. Glass is too bright."

"Have you looked at a combination of ground rock? Quartz with a little polished granite. Or something else, with glass beads thrown in to add depth."

Ronan nodded slowly. "Maybe. I'll have to play with it."

What neither of them said was that Ronan could ask their father. There was little about glass that

Ceallach Mitchell didn't know. Only he wasn't one to give advice, even to his sons, which meant it was a risk to get in touch with him. Nick knew that Ronan rarely spoke to the old man. There had to be a safer topic for the two of them to discuss.

"I heard from Del the other day," he said, thinking their oldest brother should be safe enough. "He and Maya are getting married here in Happily Inc. They're going to want some kind of theme wedding."

Ronan glanced at him. "Like a royal wedding?"

Nick snickered. "I'm going to tell Del you're talking about him wearing tights."

Ronan laughed. "Go ahead. Is there really a theme?"

"That's what the email said. Maybe I read it wrong, or he meant something else."

"I hope so."

Nick thought about the two themed weddings he'd helped out with. "They're not as crazy as you think. It's kind of fun that the couple getting married has something like that in common. You know—a memory that connects them."

"Did someone drop you on your head?"

"I'm just saying they can be nice. Especially when it's a family thing."

Not that Del would want that for himself, Nick reminded himself. His oldest brother had spent the better part of a decade avoiding his nearest and dearest. Del had left a hole in the Mitchell clan—his leaving had upset the dynamics. Nick would guess their mother had missed her oldest most of all.

Before he could stop himself, he asked, "You ever

talk to Mom?" A question bound to get a reaction because, despite being Elaine's favorite, Ronan wasn't biologically her son.

Nick only knew the basic facts about his brothers and their past. That as far as everyone was concerned, Ceallach and Elaine Mitchell had five sons; the youngest two—Mathias and Ronan—were fraternal twins. Three years ago, when Ceallach had suffered what ended up being a mild heart attack, the truth had come out. Ceallach had admitted that Ronan was the result of an ongoing affair. When Ceallach's mistress had wanted to give up her son for adoption, Elaine had agreed to take in the week-old baby.

Nick still had trouble grasping his mother's extraordinary decision. She'd had her own month-old baby at the time, which meant Ceallach's wife and his mistress had been pregnant at the same time. Yet the old bastard hadn't said a word. What kind of woman willingly took in the child of a rival and raised him as her own?

Her three older boys had been under the age of five and none of them had remembered one child miraculously turning into twins. Del, the oldest of the brothers, vaguely recalled being told that Ronan had been in the hospital all that time.

The deception was impressive, but even more remarkable was the fact that as they grew up, it was clear to everyone that Ronan was her favorite. The one child who *wasn't* hers had the tightest hold on her heart.

"She's not my mother," Ronan said, still studying the drawing.

"Don't be an ass."

"It's biology. I can't help it."

Nick wasn't one to run from a fight, and right now the idea of punching his brother seemed to make the most sense, but he knew that Ronan wouldn't hit back. He would win by simply standing there, as if asking *is that all you've got?* Which left Nick annoyed and frustrated.

"She raised you from the time you were born. She loves you and you love her. Saying she's not your mother makes you sound like an idiot. Worse, it hurts her. She has her flaws, but she doesn't deserve that."

Emotions flickered across Ronan's face but before Nick could figure out what he was thinking, they were gone.

"There's nothing to say."

Nick swore. "You never call her? You never check in?"

Ronan's silence was an answer.

"At least no one has to question whether or not you're Ceallach's son," he said. "Talk about being a dick."

There was so much more he wanted to say. Like the fact that the five of them had years' worth of memories and those had to matter. That they'd lived and fought and blown glass the way other brothers had played baseball or basketball. That even now they were each defined by their relationship with their father. Especially the three youngest—the artists. He would guess Mathias and Ronan shared his love-hate relationship with the old man, not to mention confusion about their mother—the woman who had loved her husband unconditionally—no matter what he did.

"Those alien flowers I sculpted? They're for a wedding. Nova and Joel. They were planning to get married anyway, but then her dad got diagnosed with cancer and now they're determined to have a wedding while he can still walk his daughter down the aisle."

Ronan started to speak, but Nick held up his hand.

"Don't," he said quickly. "You're going to say something we'll both regret. My point is you shouldn't wait. Mom's already had breast cancer. She beat it, but what if it comes back? What happens when they get old? Are you still going to ignore her then? Dad deserves what he gets, but she doesn't."

"She's not my mother. Everything about my life was a lie."

Nick rolled his eyes. "Dramatic much? Talk about an excuse. She loves you. That's all she's ever done. She took you in when she didn't have to and she loved you. Now you won't even call her? There aren't any words to describe how crappy that makes you."

"Get off me."

"Or what? You'll give me a long, cold stare?" Nick pointed at the drawing. "You know what's missing? Heart. Because you sure as hell don't have one."

With that, he turned and walked out of the studio. He stood next to his truck as he tried to figure out where he was going to go. Being his father's son, he knew the best place to totally get lost was in work. Because when you were in a project, the demons couldn't find you.

Pallas heard banging from the main level of the building. As she was supposed to be the only one working that morning, she started down the stairs to investigate. At the halfway point, she wondered if she should have brought something heavy along, as a defense weapon, then quickly dismissed the idea. This was Happily Inc. Nothing bad ever happened here.

She passed through the ballroom and into the big storage area and found Nick dragging support blocks across the concrete floor.

"Hi," she said when he paused to take a breath. "I wasn't expecting you today."

"I'm not here," he told her. "Or working."

"All evidence to the contrary?"

He shook his head. "Good point. I couldn't get anything done at the studio and I needed to work off my temper so I came here."

"To move impossibly heavy blocks?"

"I'll need them in place for the next panel."

*In about three weeks*, she thought, studying him.

He looked as he always did—good. Casually dressed in jeans and a worn T-shirt. But there were also signs of tension. Some tightness around his mouth and in the set of his shoulders.

"Want to talk about it?" she asked.

"No. Yes. Hell." He rubbed the back of his neck. "Family stuff."

"Ah, so it's serious."

That earned her a slight smile. "My brother is a jackass."

"Which one?"

"Ronan. We had a fight." He dropped his arm to

his side. "No, *I* had a fight. He wouldn't engage. He won't call our mother, which is pretty mean-spirited of him since she's always been on his side." One shoulder rose and lowered. "The downside of sharing workspace."

"Want to talk about it?" she asked again.

"Not really."

"Want to go for a walk? I can distract you with useless knowledge about the town."

He smiled at her. "That would be great."

They walked outside. She pointed toward the river. "Let's go that way."

The afternoon was warm and sunny, the temperatures flirting with eighty. She loved this time of year, when the heat wasn't insane and days were getting longer.

"You know our basic history," she began. "Lies told to an unsuspecting public."

"That's a little harsh."

"And yet completely accurate. Happily Inc also benefits from a weird spiritual convergence of energy, or so I've been told."

"Like Sedona?"

"That's the rumor. Mystical things are said to happen here. Oh, and people sleep really, really well. That's why we have a sleep center."

"I saw the signs when I drove into town."

"It's a big deal. We have world-famous doctors doing whatever it is sleep experts do."

"Nap?"

She grinned. "Maybe. Anyway, both of those quirks

bring in tourists, although nothing compared with the wedding trade. We are the big employers."

"Do you get a special seat at the local business association?"

"Better. We get donuts."

They crossed the street. Nick took her hand and she laced her fingers with his.

"My dad's a nightmare," he said.

She carefully pressed her lips together, wanting him to talk as much as he needed, without her interrupting.

"Genius comes at a price," he added.

"But you're normal," she blurted before she could stop herself.

He smiled at her. "Thanks, but I'm more screwed up than you realize."

"You hide it well."

"Ronan's only our half brother. Dad had an affair and Ronan's the result. Mom raised him from the time he was a week old."

Pallas came to a stop. "I thought they were fraternal twins."

"So did we."

"But how..." She didn't even know what to ask. She and Cade were fraternal twins. She couldn't imagine what it would be like to find out they weren't. That all her memories of their childhood, her feelings of connection weren't real. Except if they'd happened, then they would be real, but different.

"That isn't something you get over easily," she murmured.

"Apparently not."

They crossed the street.

"Ronan won't talk about it. Come to think about it, Mathias doesn't have much to say, either, although he puts on a better front."

They passed by The Boardroom Pub and reached the river boardwalk. Once there, they sat on a bench, Nick angled toward her.

"The thing is, we all thought Ronan was our mom's favorite."

He told her how Elaine had taken in Ceallach's bastard child and raised him as her own. Pallas listened, grateful he didn't seem to want any advice, because she didn't have any. She couldn't imagine finding out her husband had a mistress and that his mistress had had a baby within weeks of her youngest being born. Or offering to raise the other baby as her own. And for Ronan and his brothers not to know was inconceivable.

"So when Mathias and Ronan found out the truth, they moved here?" she asked.

"Yeah. The rest of us didn't figure out why until last summer. My mom had breast cancer. She kept it to herself. Not even my dad knew. When everyone found out, it all hit the fan and everything came out. Pretty screwed up, huh?"

She leaned against him. "I'm not sure there is a normal family anywhere. We all have our quirks." She looked up at him. "Although I will admit your family has more secrets than most. Is your mom okay?"

"As far as I know. She swears they got the cancer

in time and she's being monitored, so I'm guessing it's true. I know Dad worries. She's all he has."

*Not his sons? Silly question*, she told herself. She remembered what Nick had told her about growing up with the famous Ceallach Mitchell as his father.

"My mom is one of seven girls."

Nick laughed. "No boys?"

"Not until my generation. I can't imagine what it was like when they were all approaching puberty. There's fourteen years between the oldest and the youngest, so hormones would have been flying high for nearly two decades. It's amazing that Grandpa Frank survived."

"I'll bet." He shifted and put his arm around her.

She liked the feel of him touching her. The strength and heat of him. In front of them, the river flowed. Come the weekend, there would be kayakers out navigating its length. Small powerboats were allowed but only in the summer. Tourists clogged the parks along the river and filled the hotels.

"You're one of two in your family?" Nick asked.

"Yes, it's just Cade and me. My maternal grandmother died when I was a baby, so my mom moved our family in with Grandpa Frank."

Maybe that was why her father had always seemed so absent to her. He'd been living in another man's home.

"I was about two at the time, so I don't remember living anywhere else. The house is huge and old, with lots of staircases. There's a secret passage that goes from the library on the main floor up to the attic.

Cade and I would play there when we were kids. We would disappear and it made my mom crazy."

"Good for you."

"I don't get the credit. It was always Cade's idea. He's the brave one."

Nick shook his head. "I don't buy that. You're standing up to her right now. Keeping the business instead of selling it."

"I still haven't decided what I'm going to do on a permanent basis. I wish I was more like him. Cade never cared about what anyone thought. He's so independent. Here I am, living in the same town where I was born. I've barely been out of the state."

"Do you want to travel?"

She thought about the question. "There are places I'd like to see. Australia and Europe. I guess I'm not the adventurous type. I like living here. I like being here and hanging out with my friends."

"Tell you what. If I take the commission in Dubai, you can come visit me there."

"I'm not even sure where that is. I'll have to look it up on a map."

"You do that."

She couldn't imagine packing up her life and moving to a foreign country. Apparently she didn't have the thrill seeker gene.

"When do you have to decide if you're going?" she asked.

"After they finalize the commission. It's for two years. That's a long time. I like the project, but I can't make up my mind." He looked at her. "I meant what I said, Pallas. I'd like you to come visit."

His words caused her chest to tighten. Desire flickered to life and began to burn. Because visiting Nick would be about more than seeing his work. It would be about being with him. Something she very much wanted.

For a second she wished she were the type of woman who could simply tell him that. Silver would. She would grab Nick by the front of his shirt, pull him close and kiss him. Then she would take him to bed and do whatever wild things Silver liked to do. Pallas sighed—she would never be like her friend.

While she liked men, they hadn't ever been a big part of her life. Happily Inc wasn't exactly a single-guy magnet. Plus Nick was the first man in forever to really get her attention. The thing was, she wasn't entirely sure what she was supposed to do now.

Did she throw herself at him? Ask him to have sex with her? Play hard to get? Was he even interested in her? They'd kissed and it had been nice, but he hadn't exactly thrown her over his shoulder and taken her back to his room. Not that she wanted a guy who *would* throw her over his shoulder. She had a feeling it would be very uncomfortable. But in theory...

Nick leaned in and kissed her. The action totally caught her off guard, so she wasn't able to react before he drew back.

"Thank you," he told her. "For listening. It helps to have a friend to talk to."

Friend? Friend! Was that how he saw her? As a friend? They'd kissed. Didn't the kissing mean anything? She'd been having throw-over-the-shoulder images and he thought they were friends? Kill. Me. Now.

"Sure," she said brightly. "Anytime. I, um, should get back to work."

Before he could say anything *friendly*, she jumped to her feet, waved and took off at a brisk walk.

Friends! Seriously. What was up with that? Pallas couldn't decide if she should never speak to Nick again, corner him and flash her breasts, or simply accept the fact that she wasn't the kind of woman men wanted to sleep with.

The latter thought was so depressing she had to go swing by the local Starbucks to get a Mocha Frappuccino with extra whipped cream. Just to take the edge off.

She would bury herself in her work that afternoon, then reward herself with some girlfriend time. At least there she knew what was expected. She understood the rules. Stupid man. She was never speaking to him again. Or kissing him. Or flashing her breasts.

That was it, she thought as she walked into the Starbucks. No more hope of breast flashing for Nick. Starting right now.

## CHAPTER EIGHT

TWO DAYS LATER Pallas was still wrestling with her nonrelationship with Nick, and because that wasn't enough trauma in her life, her mother had invited her to lunch. Being a bad liar meant she hadn't been able to think of a reason to say no. The only bright spot was she'd insisted they go to a restaurant instead of having a depressing box lunch at the bank.

Which was how Pallas found herself with an avocado cheeseburger and the world's largest order of french fries—when in doubt, bury your troubles in food.

"You disappoint me, Pallas," Libby said firmly as she picked at her green salad, dressing on the side.

"I know, Mom."

"You do?"

"Sure. I always disappoint you. Usually I want to make you happy, but even then I fail. I'm not sure how. I'd say it's a gift, but we both end up unhappy, so it's not like it's a good thing."

She picked up a fry and ate it. Her mother studied her.

"If you keep eating like that, you're going to get fat."

"Yet another way I'll disappoint you."

"What is going on with you?"

"I honestly don't know."

Libby pressed her lips together. "What have you decided about the business?"

Until that exact second, Pallas would have sworn she didn't know. Selling versus not selling—it wasn't as if she'd had a sit-down with herself to weigh the pros and cons. Yet as soon as her mother asked the question, she knew.

"I'm keeping it."

"I see."

Two very icy words. Pallas shivered, then took a bite of her burger.

"May I know why?"

There were so many ways to answer that question, but only one that made sense to her. "Because it makes me happy."

"Don't be ridiculous."

Pallas put down her burger. "Why is that ridiculous? You don't believe me? You don't think it's possible for me to be happy anywhere else but the bank?"

"You own a small, failing business that has little chance for growth or success. How on earth can that make you happy?" .

"Thanks for the support," Pallas said with a sigh. "To answer your question, everything about it makes me happy. A week or so ago a couple came to see me. They developed a video game and they want their wedding theme to be that game. It's all the more special because Nova's father is—"

"You're making a fool out of yourself," her mother interrupted. "Everyone can see it but you."

Pallas pushed away her burger. Suddenly she

wasn't hungry at all. "You're wrong, Mom," she said firmly. "I'm not making a fool out of myself. I'm helping couples with the most significant day of their lives. I'm helping them make their wedding dreams come true. Even if they end up divorced, they'll remember their wedding and I get to be a part of that. It's good work. It's fulfilling and I like it. The only reason you can't accept it is because you didn't have a hand in picking it for me. You're upset because I won't do what you want me to. You think I should have to earn my place in the family."

Pallas stood and tossed her napkin on the table. "You know what? Today I'm not willing to do that anymore."

She picked up her bag and walked out. When she reached the sidewalk, she pointed out to herself that this was the second time she'd walked away from a difficult situation. She was going to have to make sure it didn't become a pattern. Although with Nick she'd bolted out of fear, whereas with her mother, it felt a lot more like standing up for herself—from a safe distance.

Why were relationships so complicated? She knew they didn't have to be, yet so many of them were.

Back in her office, Pallas checked her email. She had a note from Nova about more wedding details. The words were so happy and upbeat that Pallas smiled as she read. Maybe she had been dragged kicking and screaming into the alien wedding, but now that she'd committed, she knew she'd made the right decision.

Leaning back in her chair, she considered her bank statement and the business cash flow. Nova's wedding had gone a long way to making it much happier than it had been before. Yes, there was more work, but also more reward. Maybe she'd been short-sighted to want to do everything the way it had always been done. Maybe the real way to grow her business was to think outside of the box.

The idea was still unformed, but she sensed the potential. As she and Nick had talked about, the basic format for a wedding wasn't going to change, but what about all the details? They could be enhanced.

She looked at the files on her desk—each one represented a pending wedding. She looked through them until she found the black-and-white wedding—where the bride had requested zebras. Maybe it wasn't such a crazy idea after all.

She pulled out her cell phone and dialed a number.

"Hi," Carol said cheerfully when she answered. "What's up?"

"I'm working. How about you?"

"I think Millie's depressed rather than sick."

Pallas struggled to remember who Millie was. "The giraffe?"

"Uh-huh. She's listless. I know the move was hard on her, but I think she's lonely. She needs friends. Anyway, that's not why you called. What's up?"

"I have a very strange request. One of my brides is having a black-and-white wedding. She saw the zebras and would like to rent them for ambience."

Carol laughed. "Seriously?"

"You know I can't make that up."

"True. Wow. So they'd be like tea lights or balloons?"

"Sort of. We'd set up a penned area for them. I'd make sure the guests didn't touch them, although I imagine they would want to take pictures. What do you think?"

"I don't know. They're relatively tame, although still zebras, so not exactly as calm as, say, a goat."

Were goats calm? All Pallas could picture were those little baby goats jumping all over the place.

"Okay," she said slowly. "What does that mean?"

"That I'd have to think about the transportation issues and how to make sure they didn't escape. I would want a significant profit margin for the trouble and because one of the barns needs a new roof."

Pallas laughed. "Fair enough. Send me a quote. I'll pass it along to my bride and let you know. If this comes to pass, I get to have a very interesting conversation with my insurance agent."

"Zebra insurance?"

"Yup. For you, the zebras and all the guests, not to mention my facility. Should be fun."

"I also have a couple of black llamas if she'd like to use them. Maybe we could find a local white llama."

"What I would give to write that Craigslist ad. *Wanted: white llama to rent for wedding.*"

"You know someone would answer."

"Scary but true. Thanks, Carol. Send the bid over when you get it ready."

"I'll work on it right now."

"Bye."

Pallas set her cell phone back on her desk. Zebras and llamas. She wasn't sure what would be next, but that was part of the fun.

"You look happy about something."

She looked up and saw Cade standing in the doorway to her office. Pallas jumped up and ran at him. He dropped his worn leather duffel on the floor and held out both arms. She slammed into him and hugged him tight.

"You're here! When did you get back? How long are you staying? I've missed you."

"I've missed you, too, sis."

They held on to each other for nearly a minute before letting go. Pallas stared at her brother's face, taking in the new scar by his eyebrow and his tan. He looked strong and fit—a man who worked outdoors.

He had her same hazel eyes and brown hair. Somehow on him, it was more interesting. Maybe it was the cowboy thing, she thought with a smile.

She held on to his upper arms and smiled. "Don't take this wrong, but why are you here?"

"I wanted to see you."

She rolled her eyes. "Why are you in Happily Inc?"

"Grandpa Frank wants to talk to me."

"About?"

Cade hesitated just enough to make her curious. "The horse ranch."

"What?" She flung herself at him again. "Are you serious? He's finally going to let you run it?"

"Looks that way."

Cade had been obsessed with horses since he was a little kid. Grandpa Frank had a stable full of gorgeous horses outside of town. He'd raised American quarter horses for years and in the past decade or so had taken an interest in Arabian horses. As a teen, Cade had begged his grandfather to give him a job at the ranch, but Grandpa Frank had said he wasn't ready. When he graduated from high school, Cade had left Happily Inc. In part to follow his dream and in part, Pallas had always suspected, to get away from their mother.

"I'd love having you close," Pallas told him. "Can you handle having Mom in the neighborhood, as well?"

He kissed her nose. "You always had more trouble with her than me. I tune her out. You take things to heart."

"Maybe I've changed."

"I don't see any pigs flying around, so I'm going to say no."

She sighed. "One day I will. One day I'll stand up to her. You'll see."

She thought about their lunch today. While she'd told her mother what she thought, she'd also bolted rather than face the consequences. Still it was a form of progress. *Baby steps*, she told herself.

"Where are you staying?" she asked. "Want to bunk with me?"

"No, thanks. I've seen your tiny house. Plus, you have too many girlie things in the bathroom."

"You mean the matching towels and candles?"

"That would be them."

She grinned. "Afraid you'll wake up with boobs?"

He laughed. "Not really."

"So where are you staying?"

"At the big house."

Which in their family meant the Saunders/Dineen

home, not prison. Although a case could be made that there were similarities.

"Just until I find out what Grandpa Frank wants," Cade added. "If it is a job at the ranch, I'll live out there."

"Outside the county line," she said wistfully. "You're lucky."

"You left off handsome." He put his arm around her. "It's good to be me, sis. Now I'm hungry. You need to take me to lunch."

"I'd love to. Oddly, I didn't get much to eat myself. I know a place that serves a great avocado burger."

"This is the list of what we currently have out at different galleries," Natalie said, handing Nick three sheets of paper. "As per the agreement, each new gallery has six months to sell a piece. If they do, they can replace it with another. If they don't, they're taken off the preferred list for your work for at least a year. So far that hasn't been a problem." The petite brunette smiled. "You sell very well pretty much everywhere."

Good news, Nick told himself. His work was popular. He should be thrilled or at least happy. Instead all he felt was restless.

"I keep a complete inventory on my computer," Natalie continued. "At any given time, I can tell you where the works are and what we're going to ship next. I'm still cataloging your work by type and price. Different styles and mediums work well in different parts of the country and the world. There's an art to placing artists. Atsuko is an expert at it."

Natalie smiled at him. "You came to us with a huge inventory. Normally artists only have a few pieces."

"Before coming here, I hadn't had a show in over ten years," Nick admitted. "I like to keep busy, so it sort of built up."

"That's what we like to hear." Natalie turned her computer so he could see the photographs on her screen. "This is what we send to the galleries we work with. A complete profile of the work. If they're interested, we discuss terms. We will only agree to what's allowed by your contract with us."

Nick began to regret agreeing to let Natalie explain their policies to him. When he'd first signed on with Atsuko, he'd had his lawyer review the terms. When he'd been told they were fair and reasonable, he'd signed on the dotted line and promptly forgotten about the business side of things. Every few weeks he received a check. Sometimes more than one, depending on how many pieces he sold. The money flowed, he had time and space to work. He was pretty much a happy guy.

"You find this tedious, don't you?" she asked.

"Yup."

She sighed. "You'd be more interested in the business side of things if you weren't so rich," she said lightly, then sighed. "And well recognized."

He thought about the pieces of hers scattered in the gallery. "You'll get there," he told her. "Fame and fortune are right around the corner."

She pushed up her bright red glasses. "You have no idea how much I want to believe you. In the meantime, I love what I do. This job covers food and rent and anything I make on my art gets plowed right back into supplies."

He knew it was like that for most artists. They slaved away in obscurity, hoping to be "discovered" or at least turn a small profit. He and his brothers had been lucky—the upside of being one of Ceallach's talented offspring. The world already knew their names.

"Do you like working in the gallery?" he asked.

"I do. As 'real' jobs go—" she made air quotes with her fingers "—this one is pretty great. As long as I get my work done, Atsuko isn't overly concerned about when I'm here. So if I'm on a roll, I can keep working at home."

"You have room there?" He thought about the big open space he shared with his brothers and swore under his breath. "Did me showing up mean you had to move out of the studio here?"

She grinned. "While I appreciate the worry, don't bother. I'm happy in my little cubby at home. I couldn't possibly work with Mathias and Ronan. They make glass. My favorite medium is paper. Fire and paper are not a good mix."

He was about to agree, but before he could speak, he glanced out the window. Natalie's office faced the street. There were nearly always people out, walking around the shopping district of town. But what Nick didn't expect to see was Pallas with a guy. A good-looking guy who obviously knew her well. They were talking and laughing, oblivious to everyone but themselves.

His gut tightened as all his senses went on alert. Who the hell was he? An old boyfriend come to town? He started to get up, then forced himself back in his seat. Natalie saw the movement, then glanced outside, following his gaze. She smiled.

"Oh, look. Cade's back. Pallas didn't tell me. I wonder if she knew he was coming." She glanced at Nick. "Cade is Pallas's twin brother. He manages a horse ranch in Texas. At least I think it's Texas. It might be Kentucky. Either way, it's somewhere that sounds wonderful and beautiful."

"Not loving Happily Inc?" Nick asked, deliberately looking away from the window.

"I do like it here. I just always thought it would be nice to travel."

As she talked about the places she would like to see, Nick told himself that his reaction to seeing Pallas with another man didn't mean anything. Not really. Sure he liked her, but it wasn't more than that. Yes, he wanted her in his bed, but only in the short-term. He liked things controlled. Defined. Wanting was safe, but passion—too much passion—was dangerous. It consumed and destroyed. Not that it was a problem with him. He would be leaving Happily Inc in a couple of months. Leaving Pallas. Relationships with a time limit he could handle. Anything else was asking for disaster.

PALLAS SMOOTHED THE front of her light sweater before getting out of her car. She was ready. She was prepared. She was wearing mascara on a weekday.

A small thing, sure, but one that could give a girl confidence.

Any nerves she felt were her own stupid fault. She'd been the one to think about flashing her breasts at Nick. The poor man knew nothing about it. Technically, there was no reason to be embarrassed or concerned or jumpy, and yet she felt all those things. Maybe it was because being around him was confusing and a little bit more fun than she was used to. Maybe because she hadn't had a guy in her life in maybe forever. Whatever the reason, she would get through it. She would be her normal cheerful, energetic self and no one would ever guess that on the inside, she was one flirty smile away from eating an entire bag of Hershey's Kisses by herself.

She walked across the strip mall parking lot toward Wynn's graphic-printing business. Bright banners showed different styles available to customers and a giant multicolored banner offered discounted prices.

Retail was tough, Pallas thought as she went inside. Having to deal with the public all the time, getting it right or losing the business. She supposed she kind of did the same thing, but it didn't feel as intense. She had more of a relationship with her customers. Wynn had to produce a great soccer party banner, and then move on.

"I'm so excited," Wynn called when she spotted her. She wove between huge printers and met Pallas at the main counter. "I'm hoping you love this as much as I do. I'll totally admit the technical aspect was beyond me but I had the brilliant idea to go to the community college computer science department. The nice professor there gave me the name of a couple of local programming geniuses and they whipped this up in like three hours. Oh, to be that skilled."

Wynn held out a small thumb drive.

Pallas did her best to hide her disappointment. "It's um…lovely?"

"You're not good at faking it, are you?"

The question came from behind her at the exact moment a warm hand settled on the small of her back. She didn't have to turn to know who was there. Not with every cell in her body sighing in perfect synchronization.

"What do you mean?" she asked as she glanced at Nick, hoping he couldn't tell how she could feel the warmth of his hand. No, that wasn't it. The problem was how much she *liked* the warmth of his hand.

"He means you're not impressed," Wynn said with a grin. "But you will be."

She put a small laptop on the counter, then plugged in the flash drive. At first all Pallas saw was the home screen. Seconds later it went dark and familiar music from the video game began to play.

"Nova sent over a bunch of files," Wynn told them. "Separate music and graphics and all kinds of things I didn't know what to do with. I scripted what I wanted and let the geniuses do their thing."

Pallas watched a pale sun in a purple sky. As it rose, light drifted across the screen, illuminating the silhouette of a bride and groom. The wedding date and location appeared as the pan continued. Elements of the world appeared and disappeared. At the end, a hot link to RSVP filled the screen.

"I take it back." She smiled at Wynn. "That's incredible."

"I know, right? And that's only with a couple of hours. Imagine what we could do with more time. I'm thinking of taking a basic computer graphics class, just to understand what is possible. I would never want to do the formatting or whatever, but knowing a little more than I do would open up a lot of possibilities. Plus the computer guys were very excited." She wrinkled her nose. "I suspect more about being paid so promptly than because they love designing wedding invitations, but still."

Wynn pulled the thumb drive from the computer. "I'll have these ready by the end of the day. Nova's sending me her guest list so I can ship them out tomorrow. Oh, and wait until you see these."

She put a stack of slim, square books on the counter. Nick picked up one and opened it. The colors of the pages were an exact match for the game's world, but instead of a flat picture, a nearly 3-D paper image of a bride and groom rose toward them.

"A pop-up book," Pallas breathed. "You talked about it but I never thought it was possible."

"I know a guy," Wynn said. "He let me use his computerized paper cutter thingie."

Nick raised his eyebrows. "That would be the technical term?"

Wynn laughed. "Of course. Anyway, I did the design freehand. He scanned it and this is what happened. I think this is something we should think about for your weddings, Pallas. I know the brides usually have their own ideas for invitations, but these are too incredible. Pricey, but still. I made twenty for Nova, then asked her if I could run a few extras for samples. At my cost, of course."

"It's amazing. I love the idea of offering this kind of personalized invitation to my brides."

Nick turned the pages of the pop-up book. "You could precolor the pages. Shade them such that when they were cut, they had more dimension."

Pallas tried to imagine that. How would anyone know what went where? But Wynn was nodding.

"You're right. Instead of plain purple or teal, we could use gradations. Or even work with the computer program in advance and preprint the various colors so that the image was fully formed. I wonder how hard that would be."

Wynn pressed her lips together, then shook her head. "Okay—I'll play with that idea later. For now, what do you think?"

"That you're brilliant," Pallas told her. "Has Nova seen these?"

"I'm going to do a video conference with her later. The computer guys already sent her the thumb drive file and she approved that." Wynn leaned on the counter. "Don't take this wrong, but this is way more fun than new happy hour menus at the hotel bar. I hope we can do more of this kind of thing."

Pallas thought about all the possibilities. "I'm thinking we might have to."

Pallas signed the paperwork for the designs, then

took a pop-up book and thumb drive for herself. She and Nick walked out to the parking lot.

"What's next for the wedding?" he asked. "Have you talked to Alan? He's got to have some ideas for costumes for the servers. He should get with Violet. She has some interesting ideas. Want me to call him?"

Pallas looked at him. "For a guy who's just biding his time until he gets the go-ahead on his commission in Dubai, you seem invested in Nova and Joel's wedding."

He put his arm around her. "It's fun. You have a great job."

She thought about how, until now, all the weddings had been so similar. They were all variations on a theme. She had to admit this was a lot more interesting. Even the challenges were turning out to be a good thing.

Before she could say that, her phone beeped. She pulled it out of her back pocket and glanced at the screen. Her good mood evaporated when she saw the text from her mother.

"What?" Nick asked. "You're not smiling anymore."

She shook her head. "Just family stuff. My brother's back in town, which is great, but Mom wants to have a family dinner to celebrate his return. The last time I saw her, it didn't go very well. I'm not excited about sitting down to more lectures about how I'm a failure."

She shoved the phone back in her pocket and faked a smile. "Family. What can anyone do about them? I'll be fine. Anyway, I think we're on schedule for everything that needs to get done. I'm going to follow up with the vendors later today. The invitations are perfect. Hopefully everything else will be, too."

Nick studied her. "I want to tell you not to let her get to you, but I'm in no position to offer advice about families. Who all will be at the dinner?"

"I have no idea. It could be all the cousins or just a few. Grandpa Frank. It's his house. Cade, of course. I'm not sure. It could be the four of us or it could be twenty."

"You need a distraction. Something for your mother to focus on."

*If only*, Pallas thought wistfully. "Not following the rules never goes well for me. Not where she's concerned." She bit her bottom lip. "We always did a big family portrait every fall. All seven daughters, husbands, grandkids and grandparents. Every year the colors were coordinated. Drew and his family wore green shirts, we wore blue, and so on. It was a thing. The year my dad died, I rebelled. I was willing to wear a blue shirt, but not the one my mom picked out. We had a huge fight. She said I would wear what she told me or I wouldn't be in the picture."

Nick looked at her. "You're not in the picture."

"That's right," she said with a lightness she didn't feel. "It was just her and Cade." She shivered. "I don't know why it's so hard with her, but it is."

"You still need a distraction."

"Like a tattoo on my forehead? I'm not sure that would end well for me."

"I was thinking more of a who, not a what." His

dark gaze settled on her face. "Want a bring-to-dinner temporary boyfriend?"

Her heart stumbled a beat or two while her girl parts began to cheer. "Are you offering?"

He gave her that slow, sexy smile of his. "I am. I can be a great distraction. She'll be so charmed, she'll leave you alone. And if she starts in on you, I'll be there to protect you."

Unexpected tears burned in her eyes. She quickly blinked them away and told herself not to be an idiot. Having Nick offer to protect her wasn't cryworthy. Only she thought maybe it was. She couldn't remember the last time a guy who wasn't family had wanted to stand between her and potential danger.

"It's my mother," she warned, hoping her voice sounded normal and not too fraught with emotion. "There will be drama."

He lightly kissed her. "I'm an artist, Pallas. We live for drama. It's all part of the process. Tell me when and where, and I'll be there."

"Thank you."

"Anytime."

Staring up at him, she felt herself wanting to do more than flash her boobs. She wanted to tell him he was really nice and that she liked him. Which should have scared the heck out of her—and yet it didn't.

# CHAPTER NINE

THE STARBUCKS BY the river was a busy place. Pallas was happy to get a table. She pulled a second chair close and waited for Natalie to arrive. Drinking a Mocha in the middle of the afternoon was playing with fire—or at the very least risking a night of insomnia. But the dinner for Cade was that night and Nick had offered to drive. That meant Pallas could be wild and have a second glass of wine.

She briefly wondered if planning her day around lattes and wine meant she had some kind of problem, then decided she didn't care. She would face that tomorrow, *after* dealing with her mother. Surely she deserved that much of a break.

She saw Natalie walk into the store and waved her over. "I took a chance and got your favorite," she said, holding out the Dirty Chai latte. "It's the world's most disgusting order."

Natalie laughed as she took a seat. "How can you say that?"

"It's tea with a shot of espresso. You're not supposed to mix coffee and tea. It's unnatural."

"Thank you for the drink and indulging me." She set her bag on the floor. "How are things? All I hear about these days is the alien wedding. Everyone is so excited. I'm happy to have a small part to contribute."

She opened her large bag and pulled out a sketch pad. "I've been working on a mask," she said, opening the cover to show Pallas several drawings. Each of them was different, representing the different characters from the game. "I'm already figuring out how to do the folding. I'm going to make them life-size and hang them in groups."

The drawings were both beautiful and disturbing. Pallas thought they were fantastic, but wasn't sure if they were wedding appropriate.

"What did Nova say?"

Natalie sighed with pleasure. "She loves them, so yay."

"Then it's a go."

"I'm happy. How's the rest of the wedding?"

"It's coming together. Everyone's helping, which I really appreciate." Pallas frowned. "I just realized all my friends have time to help me. Is that good or bad?"

"We're making time because we're excited about the project, not because we're bored. Don't worry about us."

"I hope so." Pallas wanted the people she loved to be happy. "None of us are dating. I wonder if that means anything."

"It doesn't."

She looked at Natalie and raised her eyebrows. "Maybe you need a man."

Natalie held up her fingers in the shape of a cross. "Thanks, but no. I've sworn off men. Maybe not for the rest of my life, but for a while yet. My last relationship hardly ended well."

Pallas wanted to protest that her friend was pretty and smart and funny and kind. She was exactly who every single guy should be searching for, yet Natalie didn't look or date or even hint that she was interested in anyone, and who could blame her?

Pallas didn't know all the details, but the broad strokes of Natalie's story were that she'd been left pretty much at the altar by her jackass fiancé. With no family and no job waiting for her anywhere else, Natalie had stayed in Happily Inc while she figured out what to do next. She'd answered an ad for a personal assistant to Atsuko at the gallery and had quickly worked her way up to office manager.

She'd made friends, rented a great apartment and created beautiful pieces of art. But as far as Pallas knew, she hadn't been on a date in the past two years.

"What do you know about Nick?" she asked impulsively.

Natalie sipped her drink. "Our Nick?" Her mouth curved up in a smile. "Does someone have a crush?"

"No. Of course not." Pallas was afraid she'd spoken too quickly. "We're friends. You know he's restoring the panels for Weddings in a Box, plus he's been helping with the alien wedding. We're friends."

Natalie looked amused. "Yes, you mentioned that already."

Pallas ignored her. "Cade's back in town. There's a command performance dinner tonight. Nick offered to go with me and run interference. I was just wondering what you knew about him that I didn't."

Her friend didn't look convinced. "If you say so," she murmured, before adding, "I don't know him that well, but he seems like a very nice man. He and his brothers get along. They're not as close as Mathias and Ronan, but then they're not…" Her voice trailed off.

"I know about them growing up, thinking they were twins," Pallas told her. "Nick told me."

Natalie set down her drink. "I haven't met Ceallach Mitchell yet, but I swear he's an awful person. He's demanding and cruel. Who just blurts out that kind of information, and then doesn't tell anyone so his sons can have a little support? Their mother didn't know they'd found out, so she didn't talk to them, and Nick, Aidan and Del had no idea. Ronan and Mathias were totally on their own. They had to figure it out for themselves. It bites."

Pallas couldn't remember the last time Natalie had been so upset about something. She worked with the brothers, handling the sales of the work and who knew what else around the office, plus she was an artist, too. It made sense they'd gotten close.

"It's been really hard on everyone," Pallas said. "If I were them, I wouldn't know what to think."

"Me, either, but at least they have each other and their brothers." Natalie straightened in her chair. "Anyway, I don't know Nick as well as the others, but he seems like a good guy. He has a sense of humor and has absolutely no interest in the business side of selling his work."

"That's because he's really successful. Must be nice."

"Tell me about it." She leaned forward. "Whenever I go into the studio for something, it's like stepping into another dimension. I work with paper and found objects—it's totally different than using a chainsaw or making glass. Sometimes they intimidate me. Not that I would tell them."

"Absolutely no. You're brilliant."

Natalie laughed. "You're very sweet. I do okay. I'm in a great place and I love what I create, so that's what matters, right? It's like you at your work. You love Weddings in a Box and making people happy."

Pallas nodded.

Her friend was reminding her of something important, not to mention something else she would've had to give up if she'd gone to work at the bank. Despite her mother's claims that she'd missed her opportunity, Pallas wondered if Libby would make another run at trying to convince her to sell the business.

"What?" Natalie asked. "What are you thinking?"

"That I've always had to work to make my mother happy," Pallas admitted. "And I've always failed. With Gerald, it was different. He was such a kind man. I never expected him to leave me his business."

"He loved you like the daughter he never had. We could all see it."

"I feel guilty."

"Why?"

"Because I didn't do anything to earn it," she said, feeling foolish and defensive, even though she knew she spoke the truth. In her family—no, that wasn't fair—with her mother, love had to be earned.

"It's not supposed to be like that," Natalie said quietly. "Your mom's wrong."

"I know that in my head. It's my heart that's having trouble getting the message."

She looked up as her cousin Drew approached the table. "Ladies. Can I buy anyone a refill?"

"I'm good," Pallas told him.

"Me, too."

Drew nodded, then rested his hands on the back of the empty chair. "I'll be at the dinner with your mom tonight," he said. "If things get ugly, give me the high sign and I'll step in."

"Thanks. With Cade around, I'm sure everything will be fine. Besides, I'm bringing a fake boyfriend as my own distraction."

"A great idea. I need to look into something like that."

Natalie's mouth turned up at the corners. "Gee, Drew, I didn't know you played for that team."

"You know what I meant," he grumbled.

"Do I?"

"I'm ignoring that." He looked at Pallas. "Between the three of us, we should be able to keep Libby in line." He stretched over and ruffled the top of Pallas's head. "Gotta protect family."

She leaned out of reach and smoothed her hair. "You are sweet and annoying at the same time. How do you do that?"

"It's a gift." He grinned. "Besides, you're one of my favorite cousins."

"You say that to all the girls."

"Only family members. Otherwise it gets weird."

With that, he waved and left. Pallas smiled at her friend. "He's single and you obviously share a sense of humor. Any thoughts?"

"That I have no interest in him that way. Which is sad because I might enjoy being the queen of the manor."

"Actually that would be Grandpa Frank's house and my mom lives there, so you need to rethink your manor fantasies. Still, Drew's a great guy."

"Not for me. I wish, but there's no chemistry." Natalie's smile returned. "If you ask me, I think he's still in love with Silver."

"You know about that?"

"*Everyone* knows about that. What I can't figure out is how Silver feels about him."

"I think she's made it pretty clear she hates his guts and all his other pieces."

Natalie didn't look convinced, but then she'd only heard what had happened secondhand. She hadn't been a witness.

Back in high school, Drew had been the young prince and Silver had been the beautiful girl from the wrong side of the tracks. They'd fallen madly in love and everyone had assumed they would live happily ever after.

When Drew had gone off to his Ivy League college, he'd promised to be faithful. Three months later, he broke up with her via email and didn't return to Happily Inc for two years. When he did come back, he brought the first in a long series of well-bred, pedigreed, smart coeds. After earning his MBA, he'd returned permanently with a fiancée. Ashley Lau-

ren Grantham-Greene. She'd been as snooty as her
name, more beautiful than a perfect sunrise and as
mean as a snake. It had taken Drew until four weeks
before the wedding to figure out he'd made a horrible mistake. By then Ashley had been past the point
of forgiveness. She'd trashed his car and tried to set
fire to his house. Since then, Drew had kept his private life fully private.

For her part, Silver had spent the better part of
two years getting over Drew. Pallas remembered how
her friend had nearly been destroyed by the breakup.
Not only because she'd lost the man she'd planned
to spend the rest of her life with, but also due to everyone's assumption that he'd done it because she
wasn't good enough.

She'd moved to LA after that and had, from what
Pallas had heard, traveled with a wild crowd. There
had been rumors of jail, rehab and a Bonnie-and-
Clyde-style bank robbery. Pallas didn't believe any
of it.

One day Silver had returned to Happily Inc and
started working in her uncle's bar. When he'd wanted
to sell and travel in his RV, he'd given the bar to Silver. She'd promptly sold it and used the money to
fund AlcoHaul. As for men, there was always someone interested. From what Pallas could tell, Silver
took what she wanted and walked away when she
was finished. Not exactly the actions of a woman
still pining for her first boyfriend.

"If you don't want him, I'm going to have to keep
looking for the right woman," Pallas said lightly.
"Drew needs to be married."

"Does he know about your plan?"

"No, and it's better that way. I don't want him to freak out. Plus, right now my efforts are more theoretical. I haven't put much effort into introducing him to anyone."

"Probably better for you both."

Pallas picked up her latte. "What about you? Are you looking?"

Natalie shook her head. "Thanks, but no. Love isn't in the cards for me. The women in my family have horrible luck with men." She smiled. "Just in case you try to convince me I'm different, I'll remind you that my ex-fiancé dumped me only days before the wedding."

"That was horrible. Okay, yes, he was awful but what about the right guy?"

"I'm pretty sure he doesn't exist."

PALLAS'S FAMILY HOME sat on a hillside. Even from the large, circular driveway there was an impressive view of the town and the valley beyond. Nick ignored the play of light on the rocks at the edge of acres of landscaping, reminding himself this wasn't the time to indulge his artistic side. He was here to offer support to a very nervous Pallas.

He'd known she had trouble dealing with her mother but didn't expect her to be so obviously stressed. Despite her makeup, she was pale. He would swear she was shaking in the seat next to him and as they got out of his truck, he half expected her to collapse.

"You gonna be okay?" he asked as he closed her door behind her and put his arm around her waist.

"Maybe I'd feel better if I threw up."

"You want to do that out here or inside?"

She swallowed. "While the thought of throwing up on my mother's favorite entry rug is really appealing, I'm going to try to breathe through this." She glanced at him. "I'm sorry. I'm not usually so freaked out about seeing her. I think it's the anticipation of it all. It would have been better if she'd simply sprung the invitation on me, but no. It's not her style."

"You'll be fine." He kissed her, then squeezed her waist. "So where are we on the vomiting? Now? Later?"

She managed a slight smile. "I think I'll wait so it has more of a dramatic effect."

"That's my girl." He looked at the imposing three-story house. "At least you had lots of space to run as a kid, without having to worry about going outside."

"I know. It was magical."

"Any ground rules? Topics to avoid? Things you want me to say?"

"Just don't leave my side."

"You're on. Anything else?"

"No. Just be you. And thank you again. I can't tell you how much I appreciate you being here." She squared her shoulders. "I'm braced."

"Then let us beard the dragon." He frowned. "Do you beard a dragon? That makes absolutely no sense. There's something with a dragon, though. I'm sure of it. And a den. Or maybe a cave."

She laughed and he felt her relax.

He had plenty of crap going on with his father, so he understood how family dynamics could get completely out of whack. Still, he hated seeing Pallas like this. He'd never met Libby Saunders, but he was more than willing to take her on if necessary.

They walked up the stairs to the wide, flagstone-covered porch. Everything about the house screamed old money. He supposed that came from growing up in a banking family. He didn't know anything about that, but he'd had plenty of experience living with a legacy.

"Feel free to brag on me if you'd like," he said as she knocked on the front door. "Make up stories about how great I am. Talk about me being famous and a god in bed. Moms like to know that especially."

"Are you a god in bed?"

He winked. "You're going to have to find that out for yourself."

She was still laughing when her mother opened the front door.

Libby Saunders was in her midfifties. Well-dressed in expensive knits, with pearls at her ears and around her neck. She'd aged well and he would suspect she knew it. Funny how her cruel heart didn't show on her face.

"Hi, Mom," Pallas said quietly. "This is Nick Mitchell. Nick, my mother."

"Mrs. Saunders."

"Please, call me Libby." She gave him a tight smile and neither shook his hand nor hugged her daughter. Instead she stepped back to let them in the house. "How nice of you to join us for our family dinner."

There was just enough emphasis on the word *family* to make it clear he wasn't welcome. Pallas stiffened. He grabbed her hand and squeezed.

"Pallas always talks about you, so I've been looking forward to us meeting," he said easily. "Plus Cade's home, and who isn't excited about that?"

Libby looked momentarily confused, as if she weren't sure if she'd been insulted or not, and then was distracted by the Cade remark.

"Yes, it's wonderful to have him back."

They walked through a foyer the size of the average house, then into a big open room with a stag-sized fireplace at one end. There were multiple conversation areas, a half dozen or so sofas and a bar set up along one long buffet.

Grandpa Frank, as the older man had insisted he be called at the Concord Awaken party, came over to greet Nick.

"I heard you were coming," he said, shaking hands. "Good. The more the merrier, and if they're not family, all the better." He winked at Pallas. "How's my best girl?"

"Good, Grandpa. How are you feeling?"

"Spry and sassy."

Two men about Nick's age joined them. He recognized Cade from seeing him with Pallas. Up close Nick could see the shared physical characteristics. Their cousin Drew was a little taller, with dark hair and eyes.

After introductions were made, Drew pointed to the bar. "What can I get you two to drink?"

"I'll take a beer," Nick said, trying not to chuckle as Libby flinched.

"Chardonnay," Pallas murmured.

"I'd like a beer, too," Cade told his cousin.

"Darling, no," Libby protested. "Surely you'd like something more…" She paused when all four men stared at her. "Whatever you'd like is fine," she managed before turning away.

Pallas leaned close. "Rebellion in the ranks," she whispered. "You're the best family dinner boyfriend ever."

"I'm just getting started. Don't you worry."

The four men ended up with bottles of beer while Libby and Pallas each had a glass of white wine. Everyone sat on sofas in one of the seating areas, except for Cade, who chose a chair. Nick wondered about the staff required to run a house this big. Just keeping up with dusting would take days.

This so wasn't his style. Despite Ceallach's success, his family had lived pretty much like everyone else in Fool's Gold. The house Nick had grown up in had been a sprawling ranch style on a large lot. Nothing like this estate.

He wondered what it had been like for Pallas to grow up here. She and Cade sure would have had plenty of room to play, but had that upside come with a darker corner? Had she been lonely? Felt cut off from her friends?

Libby glanced at him. "So, Nick, what do you do?"

He smiled. "Right now I'm between gigs. I'm

working part-time as a carpenter for Pallas at her business."

Libby's mouth compressed into a moue of disapproval. "I see." She turned to her son. "Cade, darling, now that you're back, you'll have to take over one of the wings here at the house. A young man needs his freedom."

"That he does," Cade told her. "I'm going to be staying at the ranch house."

"That old place? It's practically falling down."

"I had a new roof put on it last fall," Grandpa Frank told his daughter. "Libby, Cade isn't going to live here with us. Like you said—the boy needs his freedom."

"But I enjoy having you around." Libby's expression softened. "I never get to see you anymore. You've been gone for so long. I miss our talks."

Cade shifted in his seat. "Ah, me, too, Mom. You'll see me plenty, now that I've moved back."

"It won't be enough. Nothing is right when you're not here."

Out of the corner of his eye, Nick saw Pallas flinch. No, that wasn't right—it was more as if she'd retreated into herself. Who could blame her—with Libby making it clear Cade was her favorite.

"At least your business will be successful," Libby said, still pouting. "Your sister is barely able to keep hers afloat. I offered her a chance to come to the bank, but she turned me down. Can you believe it?"

"Libby," Grandpa Frank growled. "Leave the girl alone."

"It's true," Libby protested. "Ask her."

Nick put his beer on the coffee table and leaned forward. "I'm hungry. Is there anything to eat?"

Libby turned her him, her eyes wide. No doubt she was shocked at his rudeness. His mother would be, too, but hell, someone had to be a distraction.

"There are appetizers." Libby rose. "Let me go check on them."

As soon as she left, Grandpa Frank moved next to Pallas and started talking in a low tone. At the same time Cade shifted his chair closer to Nick's.

"Who are you?" he asked, sounding more neutral than his mother.

"I work for Pallas."

"Aside from that?"

Nick held in a smile. He liked knowing that Cade looked out for his sister. "We're friends."

"Are you really a part-time carpenter?"

Drew joined them. "He's an artist. A famous one. Don't let him play you."

"What was your name again?" Cade asked.

"Nick Mitchell." He looked at Drew. "I'm not famous."

"Sure. When was the last time you needed to work a real job?"

Nick had worked as a bartender back in Fool's Gold, but that had been by choice, not necessity.

"It's been a while," he admitted.

Cade turned to his cousin. "Can you look up his balance at the bank and let me know he's legit?"

"Should we talk about the dozens of laws being broken as we speak?" Nick asked lightly.

Drew grinned. "It's two against one. You might want to get along."

"Not my style."

Cade and Drew exchanged a glance. Drew raised a shoulder. "From what I hear, he's a good guy."

"Good enough for our girl?"

Nick thought about pointing out that he and Pallas weren't actually an item. Not technically. He liked her. He liked being around her and spending time with her. She was special. He looked forward to seeing her and—

He swore silently. They *were* an item. When had that happened? He turned and saw her looking at him. He winked and she smiled.

Libby returned with a tray of prosciutto-wrapped melon, along with stuffed mushrooms.

"I hope these meet with your approval," she told him. "It's so hard to know what goes with beer."

"Pretty much anything." He reached for a mushroom. "They look delicious."

Libby's pinched look of disapproval stayed firmly in place. Cade stood and put his arm around her.

"Mom, you've got it all wrong. Nick's a great guy. He's famous."

"I doubt that."

Grandpa Frank nodded. "It's true. You've heard of his father, if not him. Ceallach Mitchell. He's that glass artist guy."

Nick was torn between wondering how Grandpa Frank knew about his father and wondering what his old man would think about being called "that glass artist guy."

"Ceallach Mitchell is your father?" Libby sank down next to him, her gaze much friendlier than it had been. "I had no idea. You're an artist, too?" She turned to Pallas. "Did you know?"

"Yes. He has pieces in Atsuko's gallery. Although technically he is my part-time carpenter, it's just because he fell madly in love with the panels at Weddings in a Box."

Her mother sighed. "As usual, I have no idea what you're talking about."

Nick squashed his flare of annoyance. "You haven't been to your only daughter's office?" he asked, deliberately making his voice thick with disbelief. "It's a great place. She's very creative and that must make you proud."

He reached for his beer. "The wooden panels that I'm restoring are exquisite. The carving is all hand done. Don't get me started on the style or details. I'll never stop talking." He took a sip. "Anyway, I'm working on them because something that special needs to be treasured. Pallas could sell them and make a small fortune, but you know her. She has too much character for that. She'd rather keep them for the business. It's one of the reasons I'm happy we're together. Because she's strong and capable and I admire her."

Libby stared at him with an uncomfortable combination of worship, confusion and annoyance. Pallas was trying not to giggle, while Drew and Cade silently toasted him behind Libby's back.

"Yes, well, that's very interesting," Libby said, returning to her original seat. "Good for you. Drew, tell everyone about the new banking regulations. They're going to change things for sure."

Predinner drinks dragged on for over an hour. By the time they finally went in to dinner, Nick was genuinely starving. Based on the couple of appetizers he'd sampled, the meal was going to be worth the wait, but still, talk about a command performance.

Fortunately, Libby hadn't turned on Pallas again, so Nick had been able to simply sit back and listen. Libby kept watching him, as if she wasn't sure if he was someone she should respect or worry about stealing the good silver.

Pallas linked her arm through his as they walked into the huge dining room. The table could have easily seated twenty. The six of them were clustered at one end.

"It's nice to know you admire me," she teased.

"I actually do."

"You're being great. I will owe you forever. Seriously, thank you for all of this."

"My pleasure." He was about to say he hadn't had to make up anything about her when he saw all the family portraits lining the dining room walls.

There were dozens of them in solid wood frames. He moved closer and saw there was indeed coordinated clothing differentiating the various parts of the family.

"Cool tradition," he said. "This is what you were telling me about."

Too late he realized his mistake as Libby walked toward him. "I'm sure Pallas hasn't told you *all* about them," she said, pointing to one of the pictures. "Like that one."

Right. The picture Pallas had been banned from because she wouldn't wear the correct shirt.

"The one where she's missing?" he asked, walking to the picture. He studied it, noting that a much-younger Cade didn't look very happy in the photograph and Pallas was nowhere to be found.

He turned back to Libby. "Looking at that must break your heart. I'm sure if you could go back in time, you'd do everything in your power to make sure your only daughter was a part of the family memory."

Libby's gleeful expression fell a little.

He crossed to Pallas and pulled out her chair. When she was seated, he sat next to her and lightly kissed her on the mouth.

"Thank you," she mouthed.

"I got this," he whispered back.

He didn't understand the family dynamics, but that didn't matter. What was important was that Pallas needed protecting and he was just the man to do it.

## CHAPTER TEN

By THE TIME they started the drive home, Pallas was feeling less smug about Nick standing up for her and more embarrassed by her family. No—not her family. Her mother.

It had always been like this between them, she thought grimly. Libby poked and prodded, looking for a weak spot, and then she pounced. Pallas didn't think her mother was deliberately cruel or mean, but there sure was something going on. Something that ended with Pallas hurt and Libby disappointed.

"You were great," she told Nick as they left the Saunders property. "I appreciate the support and the way you stood up for me." She pressed a hand to her cheek. "Which is kind of the same thing. How much wine did I have?"

"Not that much. I was happy to be there and act as your dinner boyfriend buffer." He paused. "Your mom is interesting."

"That's one way to put it."

"I wonder what happened to her when she was little."

"What do you mean?"

"Libby has some issues. A lot of what she's doing doesn't seem like it's about you. You're just the familiar punching bag, and she's reacting without thinking. Whatever demons she's wrestling are about her." He glanced over and smiled in the dim light of the car. "Of course, I'm a guy. I could be wrong about all of this."

Pallas stared at him. "Oh my God! I can't believe you said that. No, I can't believe I never thought of it before. What if you're right? What if it isn't about me at all? I could never please her but I always thought I wasn't good enough. What if it was never about me?"

She'd fought with her mother, had tried to please her mother, had thought about leaving, the way Cade had, but never seemed to find the courage. The one constant in her life had been her difficult relationship with her mother. What if none of that had been about her?

"My head is spinning," she admitted. "I'm going to have to think on that. A lot." Mostly when there hadn't been wine with dinner.

"Family is tough," he said. "I'm glad you have Drew and Cade to protect you."

"They're good guys," she said with a sigh. "Cade was always there when Mom got on me. Drew, too, although he didn't live with us. It helped a lot."

"It was the same with my brothers," he told her. "We had each other's backs. Del and Aidan weren't interested in working with Ceallach, so our dad pretty much ignored them. I knew that had to hurt. Ronan, Mathias and I got all the attention, which was both a blessing and a curse."

"Plus your dad had the excuse of an artistic temperament." Something Nick would never say, she thought. He was incredibly gifted, yet acted so normal.

"You have no idea," he said, turning by the river. "Remember when I told you about the show my dad and I did together? It was all glass. It was in New York. I'd never been, but Dad had. We stayed in a huge suite with views of Central Park. There were parties every night. My dad ate it up. He was the reason they were all there and made sure everyone remembered that."

Just hearing about it made Pallas uncomfortable. What he described was so not her thing. "But did you enjoy it?"

"At first. There was a lot of attention."

She smiled. "By that we mean women?"

"Maybe." He chuckled. "Yes. I was way out of my league. I dated my first model. They really don't eat very much at all."

"What a surprise," she murmured drily. "What about a threesome with twins?"

"They weren't twins."

She swung her head to stare at him. "Seriously? For real?"

"Yeah, it wasn't my thing."

Good to know. For a second she thought about asking how a threesome worked, exactly. Because once a man was done, he was unavailable for at least some period of time. Of course Nick had been in his twenties and it *had* been a threesome, so maybe...

"Best not to go there," he told her.

"I think you're right. So who else?"

"There was an actress. I fell hard for her. We dated for three months, then she dumped me on a national talk show. Told the host she was totally over me. I was waiting in her dressing room, along with the rest of her entourage. From their lack of surprise, I was the last one to know."

"That's horrible." Breakups were difficult enough but to have one happen that way... She couldn't imagine it.

Nick pulled into her driveway. He turned off the engine, then angled toward her. "I'm fine. It was years ago. I learned my lesson and went home. My point is all families are weird in their own way. Some just happen to be a lot closer to crazy than others."

He touched the side of her face. "At the end of the day, you're doing what you love and you're doing a hell of a job at it. You have friends and people who love you. Don't let your mom get you down."

Was it just her or was Nick the best guy ever? Before she could decide, he pulled her close and kissed her.

His mouth was warm against hers, his lips firm yet tender. He kissed her slowly, deeply, offering as much as he took. The truck console was between them, so she couldn't get as close as she would like, but even just kissing was pretty darned fun. His mouth was warm, as was his body. Plus the man had protected her—it was a powerful aphrodisiac.

He drew back and smiled at her. "So here's the thing. I'd love to come in."

Her body went on alert, then surrendered. Desire rushed through her, making her girl parts all tingly. Then panic set it. Was her house a mess? Were her sheets clean? When had she last shaved? Would he mind if she brushed her teeth first?

"But," he continued, "I have this feeling you need more time. Am I wrong?"

No! No. Of course not. Who needed time? She opened her mouth to say that, but what came out was, "A little."

She held in a groan. Had she really said that? "What I mean is—"

He cut her off with another kiss that rocked her down to her toes. Then he straightened. "You're worth waiting for, Pallas. You have to know that."

With that, he got out of the truck and went around to her side. He walked her to her door, waited for her to unlock it, then pulled her close.

His strong arms held her tight. She responded in kind, wrapping her arms around him. He was tall and broad, and when she was with him, she felt safe. Protected.

She liked being with him. She liked watching him work and brainstorming with him about her business. Funny how he'd only been in town a short time yet she felt as if she'd known him forever. Or at least a long time.

He moved his hands up and down her back, then cupped her face and kissed her. "Have a good night," he whispered.

"You, too."

"I'll see you tomorrow."

His mouth brushed against hers one more time, then he walked back to his truck and left. Pallas closed the door behind her and set her purse and keys on the small hall table. As she walked to her bedroom, she wondered why Nick had such a different and better view of her than she had of herself. It was as if he saw who she could be rather than who she was right now. An interesting concept and one she needed to consider.

THE FIRST PART of the week passed in a blur. Pallas was scrambling to get the last-minute details for the black-and-white wedding finalized. Catherine was basically a sweet person, but in the last month, she'd definitely drifted into bridezilla territory. The 2:00 a.m. texting was starting to get old.

Only seventy-two more hours, give or take, she told herself on Wednesday afternoon, as she drove to Wynn's office. Then the black-and-white wedding would be history. In the meantime she was going to be on a video conference call with Nova, Wynn, Violet, Silver and Nick. They were all bringing samples and ideas for the next stage of preparation.

She met Violet in the parking lot, struggling with two large boxes and a huge suitcase on wheels.

"Did you bring every button you own?" Pallas asked with a laugh as she rushed to help her friend.

"You mock my buttons, but they will save the day. You'll see."

"I can't wait for that to happen."

Pallas slung her tote bag over her shoulder and helped Violet wrestle the smaller box toward Wynn's shop. They were halfway across the parking lot when a familiar truck pulled up next to them. Pallas felt a little quiver in her stomach. She'd known Nick was going to be at the meeting, yet still felt a thrill at seeing him. A nice little bonus in her workday.

He rolled down his window. "Ladies, could you use a man?"

"Yes, but I suspect you're not offering that," Violet told him. "At least not to me."

Pallas ignored her friend. "I want to tell you we're self-actualized and totally capable, but some help would be nice."

"Set down the box and step aside," he told them.

They did as he requested. While Violet wheeled the suitcase into the shop, Nick carried in each of the boxes.

Wynn had a small office set up for video conferencing. There was a table and eight chairs, a dry-erase board and a large flat-screen television mounted on the wall.

Pallas helped Violet unpack the boxes. She'd brought in what looked like skirts, only they weren't that structured and they had layers of colors.

"Overlays," Violet told her. "I'm still playing with how everything should look. Nova and I have been emailing and I need her to pick a direction."

She'd also made a half-dozen sample headpieces for the bridesmaids. Wynn carried in rolls of paper that she set on the table. Nick opened a box of papier-mâché flowers. Silver arrived right after him with a large cooler in each hand.

"I feel like a slacker," Pallas admitted, taking her seat at the table. All she had was a tablet and a pad of paper.

"You'll work plenty hard the day of the wedding," Wynn pointed out. "While the rest of us are getting drunk."

"I won't get drunk until later." Silver patted her arm.

"Alcohol suddenly seems to be a theme," Pallas murmured. "Should I be worried?"

"Definitely," Violet told her.

They all took their seats at the table. At two thirty, Wynn logged in to her conference program, then turned on the television. A couple of seconds later, Nova appeared on the screen.

"Hi, everyone," the bride-to-be called, her dark eyes bright with excitement.

"Hey, Nova."

"Joel and I are so thrilled about all of this. Thank you so much for your help."

"We're loving it," Pallas told her. "This has been a really fun creative challenge."

"I'm glad. So how do you want to do this?"

Everyone turned to Pallas, as if she was in charge. Which she kind of was.

"Let's go around the table and talk about what we have planned. We're at the point where we have to make decisions and get things ordered. After you've reviewed all the options, I'll run through a tentative schedule for the day." She tapped her pad. "I sent you the file this morning."

Nova waved several sheets of paper. "I have it right here." She giggled. "It's really happening. I'm so excited."

Pallas nodded at Wynn. "Why don't you go first?"

Wynn got up and moved to the back of the conference room, where she unrolled the first four-foot by two-foot posters. It showed a landscape done in purple, teal and black, which should have been dark and creepy. Instead the plants and mountains and sky were surreal but with an elegant twist.

"Can you see it?" Wynn asked, shifting to center the poster in front of the camera.

"I can. I love it. That's perfect."

"Don't say that yet," Wynn told her. "I have three more options. Once you pick your favorite ones, I'll have them blown up into giant size, and then put in the frames we bought. They'll line the walls at the ceremony, then be moved outside for the reception."

Pallas made notes as Wynn and Nova discussed each option. Nick weighed in and in a matter of minutes, a choice was made.

"I'm next," Violet said. "Let's start with the overskirt. I've been playing with different ideas. I think some kind of belt with a hook and loop closure would work best. That way the bridesmaids can take it off for the reception, if they want."

She showed Nova the layered skirt in different weights of fabric and different color combinations.

"I also made this," Violet said, pulling a hairpiece

out of a box. The style was intricate and matched that of the female warriors in the game. Twisted braids created a series of ovals. She'd added silk flowers in the video game colors.

"I know it's kind of over-the-top, but I couldn't help myself. I also have these." She held up the more traditional headpieces with ribbons and flowers.

"Oh, wow." Nova pressed her hands together. "Can you put one on Pallas and another on Wynn? So I can see what they look like on a real person?"

Nick leaned close to Pallas. "She picked you first because you're the prettiest," he whispered. "I'd pick you first, too."

Pallas smiled at him and hoped she didn't blush. Violet got a brush out of her bag and walked around the table. After pulling Pallas's hair back into a low ponytail, she slipped the wig on her head and adjusted it. Without a mirror, Pallas had no idea how she looked, which was disconcerting, especially with everyone studying her intently.

"I like it," Nova said. "Now you, Wynn."

The headpiece sat easily on the top of her head.

"It's pretty," Silver said, her voice doubtful.

"But not as special," Nick added. "I like Pallas's better. What do you think, Nova?"

"I agree. Let me talk to my bridesmaids and find out how they're going to be wearing their hair. If they're game for the wig, we'll go that way."

Pallas pulled off the wig and shook out her hair. Nick was up next. He set three papier-mâché flowers on the table.

"I'm going to make thirty or so of each, then group them around the venue." He showed her the different colors, then explained how he would use black light paint, as well.

"I'm still working on the power orbs. I'm not sure how to make them glow."

"I love the flowers," Violet told him. "They're amazing."

"Thanks." He held up a three foot by two foot pad of drawing paper and centered it in front of the camera. "Brace yourself. Here are my ideas for your wedding dress."

"No!" Violet's voice was a whimper. "It's a designer gown. You can't paint it."

"Breathe," Silver said with a laugh. "Just breathe."

Violet covered her face with her hands. "I can't look."

Nick flipped to the first page on the pad. Everyone gasped, including Pallas. She stared at the sketch of the dress done in simple lines. What caught her attention were the bold strokes of purple, teal and black against the white lace and nude netting. Nick had followed the lines of the lace to create a swirling pattern similar to the backdrop on Wynn's posters. There were three other options, variations on design and color.

"The skin-colored background will ground the brighter tones," he said. "The colors will stand out, but I'll leave in enough white to give the illusion of a wedding gown."

"It is a wedding gown," Violet pointed out. "There's no illusion."

"Let it go," Wynn told her. "It's not traditional, but it's stunning."

"I agree," Pallas added. "But only one vote counts."

They looked at the screen. Nova wiped away tears.

"Nick, you've turned my dress into the most beautiful gown I've ever seen. I like all the options but the third one is my favorite. Can you really do that?"

He flipped back to the right page and they went over the details. Pallas studied the design and guessed it would take him hours to get the individual threads painted. If he was willing to do the work, then Nova would have the wedding gown of her dreams.

They wrapped up the meeting with a discussion of signature drink options and set a date for a virtual tasting. If Nova couldn't get into town herself, they would have a second conference call where she could see the various options and everyone would taste them and offer thoughts. By four, they were finished.

"Good work, everyone," Pallas said as they walked out of the conference room. She'd never planned so much of a wedding remotely before, but thought they had the main items handled.

"Ready for Saturday?" Violet asked.

Her happy mood faded, leaving her feeling slightly anxious.

"Yes."

"That wasn't a happy yes," Nick said. "It's the black-and-white wedding. There will be zebras. How can anything go wrong if there are zebras?"

Pallas winced. "Let's not tempt fate." She squared her shoulders and smiled at Violet. "I'm ready. It's more the bride who's the problem. She's become a bit difficult."

Violet sighed. "Better you than me. If I was working with a snippy bride, I'd be tempted to stab her with a hat pin. Of course then I wouldn't get a very good online review. It's probably for the best that it's you and not me. Let me know if I can help with anything." She wrinkled her nose. "Except for the zebras. That's more my sister's thing than mine."

Silver joined them. "If it makes you feel any better, the signature drinks are fantastic, if I do say so myself. I'll save you a batch."

Pallas laughed. "Thank you. Should things go awry, I'll comfort myself with the promise of liquor at the end of the day."

SATURDAY MORNING PALLAS woke early to an unfamiliar sound. She still had fifteen minutes before her alarm went off but the noise was so strange, she got up to investigate. Halfway down the hall she came to a stop as her sleepy brain provided the most horrifying possibility. She raced to the living room, where she tore back the drapes and screamed.

"Rain?"

No. No! It couldn't rain. It never rained. They were in the desert. She had an outdoor reception that very afternoon. And zebras. It couldn't be raining.

An hour later she stood under the Juliet balcony at Weddings in a Box and stared at the puddles forming in the parking lot. Alan drove up and waved. He joined her, offering her a take-out coffee and a pink box.

"I brought donuts. The good ones, too. No plain cake donuts for us on wedding day."

His voice was cheerful, his smile broad.

"How can you be so calm?" she demanded. "It's raining."

"No worries. The weather channel says the showers will pass in an hour or two, and then it will be sunny."

"But it's rain. We're not supposed to get rain here. We don't need rain. We get our water from an aquafer, like God intended. This is bad, Alan. It's an omen."

"You don't believe in omens."

"I've never had rain on the day of a wedding before. Not in the past eight years." Happily Inc got rain in the winter. Or on weekdays. They averaged less than six inches a year, which was perfectly fine because they had a giant aquafer with millions and billions of gallons of water. They weren't supposed to get rain. Not on black-and-white wedding day.

Alan guided her into the building. "It's all right, Pallas. We're going to drink our coffee and eat donuts, then plan out the day. By then, the rain will be gone. April showers bring May flowers."

"It's already May."

"Yes it is, Miss Grumpy-Pants. You need some sugar and caffeine. Then everything will look better."

"What if the rain is Gerald's way of saying he's mad at me for doing things differently with this wedding?"

Alan kissed her forehead. "Darling, that's not possible. Gerald loved you. You could never make him angry or disappoint him. Of that I'm sure."

The words were comforting. Pallas told herself to keep breathing and that all would be well. If not, she and Silver had a date for cocktails later.

By the time they'd eaten a couple of donuts, Pallas had to admit she was feeling a little more positive about the day. Having the rain stop helped, as did Nick showing up.

He grabbed the last donut and sat next to them at one of the reception area tables.

"Gotta love the rain," he said as he smiled at Pallas. "It clears out the air. It's going to be a beautiful afternoon and evening."

She liked that he was an optimist. She didn't believe him for a second, but she liked it. "I'm worried the rain is an omen."

Alan sighed heavily. "Someone has taken a walk on Crazy Street this morning."

"I haven't. I'm just concerned. There are a lot of moving parts to this wedding and we never get rain."

"There are always a lot of moving parts," Nick pointed out, his tone gentle. "And rain is a sign of life. In many cultures and regions rain at a wedding is considered good luck."

"Name one."

"Hindu."

She glared at him. "You know I have to go look that up, right?"

"Trust me. It's okay. The wedding is going to be great. You're good at your job. Trust me, trust yourself and relax."

Great advice, she thought two hours later when Carol arrived with the zebras, who were unamused about being transported.

"I'm glad we're doing this early," Carol told her. "They're going to need some time to settle down before people start arriving and taking pictures of them."

The three zebras had been transported in a large horse trailer. Even from several feet away, Pallas could hear the sound of their restless hooves on the floor of the carrier.

"How did you get them inside?" she asked.

Carol grinned. "All my animals will work for food. They have a favorite treat they like. Millie, the giraffe, will practically roll over for a Marionberry leaf-eater treat. The zebras were bribed."

She and Carol walked to the temporarily fenced-in area that had been installed. Pallas pointed out the huge tub of water in one corner.

"I'll make sure that stays filled," she said. "I have a special zebra watering person on duty."

"You can release that worry," Carol told her. "Zebras can go several days without drinking."

"I thought that was camels." Pallas held up a hand. "Never mind. We can explore mammals and their drinking habits later. I have a wedding to put on." She glanced at her watch and then at the parking lot beside Weddings in a Box. Right on time Cade pulled up in his truck.

"Help has arrived," she said.

Carol laughed. "Oh, good. A cowboy. Just what

I need." She walked to the trailer. "I mean that sincerely, by the way, although I have a feeling the zebras are going to freak him out."

Cade walked up in time to hear the last comment. He shook his head. "Nothing on four legs can best me."

"Brag much?" Pallas asked, giving him a quick hug. "Okay, I'm drowning. I need to know that you two will handle the zebra situation for me."

"We've got it," Carol assured her. "Go have a nice wedding. I'm already happy—the check cleared and now I can afford Millie's pricey treats."

Pallas waved at them, then hurried back toward the main venue. She'd barely reached the edge of the parking lot when a stretch limo pulled up.

Catherine was early. Pallas liked when a bride was on time and early was even better. Maybe she'd been wrong thinking the rain was a bad omen.

Only the second the rear door of the limo opened and Catherine stepped out, Pallas realized she'd relaxed just a little too soon. The tall, willowy blonde's face was red and puffy from crying. Several attendants followed, each looking more than a little shaken.

"What's wrong?" Pallas asked.

"Everything. I hate my dress. I don't know why I bought it. Have you seen the flowers? I haven't, but I know they're a disaster. I'm not even sure I still love Byron. What was I thinking? I want to call off the wedding."

Pallas ignored the sudden pile of rocks sitting in

her stomach, along with the rush of panic. She'd been through this before. Brides frequently slipped over the edge on their wedding day. She was a pro and knew exactly what to do.

She took Catherine by her arm. "Let's get you inside. Have you eaten today? You look pale. Maybe some tea and toast will help. Then we'll talk about everything that's wrong and fix it." She turned to the bridesmaids. "Is her dress in the trunk? Please bring it inside."

She got Catherine settled in the bride's room, then texted Alan. He appeared almost immediately and hurried to Catherine's side.

"Oh, my dear, what you're going through. How are you holding up?" He studied her blotchy face and straight hair. "Where are your beauty people? When are they due to arrive? Should I call and yell at them for you? I'm very good at it." He took her hand in his. "You're like ice. My goodness, who is taking care of you? Let me get you a soft blanket and some tea. You're the bride. You can't be expected to handle everything yourself. Let me help."

Catherine visibly relaxed. Pallas exhaled a breath she hadn't realized she'd been holding. Alan would work his magic on the bride, as he always did. The wedding would go forward and all would be well. The skies were clear and they had zebras. Everything was going to be just fine. She was sure of it.

THE AFTERNOON PASSED QUICKLY. Alan stayed with Catherine, the beauty team arrived and did their thing. At five, the ushers were seating the guests, and at five forty-five, the beautiful bride walked down the aisle. Pallas stood in the back next to Alan as they watched the ceremony move smoothly forward.

"See," he whispered. "It's fine."

"You were right."

"Three of my favorite words. I'm going to make you repeat them again and again."

Pallas left to check on the catering. Silver had her trailer set up and was mixing the signature drinks; the bride's specially hired DJ had already started setting up his equipment. Nick, who only needed to be a courtier for the procession, had already changed back into street clothes.

"Feeling better?" he asked.

"Much. I still think the server costumes are a little slutty, but that wasn't my call. We have food, we have drinks, we have music." She glanced over to where the DJ had set up his equipment. "I'm going to start breathing more deeply now."

"Good." Nick put his arm around her. "Want me to take your picture with the zebras?"

"Maybe later. Do they seem calm? They were tense when they arrived."

"I gave them valium. They're fine."

She spun toward him and grabbed his arm. "Don't joke about that. I mean it. I'm one crisis away from snapping."

"Sorry. No drugging zebra jokes, although that really kills my best material."

Pallas returned to the main building and waited

for the service to end. She made sure everyone made their way to the reception area and was grateful when Catherine gave her a thumbs-up.

While the wedding party took postceremony pictures, Pallas made sure the guests had plenty to drink and that the appetizers were circulating briskly. She was so focused on that she almost didn't hear the loud shrieks from the far side of the open area. Almost.

"Oh no! They're loose."

Pallas hurried to the gates just in time to see three zebras running down the road.

"Should have let me drug them," Nick murmured as Carol and Cade got in his truck and hurried after them. Pallas spotted four teenage boys laughing by the temporary fencing. She narrowed her gaze and started toward them.

Nick grabbed her arm. "Slow down there, little lady. What are you going to say?"

"That they're jerks and they have to leave."

He didn't respond—instead he held her gaze until she slumped against him. "You're right. I can't yell at them—they're with the wedding party. I hate this. The rain was an omen. What do we do now? How can we help Cade and Carol get back the zebras?"

"Aren't there horse people who work at the ranch?"

She brightened. "Yes. You're right. I'll call them. I'm sure Cade has thought of it, so I'll check with him first."

Nick took her cell phone from her. "Let me do that. You focus on the wedding."

"Thank you." She turned back to the guests only to see Silver walking toward her. Her friend didn't look happy. "What's wrong?"

"My vodka stash is missing. I don't know who took it but based on the number of bottles, we're going to have some very drunk people around in the next hour." Silver crossed her arms over her chest. "It's my own damn fault. I didn't lock the cabinet. I always lock the cabinet. I don't get it. That's not like me."

"It's the rain," Pallas told her. "I thought everything was going to be okay, but it's not."

"At least the wedding is behind us. We only have a few hours until the reception is over. We'll get through it."

Pallas hoped she was right.

The meal service went off without a hitch, as did the toast. Right before the first dance, small cups filled with rose petals were passed out for the guests to throw at the bride and groom. Sadly one of the grandmothers must have gotten into the vodka because instead of throwing rose petals, she tossed her cup of coffee right on Catherine's dress. The bride's shrieks were loud enough to wake the dead.

Pallas and Alan got most of the stain out and dried her off as best they could. She returned to the reception, ready to have her first dance. The DJ got on the microphone and asked everyone to gather around for the special moment.

"The first dance symbolizes the true love between a man and a woman," he told them. "But in this case, not so much." He pulled a handgun out of his jacket pocket and pointed it toward the guests. "This is a robbery, people. I want your money, your keys and your cell phones."

Pallas almost wasn't surprised. Who knew rain could be so dangerous.

## CHAPTER ELEVEN

PALLAS DIDN'T GET out of the police station until nearly four in the morning. By the time everyone had told their story, the DJ and his getaway driver had been apprehended and all the stolen items had been returned. The gun had turned out to be a paint gun instead of the real thing, which was a little comforting. Still, despite the almost-happy ending—how much better things would have been if there hadn't been a robbery at all—she was tired and hungry and had a killer headache. Nick walked with her, his hand on the small of her back.

While she appreciated the support and that he'd stayed with her through the incredibly long ordeal of helping Catherine and her parents press charges, as well as giving a statement, she was honestly too exhausted to express much more than a heartfelt "Thanks for staying."

"Happy to be there." He pulled her close and kissed the top of her head. "You beating yourself up about what happened?"

"Maybe. Sort of." She leaned against him. "Everything about the day was a disaster."

"Not true."

"What went right?"

"The ceremony, the weather, the food. We got the zebras back."

Cade had texted a few hours before to say all three were safely in their barn.

"They shouldn't have escaped in the first place."

"You aren't responsible for that," he told her. "Jerks did it."

"I should have thought to have a lock on the gate. Only who lets out zebras?"

They passed Catherine, crying in her new husband's arms. The harsh streetlights made the coffee stain on her dress stand out even more. Pallas looked away.

When they reached Nick's truck, he helped her inside. He drove out of the parking lot but instead of heading for her neighborhood, or even Weddings in a Box, he drove toward the highway.

"Are we running away?"

"No, we're getting you something to eat. You haven't had anything since breakfast yesterday. You're starving and probably have a headache."

"I do," she said, rubbing her temple.

"There's a fast-food place by the off-ramp that's open twenty-four hours a day."

"I'm impressed that you know that."

"Sometimes work goes late. It helps to know things like that."

"Apparently." She leaned back in her seat. "I can't believe everything that happened. Did you see the stain on Catherine's dress? I'm sure her grandmother feels horrible. Did I tell you Silver texted me to say everything was closed up? She and Alan stayed and took care of that. I owe them."

"You have good friends."

"I do." She looked out the side window at the dark and empty streets. "At least we're going to have quite the story to tell. One day this will be funny."

"It's kind of funny now."

"Not for me."

She was upset and embarrassed about everything that had gone wrong. Zebras? Really? What had she been thinking? Sure they'd been a favorite with the guests, but they'd gotten loose. She should have paid attention to the rain. It had been an omen for sure.

Nick stopped in front of the drive-through window. "They're serving breakfast. What are you in the mood for?"

She ordered an egg sandwich and coffee. Despite her exhaustion, she was going to have to go to work and check on everything. Then she could go home and get some sleep.

After paying for their order, Nick drove back to her place. They went inside and put their food on the kitchen table. Pallas started a pot of coffee because a single cup wasn't going to be close to enough.

They ate in silence for a few minutes, then Nick put down his breakfast sandwich. "What are you thinking?"

"That I should have listened to the rain."

"Was it talking?"

She managed a slight smile. "It was making noises, warning me of the danger to come." She picked up her coffee. "I feel stupid," she admitted. "I'm supposed to be good at my job."

"You are."

"The wedding got out of control."

"It didn't." He held up one hand and raised a finger. "First, a couple of guys let out the zebras, not you."

"I should have anticipated that."

"That drunk idiots would release zebras into an area where there were cars? No one could anticipate that."

"I should have locked the gate. If not to keep the zebras from getting out then to keep someone from going in."

"Carol and Cade were there. Why didn't they stop the guys?"

"They were off getting something to eat." She sighed. "I should have told them to eat in shifts." She looked at him. "I'm sorry, but you can't talk me out of the zebra guilt. It's all mine."

"I don't accept that, but I'm willing to move on. You're not responsible for what happened to the dress."

Pallas winced. "That was awful, but you're right. Not my fault."

"The DJ isn't, either. The bride and groom brought him in. You didn't recommend him."

He was right but... "How do you know?"

"You would have checked him out. You won't hire just anyone to be a vendor."

A really good point, except... "Oh, no. I hired you to be a Roman guard and I didn't know you at all. What if you'd been a serial killer?"

"You are tired, aren't you?"

"Is that your polite way of saying I'm not making sense?"

When Nick didn't say anything, Pallas got her answer. Talk about embarrassing.

"Ignoring what went wrong, did you like having different elements in the wedding?" he asked.

"I thought it was kind of fun. I'm not sure I'd do zebras again, but it was nice not to have everything be the same."

"Good. Then if there's a message from the universe, it's the alien wedding. You're being told to branch out and try new things."

Pallas wasn't sure universe messages were that clear, but she got his message. She did like working with her friends. The brainstorming was fun, as was watching it all come together.

"I do like helping them," she admitted. "Nova and Joel are darling and her dad is incredibly brave. I want to see them get married."

She sipped her coffee. "I wonder if there are special needs couples out there and if I could help with those weddings." She shook her head. "I'm not making any sense, am I?"

"You are. I think you should get some sleep, then figure it all out in a few hours."

"I have to go to the office."

"Not at five on Sunday morning."

"Oh." He might be right. After all, Silver and Alan had locked up Wedding in a Box. She could check things out later.

She collected their trash and threw it out. Nick

rose and walked around the table. He drew her close and wrapped his arms around her.

"Does that 'oh' mean you agree with me?" he asked. "That there's nothing that can't wait until sometime this afternoon?"

Before she could figure out an answer, he leaned in and kissed her. And then an answer didn't seem all that important. Her brain was so fuzzy and the exhaustion, when combined with the delicious feel of his mouth on hers, scrambled any coherent thought.

She looped her arms around his neck and leaned into him, then sighed as he deepened the kiss. His tongue caressed hers with slow strokes that made her tired brain even less lucid. Heat poured through her, chasing away a bit of the tired but not doing anything for her ability to think. She couldn't remember why going to the office had seemed so important, because it wasn't. She should listen to Nick and get some sleep. Or maybe just stay here in his arms, because that was nice, too.

His hands moved up and down her back. She liked the way he dipped lower each time until his hands cupped her butt. She arched toward him, bringing her belly into contact with his groin. It took her a second to realize that hard ridge wasn't some designer element in his jeans. It was him. Aroused.

Her eyes popped open and she stared at him. Before she could stop herself, she blurted, "You want to have sex!"

Nick gave her a sexy smile designed to bring her to her knees. "Sure. I'm with you, aren't I?"

She blinked, trying to get the words to make

sense. Because the way he'd said them, it sounded as if he *always* wanted to have sex with her. But he couldn't. She was fun and nice, but still, well in the middle of normal or average.

He leaned in and pressed his mouth to the side of her neck. His lips were warm as they moved along her suddenly sensitive skin. He paused to nibble her earlobe before dipping lower and kissing his way along her collarbone.

She was still in her regular wedding planner garb—a simple black dress that allowed her to blend into the background. It wasn't too short or too low or too anything. So why on earth...

He kissed her mouth. "Stop," he told her gently. "It doesn't mean anything."

How could he say that? It meant something to her.

"I'd like to have sex, too," she whispered, before she could stop herself.

He straightened and studied her face. His eyes were hooded and she had no idea what he was thinking.

"Is that the coffee talking or do you mean it?" he asked, his voice low and husky.

She shivered as need began to ease into her body. She was aware of the quiet all around them. The rest of the world was still sleeping. What a naughty way to start the day.

"I mean it."

The fingers cradling her butt tightened. "Do you have condoms?"

She thought of the unopened box in her nightstand drawer. She'd replaced the older, previously unopened box only a few months before. Because condoms had an expiration date and a girl never knew when a handsome man might make an interesting offer. Not that it had happened to her in forever but—

"Pallas?"

She blinked at him. "Sorry. My brain isn't working right. Yes, I have condoms. They're—"

She never got to say what they were or weren't. Before she could finish her sentence, he'd pressed his mouth to hers and started kissing her again. His hands moved up her back and paused. A heartbeat later, she felt cool air on her back and she realized he'd undone her zipper.

The man was serious, she thought, equally amused and intrigued by his action.

She lowered her arms to her side and the dress fell to the floor. She stepped out of her wedges and he quickly went to work on the buttons of his long-sleeved shirt. Seconds later they were both in their underwear. She didn't know what he was thinking, but from her end, the view was very nice indeed.

As far as she knew, Nick didn't work out. Not in a gym anyway. But his job was, by definition, very physical, and that showed. His chest was broad and muscled, his hips narrow. There were interesting little scars on his arms she would guess came from working with something dangerous like molten glass.

Technically, she'd seen him shirtless before—on the first day they'd met. When she'd asked, or rather begged him to be a Roman soldier for a wedding. But back then she'd been in work mode, far more focused on getting the bride down the aisle on her palanquin than paying attention to the honed body of a man she'd grown to like.

Her gaze dipped lower, to his obvious erection straining against his briefs. She felt her insides clench in anticipation. She could tell she was already swollen and ready. Not just because it had been so long but because she wanted to be with Nick.

Without thinking, she put her hand on his flat belly. He sucked in a breath, but didn't move. She leaned forward and pressed a kiss to the center of his chest.

She moved behind him and drew her hand with her, lightly touching his waist, then dropping it to his high, tight rear end. His back was as defined as his chest. She trailed kisses along his shoulder blades before returning to face him again.

She looked at his face. His pupils were dilated, his jaw tense. Without saying anything, he grabbed her hand and pulled her down the hall. When they reached her bedroom, he tore back the covers, then reached for her. She went into his arms.

His mouth claimed hers in a deep kiss filled with hunger and need. She dueled with his tongue, then gasped as he nipped her lower lip. She felt his fingers at the back of her bra. He unhooked it easily before tossing it to the floor.

Still kissing her, he brought his hands up to cup her breasts. He held her gently, barely moving, as if giving her time to adjust to his touch. Then a single finger brushed across her nipples. Just the one time. Fire shot through her, jolting her down to her clit. She gasped.

He did it again and again until the touch became a circling movement that had her breathing in short pants.

She wanted to squirm closer. She wanted to rip off her panties and beg him to take her. She wanted him to touch her *there* with his fingers or his mouth or anything at all. Need increased with every second that passed, but Nick seemed content to kiss her and tease her breasts until she was nearly frantic with hunger.

"Where are the condoms?" he asked as he broke the kiss.

She pointed at the left nightstand. He walked around the bed and opened the drawer. She used the time to pull off her bikini briefs and slip into the bed. He set the box on the nightstand before taking off his underwear and joining her.

She slid toward him as he reached for her, then they were a tangle of arms and legs and mouths in her bed and it was glorious. She loved the contrast of his warm body and the cool sheets and how he took her nipple in his mouth and sucked really hard. Then there was the way he managed to put his thigh between hers so there was pressure on her center and all she had to do was rock just a little bit to enjoy every blissful second of what he was doing.

He moved from breast to breast, licking and pulling deeply. She arched her back and closed her eyes and did her best to keep breathing. When he stopped kissing her breasts, she nearly whimpered, but then she felt his fingers sliding against her slickness. He found her core on the first try and began to circle.

She was so swollen, she thought hazily. So wet and ready. Every inch of her was sensitized to his touch. When he moved faster, she went with him, straining for more, needing him to take her over the edge. She wanted this, but she wanted him inside, too, filling her. She wanted his body above hers, her arms around him. She wanted to know what it was like to watch him come.

But first... Oh, but first... She sank into the sensations he created, the pleasure of what he was doing. He seemed to be able to read her well enough to know when he should move faster, press harder. She felt the moment when *maybe* became *soon* and gasped.

"Just like that," she breathed.

He did as she asked, changing nothing. She breathed into the promise, focusing every cell on the steady touch that took her closer and closer and—

She fell into her release. Muscles clenched and released in that moment of perfection. Nick continued to touch her, going slower and lighter until he was barely stroking her. As the last quiver faded, he shifted his hands so he could insert two fingers into her.

She opened her eyes and found him watching her.

"Nice."

"I believe I'm the one who's supposed to say that," she told him. "Although I would have gone with *spectacular.*"

He smiled. "I'll take that."

He moved in and out of her. She would have thought she was satiated, but instead found herself moving her hips in time with his hand. He pushed in a little deeper and touched a spot that made her breath catch.

"There it is," he murmured. "How about this?"

She had no idea what "this" was until he began to move his finger in a slow circle deep inside her. The sensation was unlike anything she'd experienced before. Arousing in a sort of less intense, but more pleasurable way. As if when she came, she would be in a state of bliss for hours. Or days.

The more he circled, the more she sank into sensations that filled her body. The more he moved, the less control she had. Her breathing increased, then turned to pants. It wasn't like before where she could push and strain to her release. She couldn't will herself to come—it had to be drawn out of her.

She opened her legs wider. She pushed her hips forward. She was close to begging and pleading because she was totally at his mercy. His gaze locked with hers. Everything about what they were doing was so intimate—she was exposed in every way possible on the verge of an orgasm and he could see it all. Yet she couldn't look away or close her eyes or stop her body from moving closer and closer.

He kept his pace steady, circling and circling. She knew she was close, although she had no idea what it was going to be like when she finally—

Her body shuddered as she fell over the edge. The ripples started from deep within and moved out. Everything was different, stronger, more intense, yet slow. She cried out—feeling pleasure and a sense of being out of control. She found herself wanting to scream and maybe cry and certainly hold on.

Her orgasm went on for what felt like hours but was probably only a minute or two. As the sensations faded, he withdrew his fingers, then turned away. She lay there, trying to get control, trying to recapture the essence of who she had been before he'd done that to her, then he was back and kneeling between her legs.

He filled her even more fully than she'd hoped. She'd thought she might be sensitive and sore, but instead, having him inside of her was exactly what she needed. She wrapped her legs around his hips and clung to his arms as he began the age-old dance of making love with her.

He moved in and out, claiming her. Their eyes locked. This time he was the one who was vulnerable, the one who let her see him getting closer. She could feel the tension in his body, hear his rapid breathing. She followed him on the journey, and as he got closer, she pulled him in more, wanting to take all of him, be a part of everything they did.

He pushed deeper and harder, then lost himself in his release. She hung on to him, savoring the shudders that claimed him. He was unexpected in so many ways, she thought as he sighed, then kissed her.

"Who knew you found wedding disasters a turn-on," he whispered.

She started to laugh, then found she couldn't stop. He joined in. He rolled to his side and pulled her close, then kissed her again.

"How about we get some sleep?" he asked.

"I think that's an excellent idea."

# CHAPTER TWELVE

PALLAS AWOKE SOMETIME in the afternoon to a handsome man kissing her shoulder. That kissing turned into a whole lot more and it was nearly three o'clock by the time they got out of her shower and managed to dress.

She was still feeling all kinds of aftershocks and tingles as she walked into the kitchen and started the coffeemaker. She glanced at the clock, turned the coffee off, then turned it back on. One cup shouldn't keep her from sleeping that night. Besides, she needed the caffeine. There was so much to do.

She had to get to work and figure out what was what—postwedding. The catering staff should have tidied up before they left and the janitorial company she hired would have already been in to put away tables and chairs and clean the kitchen and bathrooms.

But first, she was starving and she would guess Nick was, as well. She found a box of mini quiches in the freezer and started the oven. There was also a half bag of sweet potato fries that cooked at the same temperature. She had a cantaloupe on the counter.

Nick strolled into the kitchen and drew her into his arms. She went easily, liking how they fit together.

"Morning," he said, before glancing at the clock on her stove. "Or afternoon. You okay?"

She smiled. "I believe you were with me in the shower. While I'm not sure the word *okay* defines anything close to how I feel, I'm doing well, thank you."

"Me, too."

They smiled at each other.

She'd had a spare toothbrush for him, but not a razor he'd wanted to use, so he needed a shave. She rubbed her hands against the stubble.

"It's a good look on you."

"Makes me look dangerous, huh?"

She laughed. "I wouldn't go that far, but it gives you an edge."

"I'll have to remember that when I want to get my sexy on."

"Not something you need help with," she admitted. At least not with her. She pointed to the food on the counter. "It's an eclectic offering, but there are elements of breakfast. Or at least brunch."

"Works for me. What do you want to do with the rest of the day?"

As in, did they want to spend it together? Happiness joined the tingles. Suddenly work didn't seem the least bit important.

"I'd like to make sure Weddings in a Box is all locked up, but that's the only thing I have to do," she said. "What did you have in mind?"

"Maybe a movie, then dinner. After that we could go back to my place and—" His smile faded as he swore. "I live with my brother. I can't take you back to my place. I don't have a place."

She held in a giggle. "Well, you are planning to go to Dubai, so it makes sense not to bother with an apartment of your own."

"Still, it makes me feel like I'm eighteen and still living at home."

"We'll come back here. My bed seems to work for us."

He drew her against him. "Everything about you works for me."

"Nice to know."

She put the food on a cookie sheet, slid it in the oven, then set the timer before returning to Nick's embrace. He nibbled along her neck, then straightened and looked at her.

"Why aren't you married?"

She tilted her head. "It's been a while since I've had a sleepover, but I'm pretty sure that's not an expected question for the morning after."

"I'm serious."

"So am I."

Nick pressed his forehead to hers. "You're beautiful, you're smart, you're funny, you're a good person and you have a successful business. Obviously the problem isn't you. So why aren't you married?"

Was it wrong of her to want to replay the "you're beautiful" part of his list? It was all good, but somehow that one was the most appealing. She supposed that made her shallow.

"If we're going to get serious, I need coffee." She crossed to the pot and poured them each a mug. They settled at the kitchen table, where she wondered how to explain her single state.

"I'm wary about relationships," she began. "Not that I'm having to turn men away or anything, but I'm cautious."

"Because of your mom?"

"That's insightful."

He shrugged. "Parents have the best shot at messing with their kids. It's a time-honored tradition. We'll probably do it, as well."

"There's something to look forward to," she murmured, hoping she wouldn't make her children feel that they had to earn her love. "I always had to work to make her proud of me and I always failed. I didn't want to have to go through that for some guy."

"Real love doesn't have to be earned." He sounded as if he were sure.

"I've heard the rumor and I don't know if I believe it."

"You don't have to earn Cade's love."

"He's my brother—he has to love me."

"No, he doesn't. He chooses to and it's easy for both of you. I've seen you two together. You trust him to have your back."

"I want to say it's different and you're going to say it's not. Love is love." She leaned forward. "So why aren't you married?"

"Passion consumes," he said without hesitation. "I've seen my mom with my dad. She would do anything for him. He would do anything for his art. I get that love comes in many forms and most of them scare the crap out of me. It seems safe between siblings but after that, all bets are off."

"We had passion last night."

"Different kind, and yes, we did."

Their gazes locked. She felt the heat radiating from him and for a moment thought about throwing herself in his arms. Her table was sturdy—they could do it right there. But a voice in her head whispered she needed to more fully understand why he wasn't interested in getting involved.

"So you'll have sex, but you won't fall in love," she said. "What about a relationship? Say having a girlfriend?"

His mouth twisted. "In theory, yes."

She held in a smile. "If you didn't like her too much?"

"Now you're making fun of me."

"A little, but only with affection. You'll risk yourself emotionally, but to a point. Sex, yes, permanent commitment, no. Part-time commitment, maybe, if there was no risk of taking things to the next level. So I would ask why would you want to be with someone if you didn't want the relationship to have a chance of getting better?"

"If you're going to use logic," he grumbled.

She wasn't sure what she was looking for, exactly. Maybe a reminder that she had to keep her heart safe. That Nick wasn't a forever kind of guy. And while she hadn't been looking for a man in her life, now that she had one, she found she really liked it. As far as his concern—that passion consumed—she didn't mind the thought of being consumed by him at all.

For now she was safe. She liked him a lot, but wasn't in love with him. She was going to have to be careful and make sure she didn't allow herself to care too much. Even without his commitment issues, he was still leaving.

"I like that you're emotionally broken," she said cheerfully. "It keeps the playing field level."

"I'm not broken. I'm quirky."

"Is that what we're calling it?" she asked.

The oven timer dinged. Nick rose and grabbed an oven mitt. "Saved by the bell. Have you ever noticed how all of life is about timing?"

MONDAY MORNING PALLAS got to the office extra early. She and Nick had spent a lazy Sunday afternoon together. Somehow they never made it to the movies, but they had gone out to dinner. He'd gone back to his brother's for clean clothes and a shaving kit, then had returned to her place. Despite her 3:00 p.m. cup of coffee, she'd had no trouble sleeping in his arms.

She felt good, she thought as she walked through the building and checked to make sure everything had been put back in place. She'd made it through the wedding from hell and had lived to tell the tale. She and Nick were having fun. Her girl parts were very excited about all the action.

She knew the relationship was temporary and she was going to go with that. Maybe hanging out with Nick would give her the courage to find someone else after he left. A man who was interested in forever. She would like to be a part of something bigger than herself, she thought wistfully. And have kids.

A little after three, Alan strolled in. He handed her a latte, then took a seat next to her desk.

"How was prison?" he asked.

"I was giving a statement, not being arrested," she reminded him. "I should have made you go in my place. You saw the same thing I did."

"It's something I will never forget." He shuddered. "Of course, over time I'll change the story so I'm the hero and that will be fun, but dear God! I can't believe the DJ pulled a gun on us. Even a paint gun. Who does that?"

"Criminals." She leaned back in her chair. "I'm just grateful Catherine is the one who hired him. I offered her our local guy, but she wasn't interested."

"I'm sure she's sorry now. Are the zebras all right?"

"So it seems. I talked to Carol this morning and she said they're recovered and acting their normal zebra selves."

In fact her friend hadn't been all that upset about the incident. Pallas wondered if she had taken too much to heart. Maybe the rain hadn't been an omen. Maybe it had just been rain.

"I'm thinking wild animals are probably not something we should promote," she said. "But offering some custom elements to our clients might be fun."

"I wonder if anyone would like a hostage wedding." Alan chuckled. "I would have loved to have seen Gerald's face, if he'd still been with us. Can't you see him marching up to the DJ and saying very sternly, 'That simply isn't done, young man.'"

"It's funny to think about, but if it had really happened, I would have worried about him being hurt."

"Which is only one of the reasons he adored you." Alan shook his head. "I still remember when you first came to work here. You were so proud of your Disneyland experience."

"Don't mock the mouse," Pallas said sternly. "I adored working there. All the special parties were so important to the guests. It was great fun." She sighed. "And the reason I didn't do as well in one of my classes, setting in motion a series of events that totally changed my life."

"Was that good or bad?"

At the time she would have claimed it was a disaster, but now she knew being forced to leave college had turned out to be a blessing in disguise.

"I appreciate my degree more because I earned it myself," she said slowly. "And I've had a wonderful experience working here."

"Gerald was impressed with you from the beginning. After your first interview he told me you'd be running this place one day. And look, you are."

Only because of Gerald's generous and unexpected bequest. "Why did he leave the business to me and not you? You and he were close." She didn't want to define their relationship any more than that. While she knew that Gerald and Alan had been involved, she'd never been clear on the details. Friends with benefits? Partners? And asking had seemed rude.

Alan's expression softened. "He always knew that while I liked Weddings in a Box, you loved it. You were excited and passionate about every aspect. He'd created this from nothing and wanted whoever inherited it to appreciate his legacy."

"I like to think he would be happy with how things are going."

"I'm sure he is."

Pallas thought about her conversation with Nick. She'd forgotten to mention the love she and Gerald had shared. One in which she'd expected nothing and had gotten everything. Gerald had been a total stranger that first day, yet in the end, he'd changed her life. Or maybe the person to share that with was her mother. Not that Libby would get or appreciate hearing about unconditional love and generosity.

"Unless you're still thinking of selling," Alan added.

"I'm not. I'll admit that every time my mother mentions the bank to me, I get a knot in my stomach and I feel guilty. But if I wanted to work there, I would already be doing it. This is where I belong."

Alan sniffed. "Our little girl is all grown-up." He rose. "All right, darling, I'm heading back to LA. I have parties to attend. I'll be back for Nova and Joel's wedding. No one wants to miss that."

Pallas stood and they hugged. As he walked out, Silver stalked in. Pallas took one look at her friend and knew there was only one person who could put that kind of fire in Silver's pale eyes.

"What did he do now?" she asked.

"I hate Drew." Silver paced to the far end of the room and then turned back. "Hate him."

Pallas almost asked "Why this time?" because despite having broken up years ago, Silver and Drew were never quite over. Except she guessed that question wasn't exactly supportive. Instead she said, "What happened?"

Silver planted her hands on her hips. "He said he missed me."

"That bastard!"

Silver glared at her. "Do you really think this is the right time for sarcasm?"

"Sarcasm is like Jell-O. It's always the right time and there's always room."

Silver walked to one of the chairs and collapsed. She put her face in her hands and groaned. "I hate him. You remember what he did to me, right?"

"Yes, but it was a long time ago. You need to let it go."

"I can't. He's always around. In my personal space. Why can't he get married and leave me alone?"

"Why can't you get married and forget all about him?"

Silver glared at her. "First sarcasm and now logic? Why are you being so mean?"

"I'm trying to help. You need to let him go. Otherwise you'll be trapped forever. That's not healthy."

"I can't let go. I hate him. I'll never forgive him." She rose. "Come have drinks with me."

"It's barely after three in the afternoon. On a Monday."

Silver rolled her eyes. "This is an emergency. I need my friend."

*Words that could not be ignored*, Pallas thought. She grabbed her bag. "You owe me for this."

"I know. I'll make it up to you, I swear."

Pallas was more concerned about how Silver still had so much energy for Drew. The opposite of love wasn't hate, but apathy. Despite the years and miles, it seemed to her neither Silver nor Drew had found a way to move on.

"Maybe you should sleep with him again, just to get him out of your system."

"I'd rather slit his throat."

Pallas winced. "This is where I remind you he's my favorite cousin. No throat slitting."

"Can I rip out his heart and hand it to him on a platter?"

There was a visual, Pallas thought, shuddering. "Um, no. Just hate him. I think that's safest for everyone."

"I never get to have any fun."

Marla, Pallas's favorite caterer, flipped to the next page on her tablet. "I enjoy the chance to be creative," she said happily. "Vegetarian can be difficult. It's so easy to go predictable and many guests immediately turn up their noses. I wanted a nice mix of traditional foods with vegetarian options that would make everyone happy."

Pallas studied the pictures. They all looked delicious and her stomach was already rumbling. Tim, Nova's father, was a vegetarian, but neither Nova nor Joel were. That gave Marla a chance to dazzle in two arenas.

"Nova also told me that she and Joel really like the idea of a lot of finger foods," Marla continued. "In keeping with the quirkiness of their wedding. Did she tell you they're going to have game stations set up at the venue? I'd be worried my guests would find playing more interesting than the wedding itself."

"I guess they're willing to take that chance."

She handed the tablet back to Marla and pulled out her notes. "Silver said you had an idea for a signature cocktail?"

"She and I have been working together. We were supposed to get together yesterday to finalize everything, but she wasn't feeling well."

No doubt that was because of her hangover, Pallas thought sympathetically. Their afternoon of cocktails had turned into a well into the night event with their friends joining them. Pallas had known to go easy, but Silver had been all in with the liquor. Anything to forget Drew.

"You have to try Popsicle cocktails. You mix the drink and then freeze it," Marla said.

"I thought liquor didn't freeze."

"It doesn't, but if there are enough other ingredients, it gets close enough. I have several I want to try. They will be fun and different. Silver and I are going to coordinate so that everything I'm fixing goes with her signature drink."

Marla showed her a picture of a margarita pop.

"Is that dipped in salt?" Pallas asked.

"Uh-huh. We can even use flavored salts, if we want."

The outside temperatures would be warm—an icy drink would be fun. "I can't wait to hear what Nova has to say about them. I think she's going to love them."

"I hope so. Now to food." Marla propped up her tablet and began to scroll through the menu photos. "Nova said her dad is a huge fan of mac and cheese so I thought we'd do a truffle mac and cheese pop. I can make stuffed Brussel sprouts and avocado boats. One of the items I'd like to offer are mini sliders. They're about a quarter of the size of a regular slider, so truly a mouthful and that's all. We can do several kinds of hamburgers, as well as chicken burgers. We can play with the ingredients."

"I love the idea, but how do you get all the toppings on a tiny piece of meat?"

"You put the flavors into the meat itself or in the sauce."

There were also dips in shot glasses with either triangles of pita or raw vegetables, kabob options and plenty of tiny desserts.

"When do you talk to Nova?"

"Tomorrow. I'm really excited."

Nick walked into Pallas's office. Their eyes met in a quick moment of secret *I'm happy to see you* communication.

"Hi, Marla," Nick said. "Pallas."

She smiled and Marla waved.

"We're talking food," the pretty caterer said.

Nick peered at the tablet. "If there's mac and cheese, you know it's going to be good."

"Men." Marla's tone was affectionate. "I wonder if I can do a drink pop with Jack Daniel's. I'll have to try." She collected her things. "I'm off to refine before my call."

With that, she rose and left. Nick waited until she was gone to pull Pallas to her feet.

"Hey, you," he murmured.

"Hey, yourself."

He kissed her as she wrapped her arms around him. As heat warmed her, she felt herself surrendering to the moment. If she locked her office door, they could—

Her cell buzzed. She glanced at the screen, then stepped back when she saw the caller ID.

After pushing the button for the speakerphone, she said, "Hi, Nova. I just saw Marla. You're going to love everything she's come up with. We're all so excited about how the wedding is coming together."

There was a moment of silence followed by a choking sob. Pallas gripped the phone more tightly as her stomach knotted and her skin went cold.

"Nova?"

"W-we can't do this. It's my dad."

Dread joined Pallas's other emotions. "Is he okay?"

"N-no. He's taken a turn. It's bad."

Nick put his arm around her, but didn't speak.

"Oh, no. How can we help?" Pallas asked, thinking about the warm, loving father whose last wish had been to see his daughter get married.

"You can't. No one can. He's dying. They don't expect him to last the week. The wedding is off."

Pallas felt her eyes fill with tears. "Nova, I'm so sorry. Do you need anything? Do you want us to bring the wedding to you?"

She had no idea how that would happen, but there

were plenty of smart, determined people involved. They could find a way.

"It's too late. For everything. Look, I'll be in touch, but I have to go now. I need to spend every second with him."

"Of course. Give him our best."

"Thank you."

Nova hung up.

Pallas set her phone on the desk. "I barely know the man. It shouldn't matter, but it does."

Nick pulled her close and held her. He didn't speak but feeling the warmth of his embrace turned out to be just what she needed.

## CHAPTER THIRTEEN

NICK HELD THE chain saw in his hands. The weight was familiar as was the sense of waiting for the wood to tell him what it wanted. He stood in back of the studio with a five-foot-high log secured in heavy metal clamps. After circling the log a couple of times, he started the chainsaw, then turned it off. He had no idea what to do next.

He wondered why that was. Usually when he approached a piece like this, he only had to take a few minutes before he knew exactly what he was going to do. It was a symbiotic relationship as if the more he cut into the wood, the more it spoke to him. But not this time.

He didn't know what was wrong. Maybe because he'd been working with other materials since moving to Happily Inc? Maybe because he was so pissed he couldn't see straight? Neither was conducive to a good outcome, especially when he wasn't sure exactly what he was pissed at. Tim dying? The unfairness of life? Regardless, he had to get his head on straight. Practice was required for the work he did and being angry risked hurting the material or himself.

He set the chainsaw on the ground, then pulled

off his safety goggles. He dropped his gloves on the ground and stared at the wood.

It was so damned wrong, he thought grimly. All of it. Tim dying, the wedding being canceled. Pallas had been devastated. He would guess the other vendors involved were equally upset. Not only had they all wanted to pull together to create a one-of-a-kind experience for the bride and groom, they'd had something to prove to themselves. The project had brought them together, challenged them. Now it was over.

He saw movement out of the corner of his eye—Ronan stepping outside. His brother eyed him cautiously.

"You okay?"

He and Ronan hadn't had much contact in the past few weeks. From his perspective, his brother was withdrawing from both him and Mathias, but maybe he was wrong about that. It was possible that he was as much to blame.

"It won't talk to me," he said, motioning to the log.

"It will or it won't."

A statement more realistic than unhelpful. Because the medium had to have a voice. People assumed an artist simply sat down and created, but it wasn't like that. Everything they touched had come from the earth in one form or another. Matter could be changed but it was never destroyed.

He briefly wondered if people who worked with plastic or other man-made material ever heard the whispers, then shook off the question. The answer would in no way help him and he was getting tired of not knowing.

"What's going on?" Ronan asked. "Except for restoring those panels, you haven't worked with wood since you got here."

"I needed to think."

"About?"

Nick was surprised Ronan was reaching out. "A wedding got canceled."

"So?"

Irritation flared. Nick tamped it down, telling himself Ronan didn't know the details.

"That papier-mâché I've been working with—it was for that wedding."

"The one based on the game?"

"That's it. Nova and Joel needed the wedding put together quickly because her father has cancer. He wanted to walk his daughter down the aisle before he died. We just heard that he's gotten sicker and he's not going to live long enough."

Nick circled the wood, noting the placement of a couple of knots and a raw slice where a branch had been cut off.

"It's not only the wedding," he continued. "It's what it all meant to us. We were pulling together, making something bigger than ourselves. It was important to Pallas."

Which made it important to him. Not that he had to say that—Ronan wasn't stupid.

"You're seeing her?"

Nick nodded.

"Is it serious?"

"I'm going to Dubai. It's for now." And it was great. She made him laugh. She was easy to be with, and they never ran out of things to say. The sex was amazing, but he'd reached an age where he wanted more than just to get laid. He wanted…

"It's just a wedding," Ronan told him. "I'm sorry about the old man, but shit happens."

"You ever think of getting a job with a greeting card company?" Nick snapped. "Would it kill you to give a damn about someone other than yourself?"

"What do you mean?"

"Somebody's father is dying."

"Somebody's father is always dying. If you're talking about me getting involved, that's not going to happen."

"I can see that."

Nick knew the frustration building inside of him had very little to do with Ronan, but his brother had just become an easy target for what he was feeling. Despite how things were between them, he knew it was safe to let loose at Ronan. Maybe not the least bit fair, but safe.

"Why don't you care anymore?" Nick asked, approaching his brother. "Too scared?"

Ronan—his height and about twenty pounds of muscle heavier—bristled. "Back off, bro."

"Afraid someone might get inside and make you feel something. Then what? You'd have to get your head out of your ass and stop your pity party? If you didn't have to sweat how bad you had it, you wouldn't know what to do to fill your day."

His brother glared at him. "You have no idea what you're talking about."

"Then explain it to me."

"You're not worth the time or the trouble."

Nick had meant to make Ronan throw the first punch, but the complete dismissal had him swinging hard and fast. Ronan was caught off guard and took a fist to the jaw. He reacted with a quick uppercut that Nick sidestepped. As they circled each other, Nick had the thought that not only were they too old for this crap, they both really needed to work on their communication skills.

Mathias burst through the back door of the studio and stepped between them.

"What the hell is wrong with you?" he demanded.

Nick and Ronan glared at each other.

"I see. You'll fight about it but you won't talk about it. That's intelligent." Mathias pushed them farther apart. "You two done out here or do I have to hose you off like a couple of dogs?"

"I'm done," Ronan growled.

"That's right…walk away," Nick taunted.

Mathias glared at them both. "Stop it. We're family, no matter what."

"We're less than we were," Ronan told him, then walked into the studio.

Nick wanted to throw something. Or hit something, although he'd tried the latter and it hadn't helped as much as he'd hoped.

"Your brother is a jackass," Nick said.

"He's your brother, too."

"I know and he pisses me off."

"Ronan's good at that." Mathias shook his head. "Is that what started it?"

"Mostly." Nick was too embarrassed to admit he'd been looking for a fight. "How long is he going to hang on to what Dad told him? Nothing is different for us. He's still who he always was."

Mathias stared at him. "Nick, it's a big deal. To you, Ronan is exactly the same. That's probably true for Aidan and Del, too, but not to us. We thought we were twins. We thought we had a bond. Now it's gone."

"Bullshit. You have what you always had. Whatever connection you share is one you created. The only thing that changed is information."

"It's not that easy."

"It should be. We're all brothers and family. You can pretend it's different, but if that becomes true, then Dad wins. And none of us want that."

PALLAS FIGURED SHE would never be able to afford a trip to Africa, so this was the next best thing—lunch on the savanna. Well, really it was lunch on the animal preserve by the Happily Inc dump, but no one had to know that.

She and Carol sat on a blanket in the shade of a tree. Several gazelles grazed nearby. In the distance stood the small herd of zebras and Millie was in sight.

"This setting adds a level of glamor to my turkey sandwich," Pallas said.

Carol passed her a small bag of chips. "I know, right? It's hard to believe this all exists. Whatever

I have going on in my life, I can always come here, sit and just be in the moment."

"I'm glad the zebras have recovered," Pallas said.

"They were totally fine the next day. To be honest, I think they enjoyed their adventure." Carol's smile faded. "How are you doing? Everyone seems to be sad about the alien wedding being canceled. Even though I wasn't a part of things, I have the sense that I've missed something big."

"I'm okay. Of course I feel awful for Nova—she's dealing with losing her father—but I do feel bad for the rest of us. I guess we had something to prove and now we can't."

"Are you stuck with a lot of bills?"

"No. Because of the tight time frame, Nova paid for everything in advance. There are some things that can be returned, but everything custom is basically already bought. I'm going to wait awhile and see if she wants any of it."

The irony was whether the wedding went on or not, Pallas was covered, financially. She couldn't wish away the increase in her bank account, but she would much rather have put on the wedding.

"It was fun to stretch and try something different. To figure out a way to make the impossible happen." She took a bite of her sandwich. "Now it's all very sucky."

"I'm sorry."

"Thanks. Now enough about all that. How are you?"

Carol raised a shoulder. "I'm good. Still worried about Millie."

Pallas glanced at the giraffe. She nibbled leaves off a tree. Her gait was both elegant and awkward.

"She's eating. Isn't that good?"

"It is, but it's not enough. I'm concerned with how she's adjusting. I think she's lonely. She was by herself before she came here and now she's still by herself."

"Is there a Mr. Giraffe in Millie's future?"

"I don't think so. Male giraffes are solitary. The females generally live in a loose herd. I want to see if I can find a couple of female giraffes so Millie can have some friends." Her mouth twisted. "Money is going to be a challenge. Giraffes aren't cheap. Plus there's the care and feeding. Not to mention transport."

Pallas put down her sandwich. "Oh, wow. I never thought of that. Of course, you have to get them here, and how on earth do you do that?"

"It's complicated. They have to be able to travel a route without low bridges or overpasses."

"Let me guess. There's an app for that."

Carol laughed. "I sure hope so. Otherwise, I'm going to be doing a lot of really unusual research. And there's no getting it wrong. Giraffes do not bend their heads on command."

"That puts my problems in perspective." She would guess there would be a lot of back roads taken. She doubted the giraffes would be comfortable at freeway speeds. "You're going to need a giraffe wrangler or something."

"First I have to find out if I can buy any. After

that, I'll figure out how to raise the money. Then I'll worry about the wrangling aspect."

"Speaking of wrangling," Pallas said, her voice teasing, "how was it hanging out with Cade?"

"Stop trying to fix me up."

"I'm not. I'm asking. For as long as I've known you, you've never been on a date. There has to be some guy who catches your eye. I might be biased, but I think my brother is very handsome and—"

Pallas stopped in midsentence as a perfectly reasonable explanation for Carol's lack of dating occurred to her.

"I'm not a lesbian," her friend said drily.

"It's okay if you are."

"Gee, thanks. But no. And while I appreciate the offer of your brother, I'll get my own guy."

"Should I ask when?"

Carol hesitated just long enough for Pallas to lean forward and ask, "Who is he? I can tell there's someone."

"There's a guy I like but it will never work and I don't want to talk about it."

"Is he married?"

"No. And gross. He's not married." She grabbed a chip. "What part of 'I don't want to talk about it' was unclear?"

"So there is someone?"

"Yes."

"And he lives in town?"

Carol sighed. "Maybe."

"That means yes."

"Don't make me sorry I like you."

"Now I'm going to speculate. But only with you," she added quickly. "I won't say a word to anyone else." She made an X over her heart. "I swear."

"Uh-huh. We'll see. Now can we change the subject? Oh, I know—what about your love life?"

A fascinating question, Pallas thought, at least to her. "Nick and I have been hanging out."

Carol's eyes widened. "Hanging out as in going to game night or hanging out as in you've seen him naked on a regular basis?"

"I've seen him naked." She pressed her lips together. "It's very nice. All of it. Him, the naked part. I like him."

"A lot?"

"Maybe. Not that it matters. He's not going to be a permanent resident for very long." She explained about his commission in Dubai.

"You could go with him," her friend said.

"No, I couldn't. I have a business here. Plus, he hasn't asked me."

"What would you do if he did?"

Something Pallas hadn't thought about. "I don't know. It doesn't matter—he won't. We're both very clear that this is a temporary thing and I'm okay with that. When he's gone, I'll deal."

Life would return to what it had been before and she would be fine. At least she hoped she would be fine. Sure, she would miss him, but it wasn't as if she was in love with him.

As for him caring about her... She couldn't even *think* the *L* word. Because she'd been taught that

love had to be earned and she wasn't sure she had.
Or could.

"I'm glad you're having fun," Carol said. "One
of us should be."

"If you tell me who your mystery man is, I could
help."

"Thank you, but no. I'm fine. I'm strong and independent and I'll get over him, then find someone
better."

"Are you trying to convince yourself or me?" Pallas asked.

"Both."

PALLAS LEFT AFTER lunch but instead of driving back
to Weddings in a Box, she turned in the other direction and headed for the family ranch up by the base
of the mountains. Talking about Cade had made her
miss him. With Nova and Joel's wedding canceled,
she had some free time, so why not visit her brother?

Despite Carol's claims that he wasn't the man she
was secretly pining for, Pallas couldn't help but wonder if maybe he was. If nothing else, she could see if
Cade was the least bit interested in her friend. Maybe
a little matchmaking would help her feel better about
the loss of the alien wedding.

She stopped at the security gate and punched
in the code, then drove down the mile-long driveway. On both sides were fenced-in pastures. Straight
ahead was the old farmhouse and behind that was a
huge, state-of-the-art barn.

By the time she got to the house and parked, Cade

was walking toward her. She got out of her car and laughed.

"Let me guess. Some security system told you there was an intruder."

Her brother hugged her. "It said the gate had been activated by an authorized code. There's a slight difference."

"Not much of one." She looked at the weathered two-story house. The roof was new, and the structure sturdy, but it needed a coat of paint, not to mention a good window cleaning. "How are you surviving out here?"

"Good. I have all I need."

"Your saddlebag and whatever else it is cowboys require to get through their day?"

"Something like that. Come on. I'll buy you a lemonade."

"You have real lemonade?"

"Made fresh by my trusty housekeeper."

She thought of her small place and how the closest she got to having someone cook for her was when she got takeout. "You have a housekeeper?"

"I have a lady who comes in twice a week to clean, do the laundry and leave the refrigerator filled with meals."

"Obviously your salary is much bigger than mine. I'm jealous."

"I don't pay for her," he said with a grin. "She's a condition of my employment."

"Great. Now I have to hate you. *And* drink all your lemonade."

He was still chuckling as he led the way up the porch steps and inside.

As she followed him, Pallas tried to remember the last time she'd been in the old farmhouse. She must have been in her early teens.

She and Cade had both learned to ride when they were maybe five or six. She hadn't been very interested, but he'd loved everything about the ranch. In the summers he'd practically moved in with the ranch foreman, who lived in the house as part of the job.

The furniture had changed, she thought as she walked through the large living room, but was positioned the same. The stone fireplace was exactly as she remembered, as was the wooden rocking chair by the fireplace.

The kitchen hadn't been updated. There were still gingham curtains at the big windows and an antique stove some big city designer would kill to get his hands on. The refrigerator was new, as was the microwave. A farm sink, big enough for a good-sized litter of puppies to swim in, stood in front of the large bay window.

"Do you feel isolated out here?" she asked.

"Nope. I'm close enough to town to get what I need and far enough away from everyone to enjoy the quiet."

"And by everyone, you mean Mom?"

One corner of his mouth turned up. "I didn't say it—you did."

He put ice in glasses, then poured what looked to be real lemonade. Pallas took a sip and sighed. "Delicious."

"Come on. I want to show you something."

They walked out to the back porch, which was about twice as wide and three times as long as the front one. There were chairs and rockers, a swing hanging from the eaves and a rattan sofa. He motioned to the latter, then sat next to her.

"What am I looking at?" she asked.

He pointed to one of the fenced pastures. "Just wait. You'll see in a second."

She leaned back against the cushion and breathed in the warm, fresh air. Maybe it was all the grass or the pond or being closer to the mountains, but the air wasn't as dry here as it was in town. She liked the sound of the birds and—

"Look!" She pointed as a brown mare and a darling, leggy, awkward colt walked into view. "Baby horses. I want one!"

"He'll cost you about twenty grand."

She nearly choked on her drink. "Seriously? He's a baby."

"It's all about potential."

"And good advertising. Twenty grand? For a horse?"

"That's nothing. I want to buy a stallion for the ranch. He's a special guy. I'm not sure I'm going to get him, but he'll be about twenty times that."

Pallas did the math, then gasped. "Or you could just go buy an island."

"Hard to improve a breeding program with an island." Cade rested one ankle on the opposite knee. "I probably won't get him, but it's fun to think about."

"Is there an auction or something?"

"No. The owner doesn't sell many horses and I'm sure others have offered more than me."

"Who's the owner?"

Amusement filled her brother's eyes. "King Malik of El Bahar."

Pallas's knowledge of geography was sketchy at best. She knew El Bahar was south of Saudi Arabia—maybe on the water. The country was a close ally of the United States and was often referred to as the Switzerland of the Middle East. And even she had heard of their horses.

"He's hinted he's willing to sell a few horses in his stable. Rida's the only one I'm interested in. I've sent a letter to the king and heard that he'll be getting back to me in a few months. We'll see what happens."

"No offense, Cade, but why on earth would the king of El Bahar sell to you and not one of the other billion and, I'm guessing, rich people interested?"

"Because he likes me."

Pallas blinked. "You've met him?"

"Uh-huh."

"The king of El Bahar?"

"He was the Crown Prince then. His father stepped down when King Malik's oldest son turned eighteen."

Apparently her brother had quite the secret life. Of course he'd been gone close to a decade, but still. They talked regularly and texted. At no point had he felt the need to mention he'd met the soon-to-be king of El Bahar?

"Is he nice?"

"That's not a word I'd use. He's very commanding, but a decent guy. He was in Texas, looking at horses, and took several of us out to dinner. Our relationship is my only shot at getting Rida, but if I could, it would change everything."

Pallas was still trying to wrap her mind around her brother's share. "I wonder if I should look at offering harem weddings."

"Isn't that more of a guy's fantasy than a woman's idea of a good time?"

"I guess you're right, but it's interesting to think about. If you buy the horse, would you go to El Bahar to pick him up?"

"They'd probably bring him here and send someone along to get him settled. Not a problem I have to deal with now."

She touched her glass to his. "Here's hoping it becomes a problem."

He chuckled.

She returned her attention to the mare and her foal. They looked so right together, she thought. Content to simply be on this beautiful late spring day. She and her mother had never been like that. No matter what, there had been tension. Pallas had been so eager to please, but no matter how she tried, she'd failed. Even when she'd been little.

"Do you remember much about Dad?" she asked.

"Sure. He brought me out here to ride every weekend until he died."

Pallas didn't recall that happening all that often, but she must be wrong. "He's a blur to me," she admitted. "I have flashes of things, but nothing specific."

"I remember everything. When Mom told me he'd died, I refused to believe her. I kept telling her there had been a mistake. I had nightmares for weeks."

Pallas wondered how she couldn't know that. She knew that Cade had been upset, but by the time they were ten, they were living relatively different lives. She'd had her girlfriends and he'd been hanging out with the guys he knew. And he'd been gone most weekends. Riding, she thought, the past coming back to her.

"Did he stand up to Mom?" she asked.

"No, that wasn't his way." He frowned. "I don't know what they saw in each other. Moving in with Grandpa Frank can't have helped their marriage. Living with an in-law couldn't be easy."

"Was that his decision or hers?" she asked before adding, "Never mind. We were kids. How would we know?"

Not exactly a happy topic. She searched for a better one, then smiled.

"What did you think of Carol?"

"No."

She looked at him. "What does that mean?"

"You're not fixing me up with your friends. You can forget it, Pallas. I mean it."

"That's very forceful."

"Hey, I have some of Mom in me, too. It's not just all you."

She wanted to protest that she was nothing like Libby, but figured if they went too far into those muddy waters, she would end up with hurt feelings.

"She's nice," Pallas told him. "And single. You both like animals."

He sighed heavily. "And this would be you acting exactly like Mom. Give it up, kid. I'm not interested in her and she's not interested in me."

"Are you interested in anyone?"

"Not right now."

"No secret longing for a girl you left back in Texas?"

"Nope."

There was something about the way he said the single word. Maybe it was a twin thing, but she knew he was holding back. She angled toward him. "You're lying."

"There's no one, I swear."

"But?"

He groaned. "Why did you come here? I forget."

"Cade, I'm not going to let it go."

"Fine. I was involved with someone when I was in Kentucky. It didn't work out."

"Why not?"

"She was willing to sleep with the hired help but not marry him." He held up his hand before she could respond. "I got off easy. She wasn't the one and I'm glad I found out before I'd made a fool out of myself. Or worse, married her."

"But you were in love with her." Her chest hurt just thinking about it. "She hurt you."

"Not that badly. I got over her."

"Is she why you came back home?"

"No. She's why I went to Texas. I came home

because it seemed like a good time for a change of scene."

"I'm here if you want to talk."

"Thank you."

"And I could set something up with Carol."

He swore.

She laughed and leaned against him. "Fine. I'll let the Carol thing go. Maybe King Malik will sell you the horse and send a pretty horse trainer with him. You two can fall madly in love and have a harem wedding at Weddings in a Box."

"You're a freak."

"And yet you love me."

"That I do."

## CHAPTER FOURTEEN

NICK CAREFULLY MIXED the acrylic paint. He'd never been one to work with color—not this way. His wood pieces were varnished, but otherwise left natural, and with his glass, the color had been added as part of the process. Not after the fact. But papier-mâché was a whole different ball game.

He'd found the right purple, but he was still playing with the yellows and teals. So far he hadn't found the perfect combination.

"Knock knock."

He looked up as Violet walked in, pulling a large suitcase behind her. He rose.

"Hi. Was I expecting you?"

"No, and you can tell me you're busy. It's okay." She wrinkled her nose. "I just wanted to talk about the wedding."

"It's canceled."

"Yes, and yet you're painting papier-mâché flowers for it."

"I guess I can't let it go."

"Me, either."

He motioned to the flowers. "I'm going to paint them then send them to Nova. She can use them or not."

"That's what I thought, too." She lowered the suit-case to the floor and opened it. "I just couldn't stop thinking about everything that had happened. I'm sad, and I decided this was how I would deal."

The "this" was a dress. One of the bridesmaid dresses, Nick thought, staring at the garment as she pulled it out of the suitcase and laid it across his desk.

What had been a simple purple sleeveless dress—fitted through the waist, then flaring out to the floor—had been transformed. Some kind of gauzy fabric formed drapey sleeves. Beads lined the V-neck and tiny star-like decorations covered the skirt.

He bent closer and studied the stars. They weren't decorations, they were buttons, with glass centers and some kind of enameling surrounding the glass. The colors were perfect—teal and purple, with a hint of creamy yellow.

"The design is Indian," Violet told him. "They're antique—if I had to guess, I'd say they're maybe three hundred years old. Aren't they amazing?"

"Where did you find them?"

"Oh, I have buyers all over the world sending me buttons. It's a real thing," she added as he stared at her. "An expat found these in a market. They were just sitting in a box, gathering dust. So she sent them to me. I've had them a couple of years. I've been waiting for the right project." She sighed. "I'd thought this was it."

"It still is. Nova and Joel will get married."

"I know, it's just I wanted to be there to see the dresses being worn."

He walked to the sink in the corner of the studio

and washed his hands, then returned to the dress. He studied the beadwork at the neckline, then the decorations. "You have any extras of these?"

"Sure. In case one falls off or something." She pulled several headpieces out of the suitcase, then a small clear plastic box with several glittering buttons inside.

He liked the way the glass caught the light and reflected it back against the enamel. The combination of bright against dark was exactly what he'd been looking for. He hadn't known how to make it happen in two-dimensional form until now.

"The dress," he said.

Violet shivered. "You are not painting that beautiful wedding gown. You can't."

"I hadn't started when she called to cancel, but that's only because I couldn't figure out what to do. You've given me an idea."

"Then I take it back."

"Wait and be amazed."

He pulled an overhead projector on a cart out of a deep closet and wheeled it to the center of the room, facing a blank white wall. Nick used an extension cord to plug in the projector. While Violet watched, he dug a file folder out of his desk and started slapping clear plastic sheets on the top of the projector. The image of blown-up lace appeared on the wall.

"Here's the basic pattern of the lace on her dress," he said.

Violet walked to the wall. Her knee-high boots clicked on the concrete floors. She raised her hand to outline the lace.

"I thought it was a simple pattern that repeated, but it's not. See how this is almost a modified fleur-de-lis but on the other side, it's more swirly." She smiled. "You're the artist. What's the technical term?"

"Swirly works."

"So how does this relate to my buttons?"

He replaced the black-and-white sheet with one he'd painted. "The tones are off," he said as he walked to the screen. "The teal is too dull. And the yellow blows. I thought it was the paint hue, but looking at your buttons I'm thinking that's not it at all."

He opened a cabinet filled with small tubes of paint. Violet followed him and moaned when she saw the messy display. "Oooh, I want that. I could never justify the cost of so many paints, but still. I have envy."

"I've never heard that before."

"Paint envy? It's real. We don't like to talk about it much. You know—the stigma."

Violet was pretty enough, he thought absently. It would be easy to steer the conversation from friendly to flirty. All it would take were a few words and the right tone. Only he didn't want to. While he wasn't willing to put a name on what he had with Pallas, she was important to him. He would never hurt her or disrespect her.

"There's probably a twelve-step program for your paint obsession," he told her. "You could get help."

"I'll suffer in silence."

He found the color he was looking for. A milky opal that had a touch of iridescence. After grabbing a small brush and a square of cardboard, he returned to the overhead and studied the button.

"It's the way the light hits the enamel," he said, more to himself than her. "The glass and the…"

He squeezed paint onto the cardboard before dipping his brush and dabbing it onto the plastic sheet. "That's not right."

He collected more paints and a palette, then went to work blending. Violet picked up several brushes and sheets of thick, white paper. Together they worked with the teals and purples until they found the right combination of light and dark, with the slightest hint of glimmer.

Nick put a blank sheet over the painted one and quickly outlined the lace with a permanent marker. He filled in the various colors, following the sample they'd created. When he was done, he looked at the wall.

"That's it," Violet breathed. "Oh wow. That's it." She reached for the marker and touched it to the painting, creating dark dots. "I'll put the extra buttons in these spots. I have enough. They'll pick up the paint."

"Perfect." The dress would be unique to Nova and Joel's world, but elegant. "You should sew those on first. I don't know if the paint will crack on the fabric. Best not to bend it too much before the wedding."

"You have the dress?"

He nodded at a closet. "You can take it with you and bring it back when you're done."

"Should I sign a receipt or something?"

"Because you're going to steal it?"

"I guess not."

The door to the studio opened and Ronan walked in. Nick was surprised. Since the fight, they'd been careful to avoid each other. But with limited workspace, they were bound to cross paths.

Ronan took one look at him, glared, then turned on his heel and left. Violet cleared her throat.

"He doesn't know me from a rock, so I'm guessing I'm not the one he's mad at."

"Ronan and I are working through some issues."

"It's not going very well, is it?"

"No."

"Carol and I couldn't be more different, but we're still close. You and Ronan need to work out your stuff."

"Thanks for the advice."

"Fine. Ignore me. I don't mind. I'll talk to Pallas and she'll bug you about it."

"You know that we're seeing each other?"

Violet grinned. "She's my friend, Nick. In fact all her friends know. We just don't talk about it to you." Her humor faded. "But I will admit that if it comes to a floor fight, we're all team Pallas."

"So am I."

PALLAS HAD EXCEEDED her allotted mope time and yet still found herself bummed about the canceled wedding. She wasn't sure why she was so upset. Of course she felt bad for Nova losing her father so much sooner than expected, but it was more than that. She had a nagging sense of having lost something important.

Monday night she made her way to The Board-room for the weekly tournament. She was hoping some fast-paced fun would improve her mood. If nothing else, she would hang out with Nick and that was always good.

She arrived and found he had already claimed a table. He was chatting with Mathias and Natalie, which gave her the chance to simply watch him.

The man made her heart beat faster, she thought with a sigh. Not just because he was pretty to look at but because of how she felt when they were to-gether. He was an unexpected find and her feelings for him told her she wasn't as ready to give up on love as she'd thought. Somehow she was going to have to get over the whole "love must be earned" thing she had going on so she could find someone to fall in love with.

For a second she allowed herself the fantasy that Nick would stay in Happily Inc and that he would wake up and realize she was *the one*. Doubtful, but still nice to imagine.

He spotted her and smiled, waving her over. She and Natalie hugged before Nick greeted her with a kiss. Mathias held out his arm.

"After that, you and I should at least fist-bump."

She laughed and pressed her fist against his.

"I didn't know you were coming," Natalie said. "Mathias and I are already committed to playing with Atsuko and one of her friends."

"That's okay," Pallas told her. "Nick and I will find someone else."

"Maybe your board game boyfriend will show

up," Natalie teased, before glancing at Nick. "You haven't met Jasper yet, have you?"

"The resident serial killer," Mathias grumbled. "All the women go crazy over him, even though it's just a matter of time until they start to go missing."

Pallas patted his arm. "Did you lose one of your bridesmaid conquests to Jasper? Are we feeling bitter about the competition?"

"He might have had to go an entire weekend without getting any," Natalie teased. "I have no idea how he survived the pain."

"Okay, then," Mathias said. "I'm going to go back to our table and pretend this never happened."

He walked away. Natalie laughed and trailed after him. Nick led Pallas to their table.

"I thought Jasper was that writer I like."

"He is." She took the seat he held out for her. "I'll admit, I haven't read many of his books. They're a little dark for me. But they're very popular."

"For good reason." Nick sat next to her and leaned close. "Board game boyfriend, huh? So I have competition?"

Oh, if only he really were jealous, she thought humorously. "Jasper and I frequently play games together."

Nick raised his eyebrows. "Really?"

"You know what I mean."

"I'm not sure I do. What kind of games?"

"Board games."

Carol joined them. "I am partnerless. Is that okay?"

"You can take the heat off Pallas," Nick said. "Apparently she has a board game boyfriend and with me here tonight, things could get awkward."

"Jasper." Carol grinned. "I hope he shows up. He's just so interesting. It's the bad boy thing."

As if on cue, the door to The Boardroom opened and Jasper Dembenski walked in. Pallas smiled as the room went quiet. Everyone turned to look at the new arrival.

She wasn't sure what it was about him that was so intriguing. He was tall—nearly six-four—with dark hair and green eyes. Most times he sported a three-day beard, which she would guess was a whole lot more about not wanting to shave than a fashion statement. Either way, it looked good on his strong features.

Jasper wasn't conventionally handsome—he was too dangerous looking for that. Instead he was intriguing—and sexy. He wore jeans and boots most of the time. And a leather motorcycle jacket, because yes, the man rode a Harley. Even as he paused just inside the door, Pallas would swear she could hear the opening chords to "Bad to the Bone."

Jasper took off his sunglasses and glanced around the room. His eyes were a deep green, with impossibly long lashes. His gaze was as hard as his muscled body. He caught sight of her and nodded, then started toward their table. All around them women glanced at him, then away, as if he were the sun and staring too long in his direction could be painful... and dangerous.

"Here he comes," Carol said happily. "Yay us. Jasper always brings me luck."

"What kind?" Pallas asked teasingly.

"Not that kind. While he's nice to look at, he's so not my type. Too dangerous, too quiet, too everything. I like nice, seminormal guys."

Jasper stopped behind Pallas's chair and put his hands on her shoulders. "Ladies. May I?"

"Of course," Pallas told him. "Jasper, this is Nick. Nick, Jasper."

Nick rose and the two men shook hands. Jasper glanced between them, then gave Pallas a slow, I'm-so-sexy smile.

"So that's how it is. When did you two get together?"

She stared at him. "It's been eight seconds. How on earth did you figure it out so quickly?"

One shoulder rose and lowered. She took that to mean some version of *I'm a writer. It's my job and nature to observe people and pick up clues about them and their lives. Thank you for asking, Pallas. I've always enjoyed your unique wit and charm.*

Which might or might not be what he was thinking.

"What's on tap for tonight?" Jasper asked, sitting next to Pallas and across from Carol.

Pallas glanced at the sheet on the table. "We're having a Monopoly tournament," she said as she read, then she started to laugh.

"What?" Nick asked.

"It's Monopoly Junior. I want to be the cat."

Nick frowned. "I don't understand. We're playing Monopoly Junior?"

"I'm not a dog person," Carol said. "I suppose you guys want to be either the ship or the car, right?"

"I'll be the dog," Jasper told her.

"Really? Thanks."

Nick still looked confused.

"The tournaments always have a twist," Pallas told him. "We'll be playing Monopoly Junior tonight. I hope I can buy the ice-cream parlor. It's my favorite."

"I want the zoo." Carol smiled.

"You are all weird," Nick muttered. "I want to be the car."

"Of course you do," Pallas teased.

Carol reached for the ship. "My favorite piece. We are so going places."

By the first break, nearly a quarter of the people were eliminated. At their table Carol had run out of money. Under the regular rules, the game would be over, but in a tournament, the rest of the table kept playing until it was time for the break.

"We get fifteen minutes to eat and collect more adult beverages," Pallas told Nick as they rose.

"Carol is out permanently?" he asked.

"Yes. She's done for the night. Someone will join our table and we'll all start from the beginning again. With each round, the group playing gets smaller and smaller until there are just three or four left. They'll play for the night's championship." She leaned against him. "Admit it, you're having fun."

"I am." He nodded at the crowd at the bar. "I'll brave that. What do you want?"

"Hot tea."

"You're such a lightweight."

"I have to drive home and work in the morning."

He kissed her. "I'll be right back."

Pallas stretched and looked around. She knew nearly everyone in the room—a not uncommon occurrence. What must it be like for people who grew up in big cities or moved around a lot? Would it be interesting to not know everyone around, or lonely?

Drew walked over. "Hey, you. How's it going?"

She eyed him cautiously. "What? If you're going to talk about Silver, I'm not participating. She's my friend and I'm on her side."

"I'm your cousin. Family first."

"She's my girlfriend, and no."

"I'm hurt."

She doubted that.

"I actually came to talk to you about something else," he told her. "The bank."

"What about it?"

He glanced over his shoulder, as if making sure they weren't going to be overheard. "Your mom is very happy about some canceled wedding. She seems to think it will cause you to rethink your decision not to go to work for her."

Pallas tried to ignore the sudden rock in her stomach. "I don't get it. She makes all these rules and when I break them, she tells me to forget it. That I've lost my chance. So why would she care if…" She pressed her lips together. "Sorry. You have no idea what I'm talking about."

"You're right. I don't." His expression turned serious. "What I do know is you and your mom have a difficult relationship. You always have. But you're my cousin and we're close. If you want to come work at the bank, just say the word. I'll give you a job. Don't let Libby jerk your chain any more than she already has."

The rock disappeared and her muscles relaxed. "Why would you do that for me? You know she'd be pissed."

He flashed her a grin. "So what? I'm the blessed heir apparent. All goodness flows through me." The smile faded. "Seriously, you're qualified. You're a hard worker and people like you. You're exactly the kind of person we're always looking for. So it's your call. You can come see me at any time."

She flung herself at him and wrapped her arms around him. "Thank you. I appreciate the offer so much."

"There's a no in there, isn't there?"

She stepped back. "There is. I love my business. It's what I want to do with my life. I need to make that clear to my mom. But I appreciate your faith in me, Drew. I mean it."

"Unlike you, I care about family."

She sighed. "I'm not talking about Silver. Stop trying to make me."

"Does she ever mention me?"

Pallas pointed to his table. "Go."

"Does she miss me? Blink if that's a yes."

She shook her head. "You're ridiculous."

"I'm running a very successful bank, Pallas. That makes me a catch."

With that, he walked away. A few minutes later, Nick was back with a beer and a mug of hot tea.

"You're looking pensive," he said as he sat next to her.

"Drew offered me a job at the bank."

"Do you want to take it?"

"No, but I'm happy he said what he did." She rolled her eyes. "Apparently my mother has been all excited that Nova and Joel's wedding is canceled. She seems to think this will bring me to my senses. I don't get it. She wants me on her very exact terms and only on her terms. I'm not willing to do what she says, so why does she keep trying? I can't imagine she's all that thrilled at the thought of working with me. All we do is fight."

"Maybe she wants to be closer to you."

"I doubt that. Most of the time, I'm not even sure she likes me."

"Are you going to take Drew up on the job?"

"No. I want to stay with Weddings in a Box. I like what I'm doing. The black-and-white wedding kind of threw me, but I was excited about the alien wedding. I wanted to be challenged and see it all happen. That's important to me."

"Have you told your mom that?"

"What and be mature? No. I just wish…"

He waited.

"I wish she would accept me for who I am," Pallas said at last. "Without having to follow any rules or do what she says."

He kissed her. "You want your mom to love you unconditionally."

Which made her sound like a five-year-old, she thought, embarrassed. "I guess I should get over it."

"Why? She's your mother. That's her job—to love and support you. Yes, you've followed your own path. So has Cade. You want to feel supported and loved in your own family. That's not unreasonable."

Pallas knew he was right. She shouldn't have to fight her mother, just to be happy. And she should stop putting her life on hold until she received an approval that wasn't coming. Only knowing the right thing to do and standing up to Libby were two different things.

"Baby steps," she whispered. "That's about all I can do."

"You're moving forward. That's what matters."

The warning bell rang, signaling the start of the second round. Nick returned to his seat across from her. Wynn walked over.

"Everyone at my table is out," she said cheerfully. "I'm warning you, I've been on a roll."

Pallas laughed. "I think you have to worry about Jasper more than us. If the break had come five minutes later, I would have been out for sure." She waved her token. "But I'm keeping my cat."

Wynn waved her hand. "I don't care which one I am. Oh, and no one can tell Hunter what we did tonight. He's already bitter about not being able to come to the tournaments. If he finds out we played a game he considers himself too old for, he'll be devastated."

"I won't say a word," Pallas promised. She glanced

up and saw Jasper approaching. "Look who's joining us," she called.

Jasper spotted Wynn. For a second, it seemed as
if he froze in place, but the hesitation was so quick,
Pallas couldn't be sure.

Wynn and Jasper? She couldn't imagine the re-
clusive writer and the single mom together. What
would they have in common?

"Pallas has to have the cat," he said as he took
his seat.

"So I've been told." Wynn laughed. "I'll take anything. Oh, and I plan to win, just so everyone is prepared."

See, Pallas told herself. They were just friends.
Imagining anything else was ridiculous.

## CHAPTER FIFTEEN

THE HEAT FROM the blowtorch made it hard to breathe. Even through the protective gloves, Nick could feel the fire licking close to his skin. He already had a half-dozen minor burns on his arms and he and Mathias were only in day two of their metal experiment.

He waited an extra second, then turned off the blowtorch. He and Mathias quickly carried the rod to the clamps and began to twist the metal. They had a limited amount of time before the rod cooled. Once it did, they had to heat it again. Unfortunately, there were only so many times any piece could be heated and cooled before it was compromised. Something they'd learned the hard way. There were shattered and broken rods all over the concrete floor.

"One more?" Mathias asked.

Nick nodded.

Mathias turned the handle. Nick watched the rod twist, crack and go sailing out in five different directions. He and his brother ducked. One of the pieces clipped Nick in the arm. He felt a sharp pain and looked down in time to see blood trickling past his elbow.

"This might be harder than it looked on YouTube," Mathias grumbled.

Nick pulled off his gloves and goggles, then went to the sink to wash his wound. He slapped on an oversize bandage from the ones always kept in the cupboard.

"We should probably take a class or something," Nick told him. "Talk about embarrassing. Want to get a beer?"

They went to The Boardroom and ordered beers, then took a table by the window. Nick smiled as he thought about the tournament last Monday. Jasper had ended up winning it all, just like Pallas had predicted. She'd gone out in the third round, with Nick quickly following in the fourth.

He'd enjoyed himself. The people in town were friendly, which was a lot like where he'd grown up. The tourist element was also similar, but played out in a different way. Weddings instead of festivals.

Still, Fool's Gold had been a great place to grow up. He'd always had his brothers. Nick and the twins. That was how everyone had thought of the three younger boys.

"What?" Mathias asked. "You look strange."

Nick took that to be a comment on his expression rather than his face. "I was remembering when we were Nick and the twins."

"I believe you mean the twins and Nick."

"Always competitive."

"In my way."

Nick picked up his beer. "How are you getting along with Ronan?"

"We have good days and bad days. He's dealing."

"Not very well."

"Give it time."

"It's been nearly three years. He needs to get over it and move on."

"Easy for you to say. You didn't lose anything."

Nick wanted to point out that Ronan hadn't, either—the only thing that was different was information. He was still their brother and their mother's favorite. But saying that wouldn't help. Telling Mathias was meaningless and Ronan wouldn't listen.

"Ronan and I are fighting," Nick said.

"Duh."

"Still."

"You need to stop." Mathias shook his head. "I remember when all the fights were with Dad."

*Either about art or about their brothers*, Nick thought. Once Ceallach realized his two older sons weren't especially talented, he'd lost interest in them. Only the three with potential had mattered. Even as a kid, Nick had known that was wrong. While he appreciated being special, he was uncomfortable knowing Del and Aidan weren't allowed to bask in the glory that was their father.

"I can't figure out if they had it better or worse," Nick said. "Del and Aidan never had to compete, never had to deal with him. They walked away and got their own lives."

"He is both a blessing and curse."

"Where's the blessing?" Nick asked.

"Say what you want about him, it was a good gene pool. We were lucky."

Nick supposed he was right. He couldn't imagine not being able to create the way he did. Sure, things went wrong—there were plenty of shattered pieces of metal to prove that—but at the end of the day he could pick up a chainsaw and let the wood speak for him. He could carve or blow glass or, in a pinch, paint. Without that—he honestly didn't know who he would be. But there had been a price.

"You're going to say that the way he rode us hard made us better artists."

Mathias shook his head. "I don't think he made me better. I think he made me question whether I should bother. But with you and Ronan—you were able to compete with him."

A competition that had cost them dearly, Nick thought grimly. Nick had walked away from the medium he thought would be his forever. He hadn't worked with glass in nearly a decade. Mathias had given up on fine art, instead spending his time and talent making practical items like vases and glasses. The result of Ceallach's judgment on his work. When their father hadn't liked something Mathias had done, he would casually backhand it off the table so it shattered onto the floor. One day Mathias, like Nick, had stopped trying.

Only Ronan had hung in there, willing to go toe-to-toe with their father. It might have been because he was more able to handle all the crap. Or because he was stubborn. Or maybe it was because he was just plain brilliant. An asshole sometimes, but a brilliant one. Funny how that made him the most like Ceallach.

"You miss Dad being around?" Nick asked.

"No. Not even a little. You?"

"Nope. I should have left years ago. Interesting how four of us got away. Only Aidan is left in Fool's Gold."

Aidan—one of the nonblessed, or so Ceallach would say. From Nick's perspective, Aidan was one lucky guy. He had a business he loved and the woman of his dreams. Maybe the universe was compensating him for a crappy childhood.

"You talk to Mom much?" Mathias asked.

"I call her every few weeks. She's fine. All she wants to talk about is Ceallach. She barely asks what I have going on." Because her husband had always been the center of her world. No one else existed. Passion consumed. He was wise to stay safe.

"What about you?" he asked.

"We stay in touch. She always asks about Ronan."

"He won't call her?"

"Not very often."

"Someone needs to beat the crap out of him," Nick muttered.

"You made a run at it and look how that went."

Nick looked at his brother. "I wasn't trying very hard."

"Oh, sure. Is that what we're saying now?"

"He's my brother. I wasn't going to hurt him. I was trying to make a point."

Mathias looked amused. "Whatever gets you through the night."

"I know what gets you through the night," Nick said, remembering Natalie's teasing at the game tournament. "You'd better be careful. Aidan was a player and look what happened to him."

"He's crazy in love with Shelby and couldn't be happier."

"Is that what you want?"

Mathias didn't hesitate. "No."

"You sure? Aren't you tired of a different girl every night?"

"It's only on weekends." Mathias's smile faded. "Okay, sure, sometimes I think about having someone serious but I don't know. People who love you betray you."

"Not everyone. I haven't."

"I appreciate that. Okay, not you or Del or Aidan, but pretty much everyone else." Mathias's tone was offhand, as if he was perfectly all right with what had happened, but Nick knew that couldn't be true. As for the brother not mentioned—how had Ronan betrayed him?

"These thoughts are too deep for the time of day," Mathias said. "What about you and Pallas? How's that going?"

Not a subtle change of topic, but one Nick would accept. "Good. Great. I like her a lot."

"But?"

"I'm leaving for Dubai."

Mathias's mouth twitched. "I hate to burst your bubble, but you don't have the commission yet, bro."

"Come on. It's me. Who else would get it? I'm a Mitchell."

"Blessing and curse, like I said." He studied Nick. "You'll get it based on the name."

Nick glared at him. "And the talent."

"If you had any." He held up his beer bottle. "To our parents. At least we have someone to blame for screwing us up."

Nick hit his bottle against his brother's. "If life gives you lemons."

"MY FIANCÉ AND I were so impressed by Catherine's wedding," the curvy, petite brunette said eagerly. "We decided that night we had to have our wedding here."

Which was exactly what Taylor had said on the phone, Pallas thought in some confusion. How could anyone have been impressed with that disaster? "The black-and-white princess wedding," she clarified. "Where the zebras got loose and the DJ robbed the guests."

"Only with a paint gun." Taylor waved her hand. "The zebra thing was no big deal and the DJ was Catherine's fault. It's important to vet people and read reviews." She beamed. "I read all about you online. You have some excellent referrals. I was able to friend a couple of them on Facebook and then talk to them. Everybody loves you. They think you do excellent work for the price. You handle details and make sure it all comes out perfectly."

Unexpected praise, Pallas thought, hoping she didn't blush. "Thank you," she murmured.

"You're welcome." Taylor pulled a folder out of

her large Michael Kors tote. "Jake and I want an under-the-sea wedding."

Pallas stared at the picture of the mermaid-styled wedding gown and seashell dinnerware. She was less sure about the dress style on Taylor's somewhat short, round body type.

"Have you already tried on dresses?"

"Yes, and I'm so close to picking the one I want. It's fantastic." Taylor's happy smile returned. "Jake and I met by the beach. We were in a skin diving class together. I took one look at him and just knew." She sighed. "We're going to honeymoon in Hawaii."

"That will be lovely. So, um, under the sea. You do realize Happily Inc is in the desert, right?"

Taylor laughed. "Of course. We love that it's centrally located for our families and friends, with plenty of hotel space." She leaned forward and lowered her voice. "Jake is going to be a pirate. We're so excited. Could you get us a parrot to ride on his shoulder?"

Pallas's first instinct was to say no. No to the parrot, no to the under-the-sea theme, no to everything. Which was, she told herself, a reaction to Nova having to cancel her wedding. It had nothing to do with adorable Taylor and her slightly strange ideas.

This was what she wanted, Pallas reminded herself. A chance to try something different. If she and her team could create an alien world, why couldn't they come up with an under-the-sea theme?

"Tell me what you had in mind," she said as she pulled out a pad of paper.

"We want our colors to reflect the ocean. Aqua,

blue, sea green. I wish there was a way to make it feel like we were underwater. I guess big fish tanks would be expensive, huh?"

"More than that, one of the things you like about the ocean is the freedom it represents. The sea seems endless. Fish in a tank are the opposite of that." Pallas pressed her lips together. She had no idea where that had come from.

Taylor's brown eyes widened. "You're good," she breathed.

"Thanks. We can't be in the ocean, but maybe we can create the illusion of being under the sea." She stood and crossed to the bookcase on the far wall. "I have some pictures that show what I mean."

She returned to her desk and flipped through the pictures. "This," she said, pointing. One of her brides had asked for sheers to be put around the courtyard. "See how they're lit?"

"It's beautiful," Taylor said, sounding doubtful.

"I have the white sheers. Imagine if we backlit them with blues and greens. As they moved in the breeze, they could really look like water. Maybe we could look at Mylar streamers to hang down in front of the sheers." She drew on the pad to illustrate what she meant. "We could pick plants that had an ocean grass or seaweed kind of feel and put them around the edges by the sheers."

"Oh, I like that a lot!"

"Me, too. You know, it would be relatively easy to expand this theme. I'd say go with white linens. They're the least expensive and give us a perfect backdrop. Shells on the table, small message in a bottle kind of decorations instead of name cards." She caught her breath. "Oh, wow. What if you did larger message in a bottle for the invitations? They'd be harder to mail, but it might be worth it. There are shell combs for the bridesmaids' hair."

She flipped through the photo album and stopped on another page. "Silver, our resident bartender, does these fun Jell-O shots." She pointed to a picture. "I'll bet she could do a custom color to match everything else."

"I'd love that."

"And for a centerpiece, if you want to do something different, what about treasure chests? We could use glass beads and little starfishes, along with flowers. It could be unique and pretty and—"

Taylor flung herself at Pallas and burst into tears. "Thank you so much. I've wanted a mermaid wedding since I was four years old. I've been to so many other venues and everyone else told me my idea was unworkable and silly. You're making my wedding dreams come true."

Pallas hugged her back. "I'm so glad you think so. I really like your idea, Taylor. Why don't I put together a proposal, listing all my ideas, and you and Jake can look it over? Then we can meet again in person or have a conference call."

Taylor released her and wiped the tears off her face. "I would love that. Thank you. You have no idea how happy you've made me."

Pallas was feeling a little giddy herself. She got Taylor's contact information and promised to have the proposal to her by the end of the week.

This was why she did what she did, she reminded herself when Taylor had left. To make people happy on one of the most important days in their lives. Somehow she'd let herself lose a little of the magic, but she was getting it back bit by bit.

She made a few more notes, then went in search of Nick. She'd seen his truck pull up as Taylor had arrived and guessed he was here to work on the panels. It was warm these days—maybe he'd taken off his shirt.

She was still grinning when she walked around the corner and saw him bent over the huge carved wood panel. Then he straightened and she gasped as she saw a big bandage on his arm. The center was red from blood—as if the wound had taken a long time to stop bleeding.

"What did you do?" she asked as she ran over to him. "Are you okay? Should you see a doctor?"

He turned and frowned. "What are you talking about? I'm fine."

She reached for the bandage, but stopped herself before touching it, only to see about a half-dozen small burns between his forearms and the hem of his T-shirt.

"What happened?"

He touched his fingers to her chin and forced her to meet his gaze. "I'm fine. It's nothing."

"You look like you've been in a battle. Did your stove explode or something?"

He laughed. "Mathias and I have been working with metal. It's not going well, but I'm fine. It's been fun, but if we want to continue, we're going to need some training."

"And fire protection," she said, lightly tracing the burns. "Did you put anything on these?"

"Yes."

She glared at him. "You're lying. You didn't do anything."

His mouth turned up. "I put a bandage on the cut."

"When was the last time you had a tetanus shot?"

"A couple of years ago."

She put her hands on her hips. "For real?"

"Yes, I swear." He drew her close and kissed her. "But it's nice that you worry about me."

"Someone has to," she grumbled. "You were really having fun while setting fire to yourself."

"We all find our thrill in different ways. You're one of my favorite ways."

He always said the nicest things, she thought happily, enjoying the way his mouth teased hers.

He drew back just a little. "So how's your day going? Didn't you have an appointment with a potential client?"

"I did. Taylor and Jake. They want an under-the-sea wedding."

"What does that mean?"

"She dresses like a mermaid and he's a pirate."

"I'm the guy here, so maybe I'm missing the point, but if pirates go *under* the sea, aren't they dead?"

"You're reading too much into it. Don't look for the logic—just go with it."

"Okay. I will. What did you talk about?"

Pallas showed him her notes and the things they'd

come up with while brainstorming. "I want to use the sheers to create the illusion of water moving."

"You have to use pearls," he said, taking the pad from her and flipping to a clean page. He pulled a pencil out of his shirt pocket and drew what looked like a tall glass.

"There have to be some kind of plastic pearls that would float," he said, sketching several floating ovals. "We could weight them with something small. Or maybe layers of clear lacquer so they float at different levels. Then you put a votive at the top." He finished the drawing.

"I love it," she breathed. "They would be easy to put together and inexpensive. Plus we could use the tall holders for other weddings."

"You could. The food will be fun. How about a battered rowboat to hold sodas and water?"

"Perfect. And little sand dollar cookies. I have a custom cookie designer I can call. Now that you're on a roll, I have a problem for you to solve. What do we do about decorating the chairs?"

He flipped to another page and drew one of the chairs they used for weddings. After thinking for a minute, he began to fill in the back with rippling strips.

"Fabric," he told her. "Connected to some kind of band or backing. You cut it out like ruffles and edge it. Pale blue, aqua, creamy white."

She nodded, liking what he was doing. "Those would have to be custom. Unless Taylor knows someone who can edge all the fabric and then sew them together. We also thought about using a message in a bottle for place settings. I wonder if there's a way to make that work for the guest book."

He pulled her close. "It's not Nova and Joel's wedding, but it will still be fun," he told her.

"I know. That's what I keep thinking. Have you heard from her?"

"No."

"No one has. I hope Tim hasn't died. Not that I want him suffering. It's just hard."

He kissed her again. "You have a very big heart."

"How could you know them and not care?"

"Some people wouldn't."

"Then they don't have hearts at all."

PALLAS SPENT THE rest of the day working on her bid for Taylor. The more she played with different ideas, the more those ideas blossomed. While the basic wedding menu was fine, she found she really enjoyed the creative challenges.

"You're looking happy about something."

Pallas glanced up to find Libby standing in the doorway to her office. She quickly saved her computer file, then stood. "Mom, did I know you were going to stop by?"

"You did not."

Libby glanced around the office, then sighed, as if disappointed, yet again. She took the seat across from Pallas's. "I stopped by to ask what on earth you're doing."

Pallas was pretty sure Libby wasn't talking about the under-the-sea wedding. "You mean in my life?"

"No. With this business. How much longer are you

going to pretend that it's right for you? That you can make it a success? You're dabbling, which is incredibly disappointing for all of us. I'd hoped you would come to your senses on your own, but it has become apparent that isn't going to happen."

Pallas honestly didn't know what to say—which turned out to be less of an issue when her mother just kept talking.

"It's a nightmare," Libby continued. "Every time I turn around, it's worse. You are just like your grandfather."

"Grandpa Frank?"

Her mother pressed her lips together. "Who else would I mean? Bad enough that you're destroying your future, but you're taking the family's reputation down with you. Have you considered that?"

"Mom, I honestly have no idea what you're talking about."

"You were supposed to be working at the bank," Libby said, her tone sharp. "*That* was your dream. Not this wedding nonsense. I have no idea what you're thinking, but you're wrong. About all of it. You worked so hard for your degree. I was so sure you'd learned your lesson. Yet here you are, throwing everything away, and for what?"

There were so many statements, so many accusations, Pallas didn't know where to begin. She went from shocked to angry to sad in the space of a few seconds. As her mother went on and on, Pallas realized no matter what she did, she always disappointed Libby. Nothing was ever right or good enough or positive.

Nearly ten years before, Libby and her sister Margaret had decided to go on a cruise together—something they'd never done. Pallas had been happy for her mother and had spent a not-inconsiderable amount on a perfume set. Something special for her mom to take on the trip. Something to say, "Hey, Mom, I love you. Have a great time."

Libby had stared at the box before shaking her head. "Why did you buy this? I could have gotten it for half the price at the duty-free shop."

At the time Pallas had been hurt. Now she knew she had to accept the bitter truth. She and Libby would never be close. They would never just hang out and talk. While on the surface it seemed that if she just took the job at the bank, everything would be fine, she knew that wasn't true. One way or the other, she would screw up and Libby would once again be disappointed.

"You're not listening to me," her mother complained. "That is so like you."

"A constant disappointment?" Pallas asked, then didn't bother waiting for an answer. "You know what, Mom? I get it. I know exactly how it feels to be disappointed by someone again and again."

"I doubt that."

"You're wrong. I know it because that's how I feel about you."

Pallas had no idea where the words had come from, but the second she uttered them, she knew she was telling the truth. A truth that she'd been afraid to even think for far too long.

"Don't you—" her mother started.

Pallas ignored her and kept talking. "I've worked so hard to make you happy. To make you proud of me. I've kept banging my head against the wall and nothing ever changes. I'm sure you're going to say it's all my fault and maybe it is, but you know what? I'm tired of trying. I've always felt less than everyone else in your eyes. I don't know why it has to be like this but that's the way it is."

"I… You…" Libby sucked in air. "You can't speak to me like that."

"I'm not being disrespectful—I'm telling you how I feel. And I feel bad. All the time. You're not like this with Cade. I don't know if it's a girl thing or what. He never did what you wanted and you adore him. So what is it? Why can't I make you happy? Or maybe that's not the question. Maybe I should ask, why don't you care about what makes me happy?"

Pallas's chest was tight. She didn't know if she was going to cry or scream or pass out, but she kept going. She'd started this and she was going to see it through.

"Working here makes me happy. Owning Weddings in a Box is an amazing blessing and I'm grateful every day that Gerald cared enough about me to leave me this business. Yes, it's hard work and yes, I might fail, but so what? I'm going to do my best every single day, and I'm going to keep trying to make it a success. If that means you're not proud of me, then that's your problem, not mine. You've punished me before, Mom. I survived that and I'll get over this."

Pallas stood and grabbed her purse. "You're

wrong to put conditions on your love. You've done it my whole life and you've always been wrong. Families should love each other, no matter what. Sometimes I don't like you very much, but I'll always love you."

With that, she started for the door. She'd finally stood up to her mother. It had taken twenty-eight years, but she'd done it. Now she had to make her way to her car and get somewhere safe before she started shaking too much to drive. And then she was going to have wine because it had to be five o'clock somewhere.

# CHAPTER SIXTEEN

NICK HESITATED AT the entrance of the bank. While he understood the theory of separating business from his personal life, he was still pretty pissed at Libby Saunders for always coming down on her daughter.

The previous night, over a bottle of wine, Pallas had told him about her latest confrontation with her mother. While he had been impressed by Pallas's strength and courage, he wanted to confront Libby and ask her what the hell she was thinking. Pallas was a wonderful woman, a great person and any parent would be proud to have her as a daughter. Any parent except for Libby. He had no idea what had happened in the other woman's past to make her this way, nor did he care. He only knew that Libby hurt someone he cared about and that pissed him off.

The fact that she was a woman pushing sixty meant he couldn't do anything about it. Nothing physical, anyway. But he could be mad and possibly move his bank account somewhere else.

The latter thought nearly brought him out of his mood. Sure, because that would show her.

He walked inside and crossed to a teller window where he made his deposit. The young man's professional demeanor only flickered a little when he saw the amount of the check. It had been a good month, Nick thought humorously. His art was selling all over the world. Atsuko had a knack for putting the right piece in the right gallery—a talent that was making him a very rich man.

He took his receipt and headed for the door. Before he got there, he heard rapid high heels on the marble floor. The hairs on the back of his neck rose, so he turned and saw Libby approaching.

She wore a dark suit and pearls. Her eyes snapped with what even he could see was annoyance. He came to a stop, ready for whatever she had to say. A verbal confrontation would be just fine with him.

"If you would follow me," she said, without bothering with a greeting.

He didn't even hesitate, instead following her through to what he guessed were the executive offices. She went into one and faced him.

"This is all your fault," she said as he stopped in front of her. "Every bit of it."

"I have no idea what 'it' is," he told her.

"Pallas, that ridiculous business of hers. Everything was on track before you got here. Everything was going the way it should have."

"Oh, I don't know. I'd say the problem started when you punished Pallas for what happened in college," he said easily. "If you hadn't been such a hard-ass, she wouldn't have had to move home and take a job with Gerald to support herself. She would have been safely in college, earning her finance degree before coming to work here, with you."

Libby's mouth dropped open. "How dare you!"

"Tell the truth? I know hearing it can be hard. So while I'm on a roll, let me just ask this. Why do you have to ride her so hard? You're always demanding the impossible, then shutting her out. What's up with that? Where's the win? Are you going to mean her into doing what you want? You're only pushing her away."

"You have no right to talk to me this way."

"At the risk of sounding like a five-year-old, you started it."

Drew joined them. He glanced at Libby.

"You do realize everyone working back here can hear you," he said quietly. "Perhaps you'd like to take this to the privacy of your home instead of this bank."

Libby flushed. "I do not want to take it anywhere. I want this man to leave."

"This man is a customer. Libby, you need to calm down. I'll take care of Nick. If you'll excuse us?"

Libby glared at them both. Nick was intrigued by the dynamics of the complicated relationship. While Drew was Libby's nephew, he was also some high-up guy at the bank. Pallas had called him the heir apparent. Did that mean he was Libby's boss? Or that he would be one day?

He didn't get an answer from her. Instead Libby held open the door and when they left, she closed it behind them. Drew led him down the hall.

"Let me buy you a cup of coffee."

"Sure."

They went into a large, glassed-in office with a big executive desk and a couple of leather sofas in the corner. Drew opened a cabinet that held a Keurig coffee brewer and held out a tray of pods.

"What are you in the mood for?"

Nick picked dark roast. Drew dropped it into the machine, put a mug on the tray and pushed a button.

"I assume you take it black," Drew said as he handed him the full mug.

"Sure."

Drew made a cup for himself, then sat on the second sofa. "This is where I apologize for my aunt. I have no idea what got into her."

"Really? I would think it's pretty obvious to anyone who knows her and understands the dynamics between her and her daughter."

"You have a point." Drew studied him. "Anything you want to tell me?"

"You called this meeting." Nick had no idea what the other man wanted, but he could be patient and wait.

"You've been seeing a lot of Pallas."

So they were going there. Good. He wanted someone to have her back. "I have been."

Drew waited.

Nick figured that as family Drew was entitled to win this round, so he said, "She's great. I like her a lot. And I'm leaving in a few months for Dubai. I'll be there two years." At least that was the plan, he thought. Assuming he wanted to take the commission. Which he did. Why wouldn't he?

"She knows?"

"Yes. I've been up-front about it. I don't want to hurt her."

"Sometimes we do it without wanting to."

"Agreed."

"Libby's not easy," Drew said. "I don't know what her deal is, but it's pretty firmly focused on Pallas. I guess it's a mother-daughter thing. Regardless, Pallas has people who care about her."

Nick wasn't sure if he was being warned away or offered comforting information. He decided it didn't matter. "I'm glad she doesn't have to go it alone."

"Me, too."

Nick waited a second, then figured there wasn't going to be anything else. "Thanks for the coffee," he said as he put the mug on the table next to him and rose.

"Anytime."

Drew walked him out. Nick half expected another confrontation with Libby, but he didn't see her again.

*Families*, he thought as he headed back to the studio. They were complicated. In Fool's Gold he'd known the rules, but here, with Pallas's family, not so much. And then there was Pallas. He wasn't sure what to do about her. Dubai had always been the plan. Now, as he faced the fact that he would have to decide sooner rather than later, he was willing to admit that he would miss her. Miss them.

For a moment he allowed himself to speculate on what would happen if he didn't take the commission. Or if he asked her to come with him. Not that he could do either. Passion consumed. Even if it didn't, she had a life here. A business. But he enjoyed their time together and he didn't want it to end. A realization that rattled him more than he would have liked.

Neither of his brothers were at the studio when he got there. He walked over to the metal sculpture. He and Mathias had gotten to the point where there was shape, but nothing to be proud of. They were amateurs, dabbling. He thought about carving something but that didn't appeal. Restless, he prowled the huge room before stopping in front of a big storage closet. Inside was Nova's dress, which Violet had returned. All the buttons were in place—sewn by hand. He'd figured out what to do but hadn't started it yet. While Nova had given him the go-ahead, he'd waited until he felt the time was right.

Now he pulled the dress out of the closet and set the hanger on a hook on the wall. He studied the swirls of the lace, the way the pattern repeated in very subtle ways and the sparkle of light on the buttons. He crossed to his desk and pulled out the folder with the final design. Then he collected paints and a brush.

Before he made the first stroke of purple paint on the expensive dress, he thought briefly of Violet and how she would be screaming. Different from Pallas who would be all in. Still smiling, he began to paint.

"I DON'T HATE her exactly," Pallas said, passing a cookie to Silver.

"You should. If she were my mother, I'd hate her plenty. I can hate her for you, if you'd like."

Pallas smiled. "You're always a good friend to me."

"I know. Practically a saint. I should have a statue in the town square."

"We don't have a town square."

"Then we should get one and put up a plaque."

They were finishing up lunch. Silver had come by with leftovers from a shower she'd worked at the night before. The mini sandwiches and salads had been delicious, as were the cookies. They sat in the shade of a big tree in the courtyard of Weddings in a Box, enjoying the quiet before the wedding madness began in a few hours. While Pallas hadn't meant to say anything about what had happened with her mom, she'd found herself telling Silver everything.

"Libby's a bitch," Silver said flatly. "You're not going to say it, so I will. She's horrible. I'm sure she has some twisted reason, but I don't care. You're her kid. You're supposed to be nice to your kid. Especially one like you. You're productive, successful and grounded. What more does she want?"

"Me to work in the bank." That had become clear. Funny how Pallas had always felt she had to fight her mother to get a job there, but over the past few weeks she'd realized that Libby actually did want her working at the bank. She had no idea why. For control? To be able to say, "This is my daughter and she works with me?" Only that implied pride and she'd never felt her mother was proud of anything she did.

"Maybe *she* didn't want to work at the bank," Silver said. "Maybe she only did it because she thought she had to and she resents you've had the courage to follow your heart."

"I don't know. Maybe." She couldn't imagine her mother doing anything but working at the bank. It was as if Libby had been formed rather than born.

Always an adult, always responsible and dressed in a suit. "Enough about her. Let's talk about something fun."

"Like the under-the-sea wedding?" Silver took another cookie. "You gotta love Taylor's courage to just go for it. Good for her. I already have a bunch of ideas for shots and signature drinks. I'm emailing you my proposal first thing Monday."

"I'm excited about all the fun things we could do."

"I love Nick's idea about the soda and water in an old rowboat. I should be able to pick one up cheap, and then line it with plastic."

"Do they make them for kids? Because that size would be better."

Silver laughed. "See? This is so much more you than balancing ledgers and counting money. You'd hate working with your mom."

Pallas grinned. "You've never taken a finance class, have you? There's more to banking than counting money."

"Blah, blah. It's boring, regardless." She gestured to the open courtyard. "This is us. We weren't meant to conform. And screw those who don't get that."

An interesting turn of conversation, Pallas thought. "Drew?" she asked gently.

"I don't know anyone named Drew, and if I did, I would think he was a jerk. Nope, I'm over him. Totally and completely."

Pallas thought that Silver would be a lot happier if that were actually true.

"Have you thought of—" she began before Silver shook her head.

"Don't go there."

"But..."

"No. I appreciate the thought, but no. I am over him. *O.V.E.R.* We are done and I don't care." She scrambled to her feet. "Okay, I need to go prep for tonight. I'll see you soon."

Pallas collected the remains of their lunch, and then stood. She tossed the trash, but instead of going inside, she took a moment to study the building. From inside in the courtyard, there were plain stucco walls and lots of plants and trees. From the outside, there were different facades on different sides. Illusion, she thought, but the best kind. The kind that allowed silly dreams to become beautiful memories.

Gerald had given her the gift of opportunity and faith. Because he'd believed in her enough to trust her with all he'd worked for. He'd loved her and cared for her and had changed her life forever.

She walked inside. One of the wood panels was still on supports as Nick worked the repairs. Soon they would all be restored to their glorious selves. She was glad she hadn't looked into selling them. Whatever their worth, they belonged here. While they wouldn't fit in with every wedding, they were still a part of her inheritance and she was grateful.

Her mother might be a nightmare, but Pallas had good men in her life. Her brother, her grandfather, Drew, Gerald, Alan.

Nick.

He was an unexpected pleasure. Strong and kind, funny, charming and more talented than anyone she'd ever met. What he could do with nearly any medium overwhelmed her. But he didn't talk about his brilliance, or use it as an excuse. He worked the program. And soon he would be in Dubai.

Funny how at first she hadn't cared, but now the thought of him leaving made her sad. No—more than sad. More than upset. She would miss him desperately. She'd become used to seeing him every day, talking with him, making love with him. She liked that they went to The Boardroom for games tournaments and hung out with friends and had their own rituals. She liked everything about being with him. She'd been so busy scrambling to finish her degree and working and trying to please her mother that she'd forgotten what it was like to be a part of something. To care about someone that much.

Or maybe it wasn't that at all. Maybe it wasn't a timing issue, but a man issue. Maybe she'd never bothered before because no one else had been Nick. And if her feelings were specifically about him, did that mean... Was it possible...

Pallas stopped in the hallway and told herself to breathe. The truth was just there, out of reach. She wanted to know and whatever it was, she would deal. How did she feel about Nick?

The answer came immediately and most of her wasn't surprised. She loved him. She probably had for a while. She loved his smile and his mind and the way he was always touching her. She loved how he kept her safe and had been so excited about Nova's wedding. She was in love with Nick.

She waited for the fear that was sure to follow. Because love had to be earned. Only Nick hadn't earned her love. He'd simply been the man in her life. Which meant what? That she'd given love freely? That she'd handed over her heart with no expectation for reciprocation? She just loved him?

The concept was both shocking and freeing. If she could love Nick that way, with no payment required, then maybe she could start to accept that other people could feel the same way about her. Maybe she wasn't doomed to be her mother after all.

She let the knowledge of her love for Nick fill her and smiled when she felt the rightness of it. She loved him and in the loving, she was healing. It was right and it felt good. When he left, she was probably going to get her heart ripped out, but that was okay, too. It was what had to happen next. Nick was leaving and even if he wasn't, he didn't want love. He believed that passion consumed. He was wrong, but he would have to figure that out for himself. There was no way to convince him.

*Talk about mature*, she thought to herself. Look at her—all big with the emotional growth. She was pretty proud of herself. Who knew what she would conquer next!

THAT NIGHT NICK barbecued on her small patio. She had thought about telling him what she'd discovered—what she felt, but had ultimately decided that was her thing, not his. He'd never asked her to love him. If she told him, he might not understand how she meant it and he might feel trapped. She didn't want either. She wanted whatever time they had left together to be about them—not her feelings.

While the grill heated, he leaned against the counter and watched her make salad. "I saw your mom today."

She put down the lettuce. "Where?"

"At the bank. I have an account there. She's not happy."

Pallas ignored the sudden tightness in her chest. "She's never happy. What happened?"

"Nothing much. We chatted." He crossed to her and kissed her. "It took a lot of courage to stand up to her. You should be proud of yourself for doing that."

"Thanks. I am. I wish I'd done it earlier."

"Don't be. When it was right, you said what you had to. Don't take away from yourself by second-guessing the circumstances."

"Thank you."

"You're welcome. I also talked to Drew."

Her unease faded as amusement took its place. "What I would have given to be a fly on the wall."

"Everything went fine. He's a good guy."

"I think so."

"I'm glad you have people who take care of you."

"Me, too."

Dealing with her mother was difficult, but the rest of the family was pretty good.

He went to the refrigerator and pulled out the chicken she'd already put in marinade. While he went outside to put it on the grill, she finished the salad, then joined him.

"I sent back the signed contracts for the under-the-sea wedding," she said. "I'm really looking forward to all the work."

"We're going to have to figure out sea horses," he told her. "I wish there was a way to use the zebras, but honestly I don't see them in costumes."

"No zebras. They've been through enough." She held in a smile. "You could make papier-mâché sea horses. I'll help."

She expected him to groan but instead he nodded thoughtfully. "I could. I'd only need a couple of molds and now that I have the guy who can make them for me, I'd only have to do the sculpture in clay."

She put her hands on her hips. "Nick Mitchell, you are not spending your incredibly valuable time carving molds for my weddings. That's insane. You should be selling your stuff for millions."

He grinned as he turned the chicken. "My 'stuff' as you call it, already sells for plenty. Besides, projects like these are fun. I'm having a good time and so are you. Look how enthused you are. You should branch out more."

"If you can dream it, we can make it happen?" she asked, her voice teasing, before stopping and staring at him. "Oh my God! Nick, that's it. That's what I want to do. Or say. Or tell people. You know what I mean. That should be my mission statement. If you can dream it, we can make it happen."

"Not weddings in the box," he told her. "Weddings out of the box."

## CHAPTER SEVENTEEN

PALLAS HAD TO wait until after the weekend to set up a lunch with her friends. Everyone was busy with a cowboy wedding on Friday night and a smaller princess-slash-Italian villa wedding on Sunday afternoon. Monday was spent in a fog of cleanup and recovering, but by Tuesday, Pallas was dying to talk with her friends about all the possibilities for her new business. As they were a central part of the plan, she wanted to make sure they were on board. Violet had offered her place for the meeting, so at two thirty, Pallas collected her tote from her car and walked to her friend's small shop.

Violet's store was on the edge of town, in a quiet, older neighborhood. Here the roads were more narrow, the traffic lighter. Storefronts had apartments above them and old-fashioned window boxes. Violet's place was part consignment store, part antique store with an emphasis on vintage clothing. She had a section for her precious buttons and a small space to do her tailoring work.

Her loft apartment was upstairs. It was exactly the size of her store, with equally large windows. Despite Violet's love of everything old, her space was surprisingly modern. Only a screen separated the living room from the bedroom and the only walled-off section was the bathroom.

In the living room, two sofas faced each other. A big dining room table sat by the huge windows. Pallas knew that Violet used the table as much for work as for eating, so she wasn't surprised when Violet guided them there.

Violet set out pitchers of iced tea and plates of cookies, then took one of the chairs. Wynn sat next to her, with Silver next to Pallas. They all looked at Pallas expectantly.

She shuffled her notes, then pushed them aside. "My mom has been after me to sell the business," she began.

"What?" Wynn shook her head. "No, you can't."

"Libby's a bitch," Silver announced as she grabbed a cookie. "Always has been."

"I'm not going to do it," Pallas said quickly. "I love what I do."

"Good." Violet smiled encouragingly. "But? Is there a but?"

"But I haven't been happy with how things were going at Weddings in a Box. Profits were low and there's a certain sameness to the weddings. I was really sad when Nova had to cancel."

"Me, too," Violet said. "Have you talked to her?"

"No. I left her a message, but I haven't heard back. I'm sure she's busy dealing with all kinds of things." Even expected, the loss of her father would be devastating.

"We all loved working with her," Wynn said. "I've never tried to make banners like that before. What a great idea. You know, we should use them in other weddings. They're not that expensive and now that you don't have to buy the panels, we can get them together quickly. They would add a real personal touch to the event."

Wynn drew in a breath, her eyes wide. "Oh, wow, I just got the best idea. What if we took pictures as people came into the ceremony? Someone could do that and get me the file. If this was all planned in advance, I could use the same background and make a kind of collage with the pictures. It wouldn't take very long. I'm sure I could have it back to you by the time the reception starts. People could sign them and write notes. It would be a great personal memory of the event." She thought for a second. "Not that I want to be doing that every Saturday night but I wouldn't mind doing it sometimes. For someone like Nova."

"You wouldn't have to do it then," Pallas said slowly, thinking as she spoke. "What if the guest book was digital and that was how we did the pictures? It was at the reception—they got their picture taken and wrote something. I could get you the file on Monday morning and you could do it anytime over the next couple of weeks. It would be like a digital scrapbook, with the wedding theme as a backdrop. That way I wouldn't have to figure out which couples were worthy."

"I love that," Violet said. "It's fun."

"And a great moneymaker," Wynn added. "Let me get you a quote. I'll do it with a minimum number of pages, then a price for every page after that."

"This is what I want," Pallas told them. "More

creativity, more fun. Rather than weddings in a box, I want to do weddings out of the box."

"I like it." Silver smiled. "Are you changing the name of your business?"

"Yes. I'm going to file the paperwork with the city and get new business cards made. I'll have to update the website, which will take time. My point is I want to branch out. I just signed a contract for an under-the-sea wedding." She explained about Taylor and Jake's dream wedding.

"You're going to be buying more accessories," Wynn said. "And you'll need more costumes. Can you store everything in the space you have now?"

"No. We're already crammed." She hadn't thought about storage. "I'm not sure what makes sense. Those storage unit places can be expensive."

"I have an idea," Wynn said. "I want to move my business. I'm growing just enough that it's too small for me. I found a great storefront with a huge ware-house in back. I don't need that much storage and I don't want to pay for space I'm not using. I didn't want to sublease because I didn't want to have to deal with someone I didn't know, but this could be a solu-tion." She nodded at Silver. "We've already discussed Silver using a small part of it for her decorations."

"And the trailer itself," Silver added. "There's a big fenced-in parking area out back. I don't like to leave my trailer stocked when it's parked in front of my house. All I need is a couple of teenagers break-ing in, having a party, then going for a joyride. This way I can restock as needed and it's safe."

"There will still be plenty of square footage for you, if you're interested," Wynn said.

Pallas was thrilled. "That's a great solution. When can I come see the space?"

"How about tomorrow morning? I have to let the landlord know by the end of the week."

Pallas wrote down the address. Having more storage would be a big help. Right now she could barely find room for everything. Costumes were all crammed together. The caterer didn't have anywhere to set up. But if she could move everything to an off-site location, she could open the upstairs rooms for other purposes. More than one bride had asked to have the rehearsal dinner on-site, but there wasn't any room—not when she had to start setting up for the wedding the day before. Maybe one of the rooms could be modified for that. Of course with everything at a different location, she would have to get a van or something to move costumes and decorations, but why not?

"Okay, *now* I know why you asked me to come up with less-specific server costumes," Violet said. "Right now they're totally custom, and while that's great, it's expensive. You're limited by what's on hand. Some brides might be turned off by that, but if you went a different direction, you could get by with two or three server costumes that could be modified to fit any situation."

She pulled a file out of her tote. "I've thought about this. My suggestion is that you leave the guys in black pants and change out their shirts." She flipped pages to show a toga-like shirt, a shirt with billowy sleeves and a basic black shirt. "We could do a lot with vests that are easy to make and more forgiving, sizewise. I'd say dress the female servers the same. If there's enough other stuff going on, the servers will just blend into the background. You can put your decor money into other things."

It wasn't how Gerald had done it, Pallas thought, but the simpler server outfits made sense.

"The bride could still choose the look," Silver pointed out. "And hey, if she wanted to pay for custom uniforms, then she would get them."

Pallas nodded. "That makes more sense. I'd still have some costumes for specific weddings that are always popular. Like the togas for the Roman soldiers who carry in the bride. But it's not cost-effective to dress the serving staff when we're going to have so many options."

"What kind of weddings are you thinking?" Wynn asked.

"Pretty much anything," Pallas told her. "That's what I want to do—give brides their dream weddings. Of any kind."

"Zombies are very big right now." Silver grinned. "That would be a fun signature drink."

"You're gross." Violet's voice was affectionate. "How about something with wine? We could do a fake wine country wedding. Pump up the Italian thing. Or weddings based on movies."

"The seasons are nice." Wynn reached for a cookie. "A Dickens' Christmas wedding or a beautiful fall wedding with changing leaves and lots of apples."

Pallas laughed as she wrote down their suggestions. "I have to say, that's quite a range. From Zombies to a Dickens' Christmas."

"You wanted to be out of the box," Wynn reminded her.

"I do." She wanted to make her business unique. With a little help from her friends, that was going to happen.

FRESH FROM HER MEETING, an inspired Pallas stopped by Nick's studio. She practically danced from her car to the open door. Inspiration and excitement made her light and happy.

She took a second to let her eyes adjust from the bright sunlight outside. On the far side of the room, the hot glass oven hissed and roared as Mathias and Ronan pulled a long rod with molten glass from its depths. Mathias expertly spun the rod before blowing into the end of the tube. The glass grew into a circle, which transformed into an oblong shape as he spun it around several times.

The complexities of what these men did were beyond her, she thought as she glanced to her left and spotted Nick. At the sight of him, she had to hold in a sigh of general happiness. Her heart fluttered, her girl parts went on alert and the whole day just got better.

"You texted," she said as she walked over to where he was sitting at a big workbench, painting papier-mâché flowers.

"I did."

He put down the flower he was working on, stood

and held open his arms. She stepped into his embrace. Everything about being held by him was right, she thought. Everything was good. The words—an expression of how she felt—hung on the tip of her tongue, but she didn't say them. He didn't want to know and she wasn't ready to tell.

"What's up?" she asked, staring into his dark eyes.

"Can't a guy want to see his girl?"

His girl. Was she? She wanted to be. Wanted what they had to last for as long as possible. Forever sounded good. "He can, but that's not why you asked me to stop by."

"You're right."

He led her toward a door.

"Close your eyes."

She did as he requested. He took her hand and drew her forward a few steps. She sensed that she was stepping into the storage closet. A light clicked on.

"Open your eyes."

In front of her was Nova's dress—or at least some part of what it had been. Because instead of a traditional white gown, she saw swirls of color and a painted masterpiece.

Nick had combined the colors of the gaming world such that they blended and twisted and intersected. No one color dominated and there was still plenty of ivory and the soft silk. Areas had a faint shimmer. Pallas thought of the flowers she and Nova had talked about and how the dress would move. Tears burned in her eyes.

"It's beautiful," she whispered. "No, that's not

good enough. I honestly don't know a word to describe this, Nick. It's amazing."

"Thanks. There's more."

He turned on a handheld black light, then turned off the overhead fixture. The dress morphed into something otherworldly, as if the circles and waves of color had moved.

"How did you do that?"

"Black light paint. It's all blended together. We'd talked about black lights at the reception and I thought it would look cool." He flipped on the overhead light again. "I like how it came out."

"It's stunning. Nova is going to be..." Pallas thought about the reason for the postponement. She wasn't sure what Nova was going to be. "What will you do?"

"Wait a couple of days for the dress to dry, then send it to her. She and Joel will get married eventually. She'll want to have the dress."

"When that happens, I hope they come here. I'd like to help them with their wedding."

"Me, too."

She didn't bother pointing out that by then, Nick would be long gone. He already knew.

PALLAS HAD BARELY settled into her office that afternoon when Alan walked in.

"What are you doing here?" she asked. "I thought you were in LA all week."

"I wanted to see you." He sat beside her desk and took her hand in his. "I'm leaving. Not you. We'll always be close. But Happily Inc. It's time for me to settle down and I'm doing that in LA."

Pallas bit her lower lip. Alan had been a part of her life as long as Gerald. They'd been friends. Even after he'd started spending more time in Los Angeles, she'd always known she was going to see him at the weddings.

"The new guy?" she asked, when what she really wanted to say was, "Don't go!"

"Yes. Despite my handsomeness, I'm not getting any younger. I've found someone I care about and we're going to do our best to make it work." He smiled. "I'm finally settling down."

"I've heard it happens to all of us eventually."

"It needs to happen to you."

"I'm working the program."

"Nick?"

She smiled. "It's either him or you, and apparently your heart is taken."

Alan laughed. "It is. Plus, as much as I adore you, I never got the whole boy-girl thing. It's weird."

"Yes, it is." She felt her smile fade. "Who am I going to get to calm my brides now?"

"You'll find someone. It's really not that hard. Just tell them they're beautiful and that whoever is bothering them is a bitch and voilà. Happy bride."

"I think there's a little more to it than that." She squeezed his hand. "I'm going to miss you so much."

"I'll miss you. Gerald rescued us both and we'll always remember him. But now it's time for us to follow our dreams."

She stood. He did the same and hugged her.

So much was changing, she thought when Alan was gone. Less than a year ago she'd been determined to finish her degree and work at the bank. Then Gerald had died and left her the business and she'd come to realize that she didn't want to work with her mother and… And Nick had shown up. Just like that, her world shifted. Now everything was different.

Too restless to concentrate on anything, she went for a walk. It was getting hotter—a truth of the desert as summer approached. She crossed the street and headed for the river. Maybe a snow cone would help her focus. As she approached the boardwalk, she saw a familiar figure sitting on a bench. Her grandfather looked up and saw her. He smiled before waving her over.

"How's my favorite granddaughter?" he asked as she settled next to him.

"You know that's not true. You love us all equally."

"Yes, I do, but I'm careful to tell each of you you're my favorite. It makes you feel special."

She laughed, even as she was sure he was telling the truth.

"How are things with you?" her grandfather asked.

"Good. Great. I've been working hard and learning stuff."

"It's good to learn stuff. It keeps us young. You don't need that now but one day you will."

"I'll keep that in mind." She hesitated before blurting, "Why does Mom hate me?"

She hadn't meant to ask the question, but now that it was out there, she didn't call it back.

Grandpa Frank put his arm around her. "She doesn't hate you, Pallas. She loves you—in her way."

Pallas wrinkled her nose. "It's not a very friendly way."

"I know."

"Why don't I remember much about my dad? Cade does. Is it me or wasn't he around much?"

Her grandfather hesitated just long enough for her to realize there was something. She shifted so she could face him. "Grandpa Frank? What is it? Tell me."

"Your father was an ambitious man. He hadn't come from much and he was determined to get ahead. He saw Libby as a way to do that."

Pallas's breath caught as she considered the implications in that carefully worded sentence. "He didn't love her?"

"I didn't say that. I'm sure he cared. Some. But he was more interested in the bank. Libby tried a million ways to get his attention, but it was difficult." He shook his head. "He was the reason you all moved into the house. It was his idea, not your mother's. When you and Cade were born, he saw Cade as a way to secure his position."

"What do you mean?"

"Cade's a boy. Boys inherit."

"But you don't care about that. How could you? You had seven daughters."

He laughed. "Don't I know it. But your father never got that. He never saw Cade wasn't interested in the bank at all. Your father decided he would change his mind as he got older. Libby played along. Then your father died."

Pallas wasn't sure what to do with the information. On the one hand, she felt bad for her mother. On the other, she was grateful to finally find out why her father had always seemed so absent in her life.

"Do you think the reason Mom is always making me earn stuff is so I don't get hurt like she did?" she asked.

"You'll have to take that up with her."

"Oh, like that will ever happen." Still it was nice to have some answers, even though they led to more questions.

"How come you never remarried, Grandpa?" she asked.

He winked at her. "I'm a healthy, rich man of a certain age. I loved your grandmother very much and I never looked at another woman while she was alive. But now I'm single and I'm enjoying every minute of it."

Pallas winced as she tried not to get a visual. "You could have just said you didn't want to."

"I'm a big believer in the truth."

"Maybe you should be a big believer in self-editing."

He laughed. "Come on. I'll buy you an ice cream."

"Can I have a snow cone instead?"

"Of course. You can have anything you want."

They walked along the river toward the stand. Pallas thought about all she'd learned today. Some of the information changed everything and some of it... Well, she didn't know what she was going to do about her mother's past. Not that there was anything *to* do. But things made more sense now. And maybe in the knowing, there was a chance for something more than they'd had.

NICK STARED AT the FedEx envelope on his desk. He knew what was inside—the return address in Dubai made that clear. After nearly three months of waiting, a decision had been made. He turned the package over in his hands and realized he didn't want to know. Didn't want his life to change. He wasn't ready to leave Happily Inc.

No. He wasn't ready to leave Pallas.

He pulled the tab and ripped open the envelope, then pulled out the letter inside. After scanning the first paragraph, he read it again, then a third time. The words were incredibly clear.

Mr. Nicholas Mitchell, we regret to inform you the committee has decided to go in another direction for our hotel installation. I personally wanted your piece, but I was outvoted.

There was more, but none of it mattered. He hadn't gotten the job. What the hell?

He stood up, then sat back down. He shoved the letter into a drawer, pulled it out, thought about ripping it in two, then put it away again.

He hadn't gotten the job. How was that possible? Didn't they realize who he was?

As soon as he thought the question, he started to

laugh. Well, damn. He'd just been put in his place. He'd been so sure he would get the commission he hadn't considered he might not.

Both his brothers were out, so he had the studio to himself. He walked the length of it, thought about channeling his father and smashing a few pieces, but stopped himself before he could do something stupid and self-destructive.

He hadn't gotten the job. They'd turned down his idea. Did he care? Did it mean anything? Art was subjective, right? It was just...

He'd had everything on hold. He'd been waiting to decide, so he hadn't committed to a project or direction. He'd been drifting, expecting the answer to come from somewhere else and it had. Just not the way he expected. What was he going to do now?

There were dozens of choices. He could go back to Fool's Gold. He could stay here. He could move somewhere else. But the bigger question was what was he going to do with his work? Wood? Glass? Not metal—he and Mathias had yet to create anything that wasn't trash. What about—

What about Pallas? He returned to his chair and sat. Now he didn't have to leave her. Now he could be with her. They could... Well, they could... He looked around as if the answer was hidden in a corner. They could stay together. Eventually they could...

No. Passion consumed. He couldn't do eventually or forever or any of those things. He didn't want to end up like his parents. He didn't want to destroy what they had or each other. He wanted to be with her, and now he could, only he couldn't because it was dangerous. He wasn't willing to take a chance. She wasn't the problem—he was. He couldn't trust himself. But if he didn't make a move, he would lose her forever.

Not knowing what else to do, he drove over to Weddings in a Box and went to work on his panels. At least there he knew what he was doing. He had the feel of the wood. The repairs kept his hands busy as his mind raced like a hamster on a wheel. Eventually it would quiet and he would know.

He used sandpaper to smooth the edges of the long splits running vertically through the panel. He filled the larger ones with tiny slivers of wood cut to fit in perfectly. Each one took all his attention. When the questions became too complicated, he went for something easy, like cleaning the relief, inch by inch. The hours crept by. He counted them by the movement of the sun on the stone floor. When it was nearly dark and his hands ached from the work, he thought maybe it was time to give it a rest. He was no closer to an answer than he had been but—

Pallas burst into the room. She raced toward him.

"Nova called. Tim rallied. He's not dead. He's feeling better! The wedding's back on!"

## *CHAPTER EIGHTEEN*

PALLAS COULDN'T CATCH her breath. She was shaking and trying not to scream and jump up and down.

"When I saw Nova's number on my phone, I almost didn't answer," she said as she and Nick sat in her office. "I was so scared. I didn't want to hear that Tim had died. Then I told myself that made me slime. I mean, come on. I only have to hear it. She has to live it. But it wasn't bad news." She bounced in her seat. "This is the best. He's been getting stronger for a couple of weeks now. I guess there was some experimental medication and at first they thought it had failed, but now it seems to be working, so we have got to pull this together."

She looked at Nick. "You haven't said anything."

"It's great news. You're right. We have to make this work. Who should we call first?"

The words were right but there was something strange about him. Not quiet, exactly. Resigned? Was that it? "Are you mad?"

"No. Of course not. It's great news. I'm happy for them."

All the right words, but there was something. Regardless, she couldn't deal with that right now. "We have a million things to do. I want to order a zip line."

Nick's brows rose. "Excuse me?"

"Zip line. Yes, that's what I said. Why not? Nova's so happy—she said to just go for it. To order anything I thought would make the day special." Pallas sighed remembering the happy call. "She was so excited and relieved. This is the best. I think there should be a zip line to add a little spice. I think we can run it from the Juliet balcony to the ground. It won't be that fast or far, but it will make a statement."

She glanced down at her notes. "I have to call everyone. I don't know if Atsuko ever got going on her costume. I hope so. Oh, you haven't mailed the dress to Nova yet, have you? Not that she couldn't bring it back with her. Of course she could. But it would be easier if it never left in the first place." She started scribbling names. "Okay, Atsuko, Silver, Violet, Wynn. Natalie, because she said she finished the masks. I should probably call Carol, too. She's always said she's more than happy to help if I'm in a bind. Oh, and Alan. He'll want to be here."

She looked up. "Did I tell you he's moving to LA? Permanently? He's met someone, which is just so great."

She drew in a breath. "I know I'm talking too much but I'm excited. This is the best. Tim's okay and there's going to be an alien wedding." She started to laugh. "And how often does a girl get to say a sentence like that?"

Nick remained silent. He wasn't excited or pleased or anything she would have expected. Finally she couldn't stand it anymore. She placed her hands on the desk. "What?"

He looked away, then back at her. "I'll help with the wedding."

What? Of course he would help. He'd been a part of this from the beginning. He was—

She realized what was missing from his expression. The humor and affection she'd started taking for granted. The connection they had together. He hadn't looked happy to see her when she'd run in to tell him the news. He hadn't pulled her close or kissed her. He hadn't done anything.

"And then?" she asked, her voice quiet.

"And then we're done. I can't be with you anymore. The risk is too high. I'm sorry. I didn't get the commission. I don't know if I'm staying in town or not, but either way, we can't be together."

She heard the words and knew what he meant. He wasn't willing to take a chance. Not on them or on her. They were breaking up. They weren't going to be together, hang out, laugh, make love. He was moving on.

The flash of pain was so hot and so bright she thought it might blind her. He couldn't do this, couldn't mean it. She loved him. She needed him and he needed her. They were good together. How could he walk away from that? How could he not *know* what was happening between them?

Passion consumes. She remembered his words. However foolish she thought them, he believed. She'd fallen in love with him and he was moving on.

She wanted to scream he was wrong. She wanted

to beg. She wanted to run. Only she couldn't. Nova and Joel were depending on her and that mattered more than what was happening with Nick. That mattered more than anything. She forced herself to breathe deeply, then willed herself to be strong.

"Fine," she said crisply, ignoring the ache in her heart. "If that's what you want. However, I would appreciate your commitment that you won't run off right in the middle of things. If I can't depend on you to be there for the wedding, then tell me now. I'll find someone else to help. Making everything right for Nova and Joel is my priority. The rest of it can wait."

"I'll be there."

For the wedding. Just not for her.

CAROL SAT NEXT to Pallas on the sofa. Pallas wrapped her arms around her midsection, as if that would hold in the pain. She'd spent the past fifteen minutes crying and would have sworn there weren't any tears left, yet more filled her eyes and spilled down her cheeks.

Her friend was patient—waiting for her to calm down enough to speak. Carol would wait for as long as necessary. When Pallas had called, asking if she could come over, Carol hadn't hesitated. Pallas knew she could always depend on her friends. They would be there for her—no matter what. In time, that would be enough—just not today.

"I'm sorry," she said, her voice tight and thick with tears. "I'm a mess."

Carol hugged her. "Don't you dare apologize.

Ever. I'm here for whatever you need. If it's zebras, you just have to ask."

The light humor distracted Pallas long enough for her to catch her breath. She had to get control. There was so much work to be done for Nova's wedding. That was what was important to her. Not Nick and his idiocy. Only telling herself that didn't help.

"Nick and I broke up," she managed as she wiped tears from her face.

Carol continued to hold her.

"You're not surprised?"

"I'm going to be surprised if you tell me he was stupid enough to dump you. Otherwise, I had a feeling the tears were about a man. You're not usually a crier."

"I know, right?" Pallas rested her head on Carol's shoulder. "He broke up with me and I don't know why."

Carol swore. "That makes no sense. I've seen you together. You're great and I know he totally adores you. What was he thinking?"

"I have no idea." She swallowed a sob. "Why do I care so much?"

"You're in love with him."

"I know."

Pallas straightened. Carol shifted back so she could reach the pot of tea she'd brewed, then poured them each a mug.

"Start at the beginning," her friend told her.

"You mean I was born in the summer of..." Her voice trailed off. "Sorry. I just can't take it all in."

She took the offered mug of tea and sipped the

warm liquid. The familiar scent of orange and black tea offered a small measure of comfort.

"Nick told me before we got together that he doesn't believe in relationships. He thinks they cause too much emotional damage." She made air quotes with one hand. "Passion consumes. It's his thing. He doesn't get too close or too involved. He was supposed to be leaving for Dubai, so I knew it wasn't forever. I told myself that was fine. He and I would have some fun and that was all. But then it became something more—at least for me."

A wave of pain washed over her. They'd been so good together. How could he not see that?

She wrapped both hands around her mug. "When I was little, I always felt I had to earn attention from my mom. I was never good enough. Love had to be earned and I wasn't very good at getting it right. I always felt less than. It was different for Cade—he didn't have the same rules. He didn't have to try to fit in."

Carol shook her head. "I've seen how your mom acts. I hope you're not blaming yourself."

"I'm not. I was the kid—the rules came from her. But recently my grandfather told me some stuff that changes things. He said that my dad was more interested in the bank than his wife. Mom never had his attention, which is really sad. Maybe she was doing the best she could. Maybe she was trying to get me to try harder because she felt she hadn't tried hard enough. I don't know."

She drew in a breath. "Either way, I always figured it was about the rules and how I wasn't doing well following them. I was always so careful not to expect anything, except with my friends." She managed a slight smile. "You have always been there for me."

"I am pretty great," Carol teased gently.

Pallas smiled. "You are." Her smile faded. "Then Gerald left me the business. I had no idea he was going to and I was totally freaked because I hadn't earned it. He just loved me. Then Nick came along and we were so good together. I started to realize my feelings. I didn't say anything because I didn't want to pressure him. I loved him without expecting anything in return. And it felt great. Until he dumped me."

Tears burned. She blinked them away. "Maybe I should have told him. Maybe it was a mistake to not let him know how I felt."

"Only if it would have made *you* feel better," Carol said quickly. "I'm serious. This is all about you. I'm team Pallas, all the way."

"Thank you. I don't want to have any regrets."

"I don't want that, either. If you think you would feel better having him know you were in love with him, then tell him. If you are comfortable with how you handled things, then the jerk doesn't need to know." Carol grimaced. "I'm just sorry we don't have any predators on the preserve. It would be fun to let a hungry lion loose in Nick's truck. With him inside, of course."

"You're just saying that. I happen to know you're not the least bit bloodthirsty."

"Not usually, but he hurt my friend. I care about you."

"Thank you."

"You're welcome. I can't believe how stupid he is. I know I said that already, but it's true. I'm sorry things turned out this way. I know he's going to regret letting you go. He has to."

The support felt good. It would be a while until Pallas was herself again, but she figured if she'd finally learned how to fall in love she would also be able to learn to fall out of love. Eventually. Until then she had to figure out how to fake being normal and dig deep to be brave.

PALLAS HADN'T REALIZED that installing a zip line for the wedding would involve math. When the installer started his conversation with the charming phrase, "Your drop can't be more than six percent of your length," she felt the first hint of the headache that was sure to follow.

After clarifying that when he said *your length* he actually meant the length of the zip line, she waved him in the direction of the second-floor balcony.

"Whatever you can do would be much appreciated," she told him. "We're looking more for the spirit of a zip line than an actual thrill ride."

"At a wedding?"

"So it seems."

The zip line was so the least of it, but why take the time to explain? There were a thousand other details that needed her attention.

The courtyard and building swarmed with peo-

ple. The floral setup was going to take a whole day.
Wynn had already started on the printed paper panels
that would set the scene for the gaming world. Violet
and Cade and even Drew were working together to
braid different thicknesses and textures of ribbon to
hang between the panels. This was a wedding, after
all, and it required decoration.

Pallas wanted as much as possible set up today
so that tomorrow they could focus on the ceremony
and reception themselves, rather than prep work.
That meant getting tables and chairs in place this
afternoon. She would wait on the decorations until
the morning, but she had to confirm all the deliv-
eries. At two the DJ wanted to do a run-through
with the sound system. The caterer would be by to
check on the flow of the room. One hundred and
fifty guests weren't that many, but all the world-
building elements provided interesting obstacles for
serving staff.

From the corner of her eye, she caught sight of
Nick. He'd brought his papier-mâché flowers that
morning. The plants themselves were incredible—
detailed replicas of the computer-generated images
from the game. He'd matched the colors perfectly.
She happened to know there were only three different flowers, but the way he'd arranged them, it was
difficult to tell.

She did her best to avoid him. Honestly, she had
no idea what she was supposed to say. Pretending
they were just friends was impossible. With everyone running around getting things done, a personal
conversation wasn't going to happen—not that he

seemed to be in a hurry to get close to her again. Fortunately fate seemed to be on her side in the form of people asking her questions and Nick staying busy with his flowers. She was able to keep her distance without making it obvious.

A little before noon, Nova, Joel and Tim showed up. Nova's father looked pale and thin, but happy as he walked in with the bridal couple. Pallas hurried over to greet them.

"You made it," she said happily, hugging all three of them.

"We did." Nova kept her gaze on her father. "Dad's feeling good."

"I am." Tim smiled. "I've been given the gift of a little more time and I plan to use it to see my best girl get married."

Pallas watched Joel stay close to his father-in-law-to-be, offering a steady arm if Tim needed it.

"I have a lot to show you," she said. "First, some details." She turned to Nova. "Your dress was delivered to the hotel this morning. I've arranged for two of my best tailors to meet you at two. They'll work their magic and have the dress back to you first thing in the morning."

Nova'd had her first fitting before she'd shipped the dress to Nick but there were always final adjustments.

"I've tried to keep my weight steady," Nova told her. "I'd lost a few pounds, but when Dad rallied, I started eating."

"She's not kidding," Joel teased. "We went to an

all-you-can-eat buffet and the manager finally had to ask her to leave."

"That's my girl," Tim said.

Pallas pulled one of the chairs from a table and moved it close to Tim. He smiled and sat down on it.

"I can't wait to see the dress," Nova admitted. "Nick sent me pictures. I can tell it's stunning but I know it's going to be even better in person."

"You're going to be blown away," Pallas told her. "Whatever you're imagining, it's ten times better." Not only was Nick talented, this had been a project of the heart for him. Like everyone else involved, he'd wanted to make Nova's and Joel's dreams come true.

She allowed herself exactly two seconds of missing him and feeling the ache in her heart before turning back to Nova.

"We'll walk through the ceremony right now." Pallas glanced at her tablet. "It's pretty traditional, so nothing you haven't seen before. You've looked at the bridesmaids' dresses?"

"I love them."

"I do, too. So we're a go on that. Let's go inside and check out the setup there. The panels are up and we're adding the embellishments as we speak. Atsuko assures me her costume is ready, so we're good there. You've talked to the caterer already and Silver has the signature drink options ready to go."

They went into the main ballroom. The chairs were already set up in even rows. Ten-foot-high frames held printed panels representing the landscape of the gaming world. Long braided ribbons looped across the top of the panels. They were also attached to the sides of the chairs by the center aisle. A glittering white runner cut between the chairs.

Up front, where the ceremony would take place, what had been a traditional, simple, white gazebo had been spray-painted silver. Several of Nick's large papier-mâché plants nestled together. Silk flowers were scattered on the walls of the gazebo.

"We'll place the real flowers tomorrow," Pallas said, showing Nova and Joel where they would be attached by the chairs. "They're a variation on your wedding bouquet. We've also created this—"

She pointed to an arch at the far end of the center aisle. "When it's time for the ceremony to start, we'll dim the lights and turn on the arch."

She walked over and flipped several switches. The lights faded and the arch glowed. "It's black light. Nick painted your dress with black light paint. As you pass through it, the dress will change colors. Once you're on the main aisle, we'll raise the lights back up so everyone can see the ceremony."

Tears filled Nova's eyes. "We can't thank you enough."

"You can and you have. We've all enjoyed getting things ready for you. The wedding is going to be wonderful and we're all thrilled to be a part of your day."

Pallas walked them through the rest of the venue and the plan for the following day. Nova, Joel and Tim headed back to the hotel. Pallas went through her to-do list and made sure she wasn't forgetting anything.

Sometime during her meeting with the bride and

her family, Nick had left, which allowed Pallas to breathe a little easier. Just knowing he was around made focusing difficult. With him out of sight, she could ignore the throbbing pain inside of her chest and get the work done. She would mourn later, she told herself. When there was time. Right now she had more important things to do.

Which sounded just so mature, but was difficult to actually do. She walked over to one of the papier-mâché flowers and touched the lifelike petal. From what she could tell, Nick had painted it at least three different shades of yellow. He'd spent so much time, she thought wistfully. Just because he'd wanted to help—and maybe a little for the challenge. Still, he hadn't done it for glory or money, but because he was a good guy.

Not news, she told herself as she turned to look at the chairs set up for the ceremony and the panels depicting the alien world. When the ballroom was empty, it was just a big open space with high ceilings, but with a little planning and some imagination, it could be nearly anything. The great hall of a castle or an undersea cave or an alien world. She might not be in Nick's league, but in her own way, she was an artist, too. One who took words from clients and used them to create an event worth remembering.

She thought about where she'd been only a few months ago—the new owner of a business she wasn't sure what to do with. Funny how she'd been so caught up in wanting to work at the bank that she'd nearly walked away from the most wonderful gift anyone had ever offered. Only she hadn't wanted to work in the bank—instead that had represented what she'd been looking for her entire life. Acceptance. She'd wanted her mother to simply love her for herself.

Knowing what she did now, she wasn't sure that was ever going to happen. Maybe they were both too damaged. But what she did know was she was where she belonged. She was happy with her work. Blessed, and she would be grateful. No matter what.

## CHAPTER NINETEEN

NICK STARED AT the recently delivered tree trunk in front of him. It was perfect—nearly four feet across and eight feet high—straight and strong. The scent of wood drifted to him. All he had to do was figure out what the piece was supposed to be.

He stood in the afternoon sun and waited. And waited. It had been three days and he still didn't know what the hell he was going to do with it, just like with the last trunk he'd tried to work with. Instead of possibilities, there was only silence.

He'd picked up his chainsaw at least a dozen times, only to put it back down. There was no point in starting until he knew where he was going. And he didn't.

He threw the tarp back over the wood and stalked into the studio. He swore silently and felt the anger inside of him. Funny how after all this time, he understood his father a bit more. When emotion overwhelmed, acting out like a four-year-old made a whole lot of sense. Or in his case, firing a few pieces of glass against a wall would ease a lot of tension. Only he'd promised himself that would never happen again. He would handle his frustrations in another way. Although he had no idea what that was.

He was restless, confused and angry. The latter

made no sense—who was he supposed to be mad at? Himself? The selection committee? Pallas?

Not her, he admitted. She'd done nothing wrong. If anyone had the right to be pissed, she did. He'd dumped her with no warning, no reason other than he was a broken coward without the strength to...to...

He stood by his desk and wondered what he was supposed to have the strength to do. Stay? Be with her? Take a chance on them? No, not on them, on himself. Because she wasn't the problem—he was. He was the one who had looked into the depths of the abyss and sworn he wouldn't go there. *He* was the one who refused to take the chance. Not her. Never her. She was amazing and beautiful and funny and kind and sexy. She was perfect. He was the problem.

He deliberately turned his back on the racks with finished glass pieces before sitting at his desk. He pulled out a stack of drawing paper, then hesitated. Maybe he could figure out what the wood wanted to be another way. Maybe it would speak to him indirectly. He reached for a pencil and began to draw.

At first he wasn't sure where he was going but after a few strokes, everything became more clear. Long stalks of swaying seaweed. They would be easy to carve and be a simple mold. He quickly drew the alien flowers he'd created for Nova's wedding and rearranged them, placing the stalks of seaweed between groups of flowers. If he did them in blues and greens, he thought to himself, with touches of aqua and maybe a pale orange and yellow, it would be an under-the-sea garden for Taylor and Jake's wedding.

Pallas had said the bride and groom were on a

budget, so he couldn't charge them for the work, but still, the papier-mâché would add an interesting element to the decorations.

He tossed the paper on the floor and reached for a clean sheet. What about sea horses and starfish? He drew several versions of each. He wondered what Violet could do to the basic creatures with her glitter and buttons. Maybe Silver could use slices of star fruit in the drinks. There were—

An image formed, one that was so clear he could almost touch it. He stood and walked back outside. After putting on protective goggles, a vest and gloves, he picked up the chainsaw. The vision was clear. A take on Neptune or Poseidon—a god filled with energy and determination, ruling the sea.

Later he would have to do research, to get the details right, but for now, there were rough cuts to be made. He worked intently, letting his hands and arms guide the saw. He was merely the bystander, the vessel who provided the means. The wood was in control—the wood and some mysterious part of his brain he didn't understand but accepted and appreciated.

"I WAS HOPING you would be an extra," Pallas said as she sat in Natalie's office at the gallery. "There's not much to do—just be there in costume. I know you already made the masks, but still…"

Natalie held up the long-sleeved T-shirt Pallas had brought with her. It was painted, front and back, with swirling designs that matched what Nick had done on Nova's wedding dress. Violet had produced a half dozen of them to complement the servers' simple black outfits.

"Sure." Natalie grinned. "It will be fun. I like meeting new people. Count me in!"

"Yay. It's going to be a lot of fun, and there will be food."

"Where's the food?" Mathias asked as he came into the room. "Hey, Pallas. Cool shirt."

"It's for a wedding," Natalie told him. "I'm an extra."

Pallas eyed the artist, then pulled another shirt out of her bag. "Want to go? You don't have to do anything except roam around and provide atmosphere. We're going to feed everyone who helps."

Natalie rolled her eyes. "He'll say yes. Mathias lives for the weekends when he can troll for bridesmaids and have his way with them."

Mathias pressed a hand to his chest. "You wound me with your sarcasm."

"I wasn't being sarcastic. I meant every word. God forbid you should settle down with someone normal."

Mathias grinned. "You're implying bridesmaids aren't normal."

"You know what I mean."

"I do and yet I mock you. It's payback."

Pallas allowed herself a second to enjoy their banter—it reminded her of when she and Cade hung out together.

"I'm in." Mathias took the offered T-shirt. "When and where?"

She gave him the details, then turned back to Natalie. "Wynn is going to be there, along with Carol, so you'll have friends to talk to."

YOU SAY IT FIRST

As she spoke she caught something out of the corner of her eye. A movement—like a flinch. But when she glanced at Mathias, he looked as he always did—slightly amused and far too handsome for his own good.

"I'm a friend," he protested mildly.

"Not to the unsuspecting bridesmaids." Natalie shook her head. "I suppose the bright side is I'll finally get to watch you in action."

"Take notes and learn, young grasshopper."

Pallas stood. "I have to get back to wedding prep. Thank you both so much. Be on-site by four tomorrow afternoon."

She left the office and walked through the gallery to the front door. Once outside, she told herself to go directly to the car and drive back to the chaos that was Weddings Out of the Box today. That was the smart decision—the one that made the most sense. She hesitated, telling herself she didn't have time for distractions. In a mere twenty-six hours, Nova would be walking down the aisle. But instead of being sensible, she circled around the gallery and walked along the path that led to the large studio off to the side of the property.

As she approached, her stomach tightened and she found it difficult to catch her breath. She could see Nick's truck parked by the front door so knew he was there. Mathias was in the gallery, so she didn't have to worry about him. There was no third truck—most likely Ronan was working in his home studio.

She had no idea *what* she was going to say, but the need to say something, to find verbal closure, wouldn't go away. She wanted to be brave and strong and proud of herself. So much had changed in the past couple of months. If things were going to end with him, she wanted it to happen right. She didn't want regrets beyond missing him, very possibly for the rest of her life.

She walked into the studio. Thankfully, Nick seemed to be alone. He was sitting at a drafting table. Large pieces of paper lay scattered on the floor all around him, as if he was searching for the perfect image and had yet to find it.

He didn't notice her at first. She watched his sure hand glide over the paper. In a few strokes a man took shape, complete with trident and crown. Neptune, she thought, then caught her breath at the realization that he'd been inspired by the under-the-sea wedding. What would he create? Something out of wood or glass? Regardless, it would be amazing.

And she would never see it.

Pain pricked every nerve until she trembled from the ache filling her. She felt herself start to lose her breath and her self-control, then dug deep for the strength to finish this in a way that would tell Nick exactly who she'd become.

"Pallas?"

The sound of him speaking her name drew her gaze to him. She took a couple of steps toward his desk, then stopped.

He looked good. Tired, but still very much him. She knew him intimately—from the shape and feel of his body, to the sound of his laugh. She knew what moved him and, unfortunately, she knew what terrified him. She also knew that he was wrong to not trust in them, and in that moment, she knew exactly what she was going to say.

"I'm not here to change your mind," she began, her voice firm and strong. "You have to do what you have to do. I accept that. I don't like it and I think you're making a mistake, but I'm not going to try to talk you into believing me."

He watched her without speaking. She drew in a deep breath.

"You think passion consumes," she continued. "Well, it does. It's supposed to. Passion should consume, but that doesn't mean it's dangerous or bad. It's like when you put clay in a kiln." At least she hoped it was a kiln. Whatever—he would get what she meant.

"The fire and heat either make it stronger or the piece breaks. That's what passion does. It takes us to the breaking point and we either make it or we don't. I thought we were going to make it. I thought you were the one."

A muscle tightened in his jaw, but he didn't speak.

She took a step toward him. "I love you, Nick. I have for a while. I wasn't sure what to do. Should I tell you, not tell you? Because you're not the only one messed up. I'm dealing with my own demons. I believed love has to be earned, but here's the thing. You didn't earn my love. I chose to give it to you. I give it freely and I expect nothing in return."

She managed a slight smile. "Probably a good thing considering you've already broken up with me, huh?" She waited but he didn't speak, so she finished what she'd come to say.

"I love you. You don't have to love me back. I wish you would but if you don't, I'm going to be okay. I get it now. I get what loving someone is supposed to mean. It's a gift. You can accept it or not. That's up to you. It doesn't have to be earned and there's no time restriction. It just is. Whatever happens, whatever you decide to do, I hope you're happy. I hope you find what you're looking for."

*I hope it's with me.* But she didn't say that because what was the point? They both already knew that.

She turned and left. The tears waited until she was in her car. She accepted them, along with the sense of emptiness in her heart. Both would pass. She was stronger than she'd ever been. She was proud of herself in so many ways. As for Nick, he would either get it or he wouldn't. She loved him, she wanted him, but she didn't *need* him to be happy. She'd found that strength within herself, and no matter what, she was going to be okay.

SATURDAY MORNING PALLAS was up at five. She'd slept surprisingly well and woke with a sense of happy expectation. Everything was going to go smoothly today, she thought as she showered and dressed. The preparation and hard work would pay off in the form of a beautiful, memorable wedding. Tim would get to walk his daughter down the aisle, Nova and Joel would be married, and all the guests would leave with a sense of having been a part of something wonderful.

By six, she was on her way to Weddings Out of the Box. There was no traffic and she arrived in less than ten minutes. She'd barely gotten to her office when Nova texted her, saying they were all awake and so excited.

Me, too. Try to eat and drink lots of water this morning. See you at one.

Not that brides listened, she thought humorously as she tucked her phone in her back pocket and ran down the stairs to double-check the ballroom.

By nine she'd been over every square inch of the building. The caterer had arrived to start setting up the outdoor tables, while the florist was busy unloading centerpieces, decorative sprays and bouquets. The ceremony was at five, the dinner at six thirty, with dancing and the zip line to follow. Sunset was just before eight, which meant there would be lots of romantic time in the dark. The colored twinkle lights would have their chance to add Concord Awaken ambience.

She was heading back to her office when she saw a familiar yet unexpected car pull up in the parking lot. She jogged toward it as Alan stepped out and held open his arms.

"You came!" She hugged him tight. "Thank you, thank you."

"I couldn't let down my favorite girl. Plus there was no way I could miss this wedding. It's going to be your best one yet."

A tall, redheaded man who looked to be about forty stepped out of the passenger side. Alan beamed. "This is Bryant. Bryant, this is Pallas."

"Hi." Pallas leaned close to Alan and lowered her voice. "He's very handsome."

"I know. Aren't I lucky?" Alan linked arms with her. "Come on, Bryant. The gang's all here. Let's put on a show!"

Nick parked his truck next to several cars, then walked around back and pulled off the tarp. He'd spent most of the night making a long papier-mâché vine to wrap around the gazebo being used in the ceremony. He would get it in place, then touch up the paint. The backdrop would continue the theme and make Nova's dress even more eye-catching for the pictures.

He carried in the first section of the vine. Workers were everywhere. Silver had set up her trailer and was putting out chairs covered in black cloth. The tables were set, and purple, teal and yellow flowers were everywhere.

He did his best not to look for Pallas. Her words had haunted him all night, and despite thinking about nothing but what she'd said, he was still confused.

He believed her. She loved him. Pallas. He knew he didn't deserve her or her feelings, but he supposed that was the point. Freely given, she'd told him. With no expectation of anything in return.

He wanted to give back, wanted to tell her he felt the same. Only he couldn't. Because of what could happen. Passion...

He knew the next line. Passion consumed, destroyed, whatever. He'd believed that most of his life. Yet without passion, what was the point? As she'd pointed out, without love, weren't they all just going through the motions?

He walked into the ballroom and stopped to let his eyes adjust to the relative dimness of the huge room. Then blinked when he saw glowing glass orbs surrounding all the papier-mâché flowers he'd set out previously.

They were exactly as he'd drawn them. Light seemed to emanate from the very center. They were scattered on the runner in the center aisle and on the steps to the gazebo. Ronan walked in from the far entrance, an orb in each hand, and stopped when he saw Nick.

"You never got around to these," his brother said with a shrug. "I figured they were important, so I made a few."

There were more than a few, Nick thought as he glanced around at the glowing objects.

"That took some time," he said.

Ronan shrugged again. "I didn't mind. I figured out how to get the glow and the rest was easy. All anyone talks about is this damn wedding. I thought I'd help."

He set down the two orbs he was carrying and crossed to Nick. After taking one end of the vine, he said, "Before, when we were fighting. I never meant you weren't my brother. Just that we're different."

"Why didn't you say that?"

"Because I can be a stubborn ass."

"You got that right."

Ronan grinned. "Come on. Let's get this in place. I hear there's going to be a wedding."

# CHAPTER TWENTY

NICK HONEST TO God didn't know where to look. Yes, technically Nova was covered, but not in a way that made him comfortable. The thong was way too... thong-y and the corset bra thing wasn't supposed to be seen by the likes of him. Her silk robe kept sliding off her shoulders and she didn't seem to notice. Not that he was interested. He was a Pallas guy all the way, but still.

"Get over it," Violet muttered as she pinned glittering fabric braids into Nova's avant-garde hairstyle. "You'd see more if she were wearing a swimsuit."

"She's in her underwear," he grumbled. "It's not right."

Nova sipped her glass of champagne. "Breathe," she told him. "Joel knows you're here and he's fine with it."

Words that allowed him to relax. "Okay then."

Violet rolled her eyes. "Seriously? That's all you needed to know?"

"Sure. You don't hit on another guy's woman and you sure don't stare at her in her underwear on her wedding day."

"But the fact that he knows you're here makes it

all right? Unbelievable." She looked at Nova. "How did you think to say that?"

Nova smiled. "I work with guys all the time. After a while, you pick up a thing or two."

Nick handed Violet another braid. She started to place it, then glanced at him.

"Over an inch," he said. Not that he knew anything about hair, but he was pretty good at symmetry, which was why he was in the bride's room two hours before the ceremony.

Except for long bangs, all of Nova's hair had been pulled back tight against her head. Individual braids of hair created circles in an almost spiral design. The fabric braids were added, going the opposite direction. Once they were in place, Violet would sew in sparkling teal and yellow buttons, adding flash while also securing braids in place.

"You've all been so amazing," Nova said. "I can't thank you enough."

"It's been fun," Nick told her. "We've enjoyed the challenge."

"It's true." Violet pinned another braid in place. "Pallas is changing her whole business model. We're going to do more crazy weddings. I, for one, can't wait. You inspired us. You and Joel and your dad."

Nova's eyes filled with tears. "I'm so happy he can be here."

"No crying," Violet told her. "You can't ruin your makeup until after the ceremony. And the pictures."

Nick watched as Violet placed yet more braids. He walked around Nova and checked her hair from every angle. When it was time to get her in her dress, he looked away as she was hooked into a complicated hoop slip creation, then carefully held up the dress so Nova could scoot under it.

There was plenty to do. Fastening and adjusting and handing Violet buttons, but all the while he kept thinking about Pallas. How she had made this happen. She'd taken an idea and created magic. No one else was willing to do the work to help Nova and Joel, but Pallas had done it. She put herself out there and this was the result.

He missed her, he admitted to himself. He missed being with her and talking to her. He missed her smile, her laugh, her quick mind. He missed holding her. There was nothing about her he didn't like. But the damn demons… How was he supposed to forget about them? How could he trust himself, trust them?

If only she hadn't said she loved him. Then he could have walked away without looking back. But now…that gift was there. Waiting for him to grow a pair and claim it. She loved him. How had he gotten so lucky?

"Nick, I'm going to crawl under her dress and adjust the slip. I need you to hold it up for me."

"Hell of a way to spend a day," he said.

They both laughed.

He told himself he would get through the wedding, then he would head up into the mountains for a few days and figure out what was going on. He would either get over Pallas or surrender, because being where he was—so close and yet so incredibly far from what she offered—was impossible.

THE PANELS LINED the ballroom, creating the illusion of an off-world location. With the subdued lighting, every reflective surface shimmered. The glass orbs seemed to glow from a mysterious power source and the origami masks added to the otherworldly air.

Pallas stood by the door, waiting for the music cue. Next to her was Atsuko in slim black pants and a traditional Chinese jacket in purple and teal. The unexpected combination blended perfectly with all the decorations and colors.

Behind her were the bridesmaids in deep purple and teal dresses. The gowns themselves were simple, but the gauzy, floating overlays added dimension to the style. Beads lined the V-neck and tiny stars dotted the skirts.

Their bouquets were traditional earth flowers, enhanced by Violet's buttons. Their headpieces were small, simpler versions of Nova's hair.

Nova and Tim were last in line. Tim had gone with a tuxedo while Nova stunned in her amazing, painted gown. Even in the unflattering light of the hallway, she was a vision of color and beauty. As she moved, the gown seemed to twist and glow with a life of its own.

The music quieted, then the first of three songs started. Pallas nodded at Atsuko, who started down the center aisle. The bridesmaids followed. Right before Nova and Tim started for the archway, Nova reached out her hand.

"I can never thank you enough."

Pallas blinked away tears. "You already have."

THE CEREMONY WAS FLAWLESS, the dinner delicious and the sun set right on time. Pallas allowed herself to breathe a sigh of relief. There was still the first dance by the bride and groom, the father-daughter dance, which should make everyone cry, then cutting the cake. Only a couple more hours until she could know everything had gone perfectly.

Pallas was about to relax when she saw Alan heading toward her. His purposeful stride made her want to whimper.

"What?" she demanded. "Just say it. Don't hint, don't try to make me feel better, just come clean."

"You can be very bossy."

"Alan!"

"Your mother is here, and your grandpa Frank."

Her mother? What on earth?

"Your look of shock tells me you didn't know. Nova invited Grandpa Frank and I'm guessing Libby's his plus-one. That's all I can think of."

"It's been three hours. How could I not have seen them before?"

Alan patted her arm. "You've been busy. It's all right. We're all here. You'll be fine."

Her mother at the wedding? Her mother had never come to one of her weddings before. Why now? Why this one?

She pushed the questions from her mind. She had enough to deal with. The last of the details, the fact that Nick was still here and making her want to fling herself at him every time she saw him. Not that she wanted him to go. She liked knowing he was in the room even if they weren't together anymore. Which probably made her in need of therapy, but it was true.

"Thank you for the warning," she said. "I'll do my best to stay out of her way until all this is over."

"Good plan. If I see her heading your way, I'll try to run interference." Alan flashed her a smile. "I'll ask her to tango."

"That will certainly get her attention."

The music quieted, then the first dance song began. Joel and Nova walked to the wooden floor put down by the front of the open space. Behind them twinkle lights flashed and the orbs Ronan had created glowed. Everyone collected to watch the happy couple.

When they were done, Tim approached his daughter. But instead of starting to dance, he picked up a nearby microphone and began to speak.

"Thank you all for being here to witness my daughter's marriage to Joel." He looked around at the guests. "I know what you're thinking. How awful you feel because I'm dying. But you're wrong. It's not awful. I have the gift of knowing how much time I have left. I have the privilege of knowing nothing will go unsaid. I tell my daughter I love her every day. I hear the words from her. I spend time with my friends. We talk about our passions and loves. We talk about life. I am blessed in every way possible."

He turned to Pallas and smiled. "I want to give a special thank-you to everyone who worked so hard to make this wedding come true exactly how Joel and Nova imagined it. Pallas, you're a miracle worker and I will always be grateful for the privilege of walking my daughter down the aisle. You've made our dreams come true."

Pallas mouthed, "You're welcome," all the while fighting tears. Tim was right. Love was what mattered most. Caring and being cared for—knowing there were those who needed you in their day to make things better.

"Thank you all for being a part of this special day," Tim concluded, then handed the microphone to Joel and began to dance with his daughter.

Pallas cleared her throat, then went to check on the cake. *What a wonderful family*, she thought. Thank goodness she'd taken on the project. How very sad if she'd refused the challenge—she wouldn't have known this was what she was meant to do. In her own small way, she would spend the rest of her life making dreams come true.

"Pallas?"

She turned and saw her mother approaching. Alan hurried up behind her, waving his arms as if he was going to distract Libby, but it was too late.

"Hi, Mom."

Pallas told herself she would give her mother exactly two minutes to tell her everything that was wrong with her, then excuse herself to see about the cake. "Did Grandpa Frank bring you?"

Her mother nodded, then surprised Pallas by blinking away tears. "That man…Tim…what he said. It was so wonderful. I'm sure your grandfather cared about me, but never like that. He had seven daughters. We had to be interchangeable."

"Mom, no. Grandpa Frank loves you. He's a good guy."

"Oh, I know that, it's just…I never felt special. Not with him and not with—"

She stopped speaking but Pallas could fill in the rest of the sentence. *Not with your father.* Because he hadn't married Libby for the right reasons. He'd wanted an in with the bank.

"I always thought if I did better," Libby continued, "if I was smarter or more successful, then I would have his attention. If I was everything I was supposed to be. But it was never enough for him."

Pallas didn't know which "him" they were talking about. Grandpa Frank or her father. Then she realized it didn't matter. Libby had suffered at the hands of all the men who were supposed to love her best. Perhaps intentionally, perhaps not. At the end of the day, the pain was still there.

"That's why I was so hard on you," her mother told her. "To make sure you were everything you could be. But what you said before, about how I was supposed to love you unconditionally, that hurt me. Only I began to wonder if you were right."

They stared at each other. Pallas sensed she was supposed to say something but she had no idea what.

"I do love you, Pallas."

Unexpected words that were oddly comforting. "I love you, too, Mom."

"Maybe if you came to work at the bank we could—"

Pallas shook her head. "That's not going to happen. This is what I do. I love my work and I make people happy. There's not going to be any bank for me."

Her mother pressed her lips together. "You're probably right. We'd fight all the time anyway and Drew would take your side, which I would find annoying."

Pallas smiled. "I'm one of his favorite cousins."

"So he tells me on a regular basis." Libby studied her. "Are we okay?"

"We are. Will you try the zip line?"

"No, but your grandfather will, I'm sure. The man thinks he's seventeen. He's going to break his neck one day."

Before Pallas could say anything, her mother pulled her close and hugged her. Pallas hugged her back. She didn't think their relationship was magically fixed but they'd made a start and for now that was enough.

NICK KEPT TELLING himself he should leave, but here he was—still at the wedding as the happy couple cut the cake.

Everything had gone according to plan. Pallas and her team had done a hell of a job. He'd only played a small part and didn't think he deserved any credit. He'd painted the dress and made a few flowers, but Pallas had done so much more.

Nova and Joel were practically floating with happiness. Grandpa Frank had been the first down the zip line and in a move that was both confusing and unsettling, Tim and Libby were sharing their third slow dance.

Nick circled the party, unable to shake the restlessness that drove him to keep moving. He was looking for something and didn't know what. Or who. For maybe the millionth time, he sought out Pallas, watching her chat with a guest.

She was amazing. The way she'd handled everything, how she'd totally been there for Nova and her family. She cared about people and they cared about her. How could they not?

He thought about what Tim had said earlier. The man had been all about the love. For him passion didn't consume, it was his reason for hanging on. He supposed it was like his art. When he didn't give 100 percent, the piece had no soul. It was simply inert. But when he put himself into it, then there was a chance it would live and breathe. He had to be willing to take the chance or he was just wasting his time.

He stopped and watched Pallas talking to Silver. The two women laughed together, then Silver handed Pallas a drink.

He liked looking at her, he thought. Being with her. He missed her desperately and wished…

What? That he wasn't afraid? That he could believe? That he was willing to take a chance on them? Because it was all right there, waiting. Pallas had offered her heart and he'd walked away. Walked away from the one person he wanted to be with for the rest of his life.

The truth slammed into him where it stabbed his soul and left him gasping for air. He wanted to be with Pallas always. He loved her and he trusted her. She was… She was everything!

He crossed the grass, took the drink from her

hands, then cupped her face and kissed her. When he drew back he stared into her eyes.

"I love you. I'm sorry I've been such a jackass. I love you, Pallas. Please give me another chance."

Her gaze searched his, then she smiled. "I told you there weren't any conditions. I'm all in, Nick. I have been from the first."

The tight band around his chest loosened and he knew they'd been damned lucky to find each other. No. He'd been the lucky one. For reasons he would never understand, Pallas had chosen him. He only knew one thing to do—hang on and never let go.

"I'm all in, too," he told her. "For always."

They walked to the dance floor and held on to each other as they swayed to the music. Certainty washed over him—certainty that this was the best thing he'd ever been a part of. Loving Pallas, being loved by her—it was right.

*Three months later*

"I HONESTLY DON'T know what to say," Taylor breathed as she stared at the life-size—assuming Roman gods were six foot four—wood carving of Neptune in the center of the courtyard.

He dominated the space, his arm raised. The tips of the trident gleamed, probably because they were gold plated. His cape seemed to move in the breeze. At any second he would step down and join them for the upcoming party.

"The artist, Nick, he's famous," Taylor added in a whisper. "We can't afford this."

Pallas held in a grin. "You don't have to. I told you—Nick's loaning you this big guy for your wedding because you inspired him. Then Neptune is off to some hotel in Italy where he will find his forever home in the lobby."

A fact that was exciting to her, mostly because Nick was overseeing the installation and she would be joining him for a two-week Italian vacation. She couldn't wait to be alone with him somewhere that beautiful.

The summer had flown by in a flurry of weddings, work and being madly in love with the greatest guy ever. Nick was an incredible boyfriend. She'd thought he was good before but once he committed himself, he was focused, attentive and so sweet. The only surprises had been good ones. Like the time he'd...

She told herself this was not the time to daydream about her good fortune in the love department. Taylor's wedding was in two days and the bride needed her full attention.

They walked through Weddings Out of the Box and went over every detail. The under-the-sea theme had played out beautifully.

"You've been to see Wynn?" Pallas asked.

"Yes. The panels." Taylor's voice was dreamy. "They're wonderful. She's so talented."

"She did a great job. We'll have them up in time for the rehearsal tomorrow night. I just love all the little touches."

"Me, too." Taylor hugged her. "You've been so

wonderful. Thank you. Jake and I are getting our dream wedding and you're the reason."

"It takes a village." Pallas glanced at her watch. "I believe you have a massage in half an hour. You need to head back to the hotel."

Taylor shrieked. "I don't want to be late for that. After I get my special manicure."

Pallas had started coordinating with the local hotels to offer spa packages for her brides, including mani-pedis that included polish coordinated to the wedding colors.

Taylor hugged her one last time before dashing out. Pallas laughed as the other woman ran to her car. The few days before any wedding were always insane, but she loved every second of them. Of course these days she loved almost everything in her life.

She walked into the ballroom and watched as Nick assembled the lightweight wooden frames he'd constructed for her. The aluminum ones had been delivered, but he'd hated them on sight and insisted in making her something custom. Now she walked over to study the dark wood.

There was something on it, she realized. A pattern. She moved closer and saw that it wasn't a pattern at all—at least not in the traditional sense. It was their initials looping together, along with tiny hearts.

She rubbed her fingers against the wood, then looked at him.

"You did this. It's beautiful, but what were you thinking? You're an important artist. You can't waste your time decorating screen frames for me."

"It wasn't a waste of time, Pallas. The wood told me what it was supposed to be. I just did the work."

She fought against tears. There had to be dozens of hours in the project. Maybe hundreds. "When did you find the time? You were supposed to be finishing Neptune."

"I did both. I'll admit I didn't get a lot of sleep, but that's okay. You're worth it. Do you like them?"

She looked at the huge frames that would be filled with Wynn's panels. "They're wonderful. Just like you."

"I'm glad you think so."

He surprised her by dropping to one knee and taking her hand. Um, no. Surprised was not the word. Stunned was better. She stared at him.

"Nick?"

"I love you, Pallas. Thank you for taking a chance on me, on us. Being with you is the best part of my life. I want to make you happy and be with you for as long as possible. Marry me. Please."

She couldn't think or breathe or see anything but the amazing man she'd had the good fortune to fall in love with.

"Yes," she breathed. "Yes, I'll marry you."

He stood and drew her against him, then kissed her. They hung on to each other before he stepped back and pulled a small Tiffany box from his pocket and opened it. Inside a beautiful diamond solitaire winked *hello, gorgeous*.

Pallas's hands were shaking as he slid the ring into place.

Nick kissed her again. "So, I was thinking. What are your thoughts on planning your own wedding?"

"No, thanks. I do that for a living." She bit her lower lip. "Unless it's important to you. I should have asked first. Whatever you want is fine."

"I'm thinking elopement."

"Really? Because that would be great."

He smiled and touched her cheek. "It turns out Atsuko is friends with the US ambassador to Italy. He's put me in touch with someone who can make all the arrangements. If you'd like to get married in Italy."

She started to laugh. "Gee, let me think about that for a second."

He kissed her. "So Italy, then."

"Anytime, anywhere."

"That's my girl."

He kissed her again and she hung on as if she would never let go. Which was kind of the plan.

\* \* \* \* \*

*Visit HappilyInc.com to discover more about the wedding destination town founded on a fairy tale!*

*Can't get enough romance?*
*Keep reading for an excerpt from*
*SECOND CHANCE GIRL,*
*the next great read in the* HAPPILY INC *series*
*by #1* New York Times *bestselling author*
*Susan Mallery!*

# CHAPTER ONE

GETTING KICKED IN the stomach by a gazelle was never pleasant, but at one thirty in the morning, it was especially hard to take. Carol Lund glared at Bronwen and the gazelle glared right back.

"You don't get to have attitude, young lady," Carol told her. "I'm not the one who insisted on going out by the rocks. I'm not the one who got scraped up, yet here I am, in the middle of the night, checking on your leg to make sure you don't have an infection."

Bronwen was notably unimpressed by Carol's presence and dedication. She stomped her front hooves and turned away.

"You say that now," Carol grumbled. "But just wait until feeding time. Suddenly I'm your best friend. You're incredibly fickle."

Carol packed up her supplies. Bronwen's leg seemed to be healing nicely. With luck she wouldn't require a second night's visit tomorrow and Carol could catch up on the sleep she was missing.

She left the gazelle barn and started for her Jeep. The night was clear and cool and there were a million stars in the sky. While Carol would have preferred that Bronwen hadn't been injured and that they'd both been able to sleep through the night, she had to admit that staring at the perfect sky was a very cool compensation. If she didn't look at the horizon, or try to pick out individual constellations, she could be anywhere in the world—literally. Because the night sky was a constant.

Oh, sure, there were differences between the hemispheres and at certain times of the year, but still...stars!

She climbed in her Jeep and drove toward her small bungalow, then pulled onto the shoulder before she got there and cut the engine and lights. She got out of the Jeep, sank down onto the ground and gave herself over to the nighttime view.

It was October in the desert, which meant warm days and pleasant nights. Rain was an unlikely possibility—that was more a spring-summer thing. The closest town was Happily Inc and it wasn't all that huge, so it wasn't hard to get away from the streetlights and into true darkness. Here, on the road, she was flanked by the mountains and the golf course, with the rolling hills of the Happily Inc Animal Preserve just behind her. And the stars.

She draped her jacket on the ground so she could lie down and get the best view of the wonder overhead. She had no idea how long she'd been lying there when a pair of headlights cut through the darkness and briefly illuminated her.

Carol sat up as a swoopy midnight blue Mercedes sedan pulled in behind her Jeep.

Of all the gin joints in all the world, she thought. She watched a tall, dark-haired man step out of his car and walk toward her. It had to be after two in the morning, yet Mathias Mitchell looked more alert than sleepy. No doubt the lingering effects of the hunt, takedown and getting laid.

He stopped a few feet from her. It was too dark for her to read his expression, but if she had to guess, she would say he was amused. Mathias seemed to find the world a delightful place. She supposed given who he was, with his combination of good looks, easy charm and career success, there was no reason he should think otherwise. To mix metaphors and clichés, the world was his oyster and Mathias dined well.

She, on the other hand, was simply a woman with looks and a personality as ordinary as her name.

"Lose a contact lens?" he asked drily.

"Bronwen hurt herself, so I had to go check on her. On my way back, I stopped to look at the stars."

He sank down next to her and raised his gaze to the sky. "Why not wait until you got home?"

"This is the best view in the area."

"Because you've tried them all?" He sighed. "You're an odd woman, Carol Lund. Who's Bronwen? One of the zebras?"

"Gazelle."

"Fancy name for a cow."

Carol felt her lips twitch and was grateful he couldn't see her trying not to smile. The conversation was familiar. Unlike most of the citizens of Happily Inc, Mathias had no romantic notions about the animals grazing just outside of town. "Gazelles aren't cows."

"They're close. Oh, I'll give you that they're more

elegant, probably faster, too, but still, under their pretty outsides, they're cows. Just like your precious Millie."

Carol glared at him. "Don't you say that. Millie's wonderful."

"I'm not saying anything about her character, just pointing out that despite her being adorable and very tall, she is, in fact, a ruminant." He leaned close enough for her to smell the perfume clinging to his body. "Which makes her just like a cow," he added in a stage whisper.

She waved her hand in front of her face. "There's a smell."

Mathias nodded. "Yeah, she did get a little heavy with the scent."

"Did the big boobs compensate?"

"I'm not actually a breast man. My requirements are more about general appeal."

"If she's slutty, you're in?" She cleared her throat. "So to speak?"

"You wound me. There's a process."

"Not a very good one. You really need to shower before you go to bed tonight or your sheets are going to reek."

"Excellent advice. Thank you."

"My neighbor, the man whore."

She made the statement without a whole lot of energy—mostly because there was no point. Almost nothing ruffled him. Despite what he did for a living, he was the opposite of a brooding artist. Except for his questionable taste in sexual partners, there was little not to like about Mathias and she had to admit that in her heart of hearts, she was a fan.

"Have you considered that nearly all the derogatory terms about a person being promiscuous are directed at women?" He glanced at her. "Slut, whore. We have to modify them to make them apply to a man."

"What about a player or a sugar daddy?"

"No guy minds being called a player and I'm not sure any human has used the term 'sugar daddy' since 1979."

She chuckled. "That's not true. People say it all the time."

He looked at her, but didn't speak.

"Okay, maybe not *all* the time, but lots."

"Carol, Carol, Carol, you are such an innocent."

"That must be refreshing after a night with one of your women."

"It is, although I have to say, I don't understand your dislike of bridesmaids."

"I don't dislike them. I simply don't understand what you see in them. Or what they see in you."

The last was a lie. Mathias was funny enough to be charming and sexy enough to be irresistible. She would admit that even *she* had had the odd fantasy or two about him. Not that she would ever bother to act—she knew her place in the world. She was the plain peahen, while Mathias was the classic peacock. There was no reason for him to notice her and even if he somehow did, he only did one-night stands and that had never been her thing. She was much more a fall in love first kind of girl.

"What I see in them is that they'll be gone in the morning," he said as he stood. "As for what they see in me, isn't that obvious?"

He held out his hand. She reached for it and he pulled her to her feet. As soon as she found her balance, he released her, then reached down and grabbed her jacket. He put it around her shoulders.

"Come on, my little animal warden friend. We need to get you into bed. Morning comes early and cows expect to be fed."

"I should slug you really hard in the stomach," she grumbled as they walked to her Jeep.

"Such violence. You're not embracing the cow mantra of being one with nature."

"If you say cow one more time, I swear I'm going to—"

He held open the driver's door and she slid onto the seat. They were nearly at eye level.

"You're going to what?" he asked.

The dome light illuminated his features. His eyes were dark and his smile nearly blinded her with its brightness. He had broad shoulders and the honed body of a man who used muscles every day in his work.

As happened every now and then around him, she remembered that she was a healthy woman in her twenties who hadn't been with someone in way too long. Mathias had to know what he was doing—he certainly had enough practice.

Not that he would be interested in her. Not only didn't she fit his "You must be leaving town" criteria, she wasn't, you know, special. Or at least not special enough to tempt the likes of him.

"I'm going to start training the zebras to poop in your yard. Have you smelled zebra poo? It's going to make that perfume seem like nothing."

He flashed her a smile. "Time to say good-night, Carol."

"Good night, Carol."

He closed the door and walked to his sedan. She started down the road, the Mercedes following closely. A couple of miles later, she pulled into her driveway. Mathias flashed his lights, then kept going. For a second, his car disappeared as he rounded a small hill, then she saw him as he came out the other side. The lights turned as he drove onto his property, flashed twice again before disappearing into his garage.

She continued to stand in the darkness until more lights appeared, this time in his massive house on the edge of the animal preserve. There was humor in the fact that her twelve-hundred-square-foot bungalow could fit comfortably in his five-car garage with room to spare, yet he was her closest neighbor. There she was—living on the edge of the world of the "haves" and more than happy to stay on her side.

Carol unlocked her front door and went inside. She toed off her boots, then went directly to her bedroom and barely pulled off her jeans before sinking onto the mattress and sighing.

Morning would come way too early, thanks to Bronwen. Unlike some people who lived in big mansions with views, she had to get up with the sun. Her herd didn't like to wait for breakfast.

Carol quickly fell asleep only to find herself tangled in a strange dream of flying cows and Mathias begging her to kiss him. She woke to the insistent sound of her alarm and the knowledge that of the two scenarios, flying cows were by far the more likely to happen.

MATHIAS WALKED BAREFOOT across his patio. It was still early and a light mist clung to the ground—no doubt the result of early-morning watering, but he preferred a more romantic explanation. It was the artist in him.

He took his favorite chair, set his coffee and sketch pad on the table beside him, then prepared to wait.

He wasn't sure how long ago the ritual had started. Shortly after Millie had arrived, maybe. He didn't know why she got to him more than the others. She was just a giraffe. Shouldn't he find beauty in the swift-footed gazelles or majesty in the water buffalo?

While he'd been aware of the animals when he'd purchased the house, he hadn't really noticed them for the first few months. He supposed they'd crept into his consciousness after he'd met Carol.

Most towns hid their dumps behind gates or far away from any suburban sprawl. Happily Inc had planned differently, putting it just southwest of the population center, carefully downwind.

In addition to running a recycling and reclamation program that was one of the best in the nation, the two men who owned and ran the dump had also purchased hundreds of acres around the landfill. Grasses and trees had been brought in. Once they'd taken root, the animals had appeared. The gazelles had been first, then the zebras. There were a few wading birds, the water buffalo and lastly, Millie.

Mathias knew the basics—the two men who had created a unique African savanna on the edge of the California desert were Carol's father and uncle. When she'd completed her degree, she'd come to work at the preserve. A year ago, the old man in charge of the animals had retired, leaving Carol to take over. A few months after that, Millie had arrived.

Mathias didn't know why the giraffe and the woman were so closely linked in his mind, but they were. Now, as he watched the morning fog slowly dissipate, he saw Millie stroll into view.

She was a reticulated or Somali giraffe, nearly fifteen feet tall, with traditional markings. Her face was almost heart shaped, with widely spaced eyes and an inquisitive gaze.

Mathias sipped his coffee before reaching for his sketch pad. He already had hundreds of drawings of Millie and Carol, but he hadn't yet found *the one*. He would know it when he saw it, so every morning he waited.

Carol appeared when they cleared the trees. She barely came to partway up Millie's shoulder. In the morning light, her short red hair seemed almost blond. She was strong and wholly herself—a contrast to his usual type of woman, so he shouldn't have found her appealing…only he did. There was something about her lack of artifice, something about the way she was so comfortable in her own skin that made him pay attention.

Carol and the giraffe strolled together like this most mornings, after the other animals had been fed. At first he'd thought this was Carol's way of making Millie more comfortable with her surroundings. But the walks had continued long after Millie had settled in to her new home. When the small donation jars had started popping up all over town, he'd realized Carol was attempting to fulfill Millie's need for companionship.

A few minutes on the internet had taught Mathias that while male giraffes were mostly solitary, female giraffes lived in a loose group. Mothers often took on babysitting duties so they could each go forage for food. Carol's morning walks were her attempt to help Millie feel as if she had a herd.

He watched them for nearly half an hour then went inside. Before heading to the studio, he went to his sunroom where he worked from home. Not with glass—that setup would require more equipment, not to mention a very understanding insurance agent—but with pencil and pad or even paint and canvas.

He flipped through the drawings stacked on a shelf. Millie alone, Millie and Carol walking, Millie with the zebras. It was there, he thought, doing his best to ignore the ever-present frustration. He'd been close a couple of times, nearly capturing the image he wanted. It would come—he had to believe that. And when it did, he would create it out of glass. Assuming he still had what had once been his reason to live and breathe.

ULRICH SHERWOOD, Duke of Somerbrooke, stared out of the eighth-floor conference room window of the Century City high-rise. To the west was Santa Monica and the vast Pacific Ocean, to the east were haze-covered mountains...or maybe that was smog smudging the outline. He'd only been in Los Angeles twice before and hadn't enjoyed himself either time. This visit was to meet with lawyers—something else he didn't enjoy but which was in this case a necessary evil. A very well-financed TV producer wanted to set a modern-day *Downton Abbey* in England and Ulrich's home of Battenberg Park had been chosen as the location. Not only did the use of the rambling estate mean a hefty fee, Battenberg Park would also receive a "spruce" as the lawyer had called it. For their purposes, that meant fresh paint and a significant upgrade in landscaping. Combined, the fee and the "spruce" had made a trip to Los Angeles more than worth the time and effort.

Linda, the forty-something attorney, returned to the conference room and smiled at him. "Your Lordship."

"Ulrich, please," he murmured, knowing there was no point in correcting her to use the more accurate "Your Grace." Not only did he prefer to keep that sort of formality to a minimum, he was in the States. Here, true royalty came in the form of movie stars. What did anyone care about lineage, titles or peerage?

"Here's your copy of the contract," Linda said. "Along with a receipt for the first payment. As you requested, we wired the money directly to your bank."

"Excellent."

Linda had the firm, slim body of a woman who took fitness seriously. She looked at least a decade younger than what he would guess to be her age and he was sure, when it came to playing the game, she was far more experienced than he. He'd married young, divorced only two years ago and since then had avoided entanglements. He supposed he should have been flattered and perhaps intrigued when she said, "Now that our business is complete, I'd love to take you out to dinner. I know a great little place not far from my condo."

Ulrich knew he could easily take advantage of what was being offered. He was single, out of the country and no one would ever know. He doubted Linda wanted or expected anything other than the one night. What could be more perfect?

Only he couldn't summon the interest. It wasn't that she was nearly a decade older, it was…well, everything.

"Thank you for the invitation," he said, offering a polite smile and a tone of genuine regret. "I'm afraid I have pressing business in the eastern part of your state and I must get on the road right away."

"Where are you heading?"

Ulrich did his best not to curl his lip in disdain. "To a town called Happily Inc."

She laughed. "I've been there. A friend had a destination wedding at a place called Weddings in a Box a couple of years ago. It's cute. An interesting choice for a man like you. Are you getting married?" She sounded more intrigued than put off by the idea of his pending nuptials.

"What? No. I have, ah, family business in the area."

An American shyster stealing from his grandmother, to be exact.

Linda regarded him thoughtfully. "I'm sorry we won't be able to spend the evening together."

"As am I," he lied. "Truly." He waved the folder. "Thank you for this."

"You're welcome."

Ulrich nodded and left. Twenty minutes later he was heading east on I-10. His rental car's nav system promised him an arrival at his destination in less than four hours.

On the seat next to him was his briefcase. Inside, along with the contract from Linda's production firm, was a name and an address.

For the past half dozen or so years his eighty-year-old grandmother had been sending packages to one Violet Lund. At first Ulrich hadn't noticed or cared, until the head housekeeper had mentioned that items from the estate had gone missing. A pair of candlesticks here, a small painting there. Individually the items were of little consequence, but in the aggregate, they were significant.

He'd found out about the packages, but when he'd questioned his grandmother, the dowager duchess had informed him it was none of his business.

Ulrich had very little family left—Winifred, his grandmother, was his closest living relative. She'd helped raise him after his mother had died, they'd comforted each other when his father had passed a few years before, and he loved her deeply. There was no way he was going to confront her directly, but that didn't mean he couldn't go around her and find out about the disgusting human being who would prey on a helpless old lady.

For a second Ulrich mentally paused to appreciate the six or seven thousand miles between him and his grandmother. Because if she ever knew he'd thought of her as helpless or old, she would grab him by the ear and give him a stern talking-to. She wouldn't care that he was thirty and the Duke of Somerbrooke.

Fortunately he didn't plan to tell her. Instead he would confront the con artist and sever the contact. Then he would fly back to England and retreat to his beautiful if slightly needy home and brace himself for the Hollywood invasion.

Nothing about his mission was pleasant, but that didn't matter. For centuries, his ancestors had been riding or sailing or in his case, driving into battle. Not for glory or personal gain, but because it was expected. He had been raised to do the right thing— damn the inconvenience or short-term consequences. Or in this case, the thieving ways of the mysterious Violet Lund.

## CHAPTER TWO

MATHIAS HELD THE form in position. Ronan focused intently as he heated the glass to a molten state. Timing was everything. The material had to be hot enough to shape, but not heated too much or it would become a blob and he would lose all the work he'd already done.

A sketch of the completed piece was pinned up on the wall of the brothers' giant studio. The finished installation would be nearly thirty feet across and ten feet high. On the left was a perfect green dragon—on the right was an elegant white swan. In between the two were morphing shapes as one became the other.

Ronan had just started the piece. He had a year to complete it and then he would oversee the installation of it in an upscale hotel in Japan. While these days he mostly worked in the privacy of his studio at home, aided by assistants and interns, he often started a project at the studio they and their brother Nick shared. Mathias liked to think Ronan wanted the comradery and the shared energy, but maybe he was fooling himself. He and his brother had once been close. A few years ago, all that had changed.

Ronan pulled the glass out of the oven. Mathias stepped into place and held the form as Ronan spun the rod. Nick applied pressure with a sharp edge. The glass yielded.

The heat was intense, as was their concentration. Success or failure was measured in seconds as the material hardened in the breathable air. Ronan studied what they'd done, then returned the piece to the oven, only to pull it out again and watch it cool and harden.

The commission would be done in hundreds of sections all carefully joined together, like a giant glass puzzle. It would consume him for weeks at a time. Mathias had seen it happen before. The start was slow, then the project picked up momentum. Usually Mathias had been a part of that. This time, he was less sure.

In his head, Mathias understood why. Everything was different now. They were no longer two of the five Mitchell brothers. He dropped the form back into the bin and walked to his work area, then shook his head. Okay, that wasn't true. They were still the Mitchell brothers, but he and Ronan, well, that was gone forever.

He studied his own morning's work. Two serving bowls in a dozen shades of amber, moss green and yellow. Unlike Ronan's creation, Mathias's was practical rather than esoteric. He made light pendants and giant vessels that were used as bathroom sinks. He created vases and platters and dishes. The latter were done in various colors to reflect the seasons. White, blue and silver for winter, pale green, pink and peach for spring, red, orange and purple for summer and amber, moss green, chestnut and yellow for fall.

There had been a time when he, too, had created art, but he'd figured out this was his path. He liked what he did—he brought beauty to people's everyday lives. If every now and then he yearned for something more, well, what was the point? Yes, he had some of their father's talent, but Ronan and Nick were the artists. He was just a guy who worked with glass.

He studied the bowls, pleased with the outcome. Every year he tried to do something to challenge himself. For this year, he'd decided to add a shape to the serving pieces. The fall bowls had the outline of a leaf. Summer had been a strawberry and spring, a daisy. For winter, he would take on a snowflake—something he still had no idea how he was going to create. Every attempt had been a disaster, but that was half the fun.

His phone chirped. He glanced at the screen and saw he had a text from his mother.

"Incoming," he said aloud, then glanced at his brothers to see if either of them had heard from her.

Nick reached for his phone while Ronan ignored him.

"Nothing," Nick said. "Guess it's your lucky day."

"Sure it is," Mathias grumbled as he read the short message.

I'm coming to see you.

An interesting statement that would have made him uncomfortable if his mother hadn't been over four hundred miles away.

When?

What he expected was for her to say sometime next week or at the end of the month, when his brother Del was getting married.

In about ten minutes. I'm in town.

Mathias swore. His first thought was "Why me?" followed by "Hell, no" followed by "Run!" Instead of following his instincts, he reminded himself that he loved his mother, even if he found her difficult, and that not dealing with her wasn't an option.

Great, he texted back, telling himself it wasn't an actual lie. More of a hedge.

"What?" Nick demanded.

"She's on her way."

His brother relaxed. "That gives us about eight hours. Why is she coming here?"

"I have no idea." He swung his attention to Ronan. "She's ten minutes away."

Mathias watched the play of emotion on Ronan's face. They were easy to read. Shock, annoyance, the need to disappear. Not all that different from his own reaction.

Five years ago he would have said the similarity was because they were twins. Fraternal, but still. They shared a bond that time and space couldn't break. Only they'd discovered they weren't twins at all—they never had been. It had all been a lie and nothing had been the same since they'd had that particular truth thrust upon them.

Ronan set the still-cooling glass on the heatproof bench, grabbed his keys and bolted.

"We're not going to see him for three days," Nick grumbled. "He's got to face her sooner or later."

"You're telling the wrong guy."

Mathias walked to the entrance to the studio and

waited. Ronan was already backing out of the parking space. He turned right on the street and headed for the hills. Or in his case, the mountains. Nick was right—they wouldn't see him for days.

The October afternoon was warm and clear. Rain rarely came to the desert and this wasn't the season. From now through the holidays there wouldn't even be a cloud in the sky. Come spring, the weather got a little iffy, but not often and not for long.

Happily Inc sat in the middle of the California desert, with Arizona to the east and Mexico to the south. An underground aquifer provided more than enough water for residents and visitors alike. There were mountains for those who preferred that topography, as well as an odd convergence of energy that made Happily Inc a special and magical place for those who believed in that kind of thing. More significant to daily life was the fact that the town was a destination wedding location with most of the local businesses focused on all things nuptial and tourist. The only large-scale exceptions were the sleep center north of town and Carol's animal preserve to the southwest.

An unfamiliar car pulled into the parking lot and took Ronan's spot. It was a nondescript sedan, a rental. His mother was behind the wheel and his father was nowhere to be seen. Unless Ceallach was hiding in the back seat, maybe this visit wasn't going to be so bad after all.

"Hey, Mom," he said as Elaine Mitchell got out of the car and hugged him.

"What an adorable little town. And so easy to navigate. I wasn't sure I could find my way from the airport, but it all went just fine." She turned back to the car. "Come on, sweetie."

Mathias had a second of panic, thinking his joke about his father hiding had tempted the fates just a little too much, only instead of the family patriarch stepping out onto the pavement, a brown-and-white beagle jumped down and immediately raced over to him, her ears flapping and her long tail wagging happily.

"Hey, Sophie," he said as he crouched down to greet the dog.

She ran in circles around him before jumping up to put her paws on his shoulders and thoroughly kiss his face. He laughed, then stood to get out of the wet zone.

Nick stepped out of the studio. He looked at Mathias, who shook his head. His brother relaxed as he approached their mother.

"Mom," he said warmly. "You're a surprise." He bent over to greet Sophie.

"I know. I should have called, but I didn't."

Mathias had the uncomfortable thought that she'd deliberately not given them much warning because she'd known they would scatter if given the chance. Which sure didn't say much about them as sons.

The problem wasn't her, he thought grimly. It was their father. The man they wouldn't have to ask about because Elaine would happily tell them everything and more.

The three of them walked into the studio, Sophie bringing up the rear. At the last second, Mathias thought about all the tools, glass and ovens in the room and grabbed Sophie's trailing leash. Elaine glanced around, as if looking for someone, then her happy smile faded a little.

Mathias silently called Ronan five kinds of bastard for hurting the woman who had always loved him. But his brother wouldn't see it that way and no one had been able to get through to him, despite how they'd all tried.

"This is nice," she said with false enthusiasm. "Big and open. You all work here?"

Nick and Mathias exchanged a glance, as if hoping the other would speak first.

"Ronan has his own studio at his place," Mathias finally said. "He works there a lot."

"I see. And the gallery is close?"

"Across the parking lot. You should meet Atsuko before you go. She's the one selling our work."

"I will next time. I'm on my way back to the airport to catch a flight."

Before Mathias could ask why she'd bothered to come by, she continued, "Your father and I are heading out on tour. He's going to be lecturing and giving demonstrations. It's all very exciting to see him get the attention he deserves."

Mathias did his best not to roll his eyes. The last thing Ceallach Mitchell was lacking was attention. In his universe, he was the sun and everyone else revolved around his greatness and light.

"We'll be gone about a month and then come back here in time for Del and Maya's wedding."

"That's great, Mom," Nick said. "So, ah, why did you stop by?"

Elaine turned to Mathias as if it was obvious. "Someone has to look after Sophie while we're gone."

Mathias dropped the leash he was holding. The dog immediately took off exploring. "No. No way. I can't."

"Yes, you can. She's adorable and you love her."

*Love* was strong. He liked the dog…from a distance. It wasn't that she was a bad dog—not exactly. It was more that she had an adventurous spirit and only listened when it suited her purposes. If there was trouble within a five-mile radius, Sophie found it, rolled in it, then brought it home as a prize.

His mother's gaze sharpened. "Nick can't take her. He and Pallas are newly in love and Sophie would only get in the way."

Nick's expression turned smug. "That's true."

"You have that big house," his mother went on. "With a yard. Sophie will be fine with you and it's only for a month. Besides, taking care of her would be good for—"

The sound of glass shattering cut through the afternoon. They all turned to stare as Sophie yelped and raced away from the rack filled with finished plates, bowls and glasses. Mathias hadn't seen what had happened but he would guess Sophie's everwagging tail had been the culprit.

Elaine hurried toward her dog. Mathias swore and followed. They had to keep Sophie away from the glass so she didn't hurt herself. But as they approached, the happy beagle decided this was some kind of glorious game and darted away.

"I've got her," Nick called as he lunged.

Sophie sidestepped, whacked one of the two bowls Mathias had completed that morning with her tail and then took off for the other side of the room. Mathias managed to get close enough to stomp on her leash, which brought her to a quick stop. He grabbed her in his arms and hauled her up to safety. Sophie relaxed and gave him a doggie kiss on the chin.

Elaine smiled. "See. You're going to do great with her."

Not exactly the words he would have used. Still, he was smart enough to know when he'd been bested. He could yell and complain and generally make a fool of himself but at the end of the day, Elaine was his mother, he loved her and there was no way he could tell her no. Which meant today, it sucked to be him.

MONDAY NIGHTS WERE tournament nights at The Boardroom Pub. With weddings running the local economy, Happily Inc worked on weekends. Monday was the town's traditional party night, such as it was, and many of the residents made it a point to get out for a little fun before the next batch of wedding folk blew into town.

The Boardroom, a pub devoted to every board game known to man, celebrated Mondays with different challenges. There had been a Monopoly Junior competition over the summer. Hungry, Hungry Hippo night, along with board based trivia games, checkers, chess. If there was a board used at any point in the game, it could be found in The Boardroom.

Carol liked Monday nights. In the past, she'd enjoyed the chance to hang out with her friends and have fun. Lately, she was just as interested in the big crowd that showed up for the tournaments. Ever since she'd come up with the idea of buying a herd for her lonely giraffe, she'd been in fund-raising mode. There were donation cans all over town and on Monday nights, a percentage of the proceeds at The Boardroom went to the "buy Millie a herd" cause.

As she wove between the tables, she called out to people she knew. Once she reached the bar, she shook the giraffe-print-covered can and was delighted to feel the weight of it. Yes, the money was flowing slowly, but at least it was flowing. Buying giraffes wasn't cheap, nor was the very tricky transportation to get them to the animal preserve. There would be the costs of additional housing, not to mention feeding. Millie's favorite marionberry leaf-eater treats were pricy.

Still, progress was being made and that was what mattered. Carol needed her favorite girl to be happy.

After confirming the full can, she looked at the chalkboard to find out the challenge of the week, then grinned.

"You look happy," her friend Pallas said as she approached. They hugged.

"I love Clue."

Pallas, a hazel-eyed brunette with an easy smile, groaned. "Let me guess. You can always figure out who did it and where. I never can. There's too much to keep track of."

"That's why you take notes."

"It's not a game if you're taking notes. Want to sit with us tonight?"

"Sure."

They made their way to a table. Seconds before they arrived, Carol remembered that Pallas would most likely be sitting with her fiancé. Nick was a great guy—Carol liked him a lot. The problem was his brother. Because Carol wasn't sure she wanted to spend the evening sitting next to the ever dreamy Mathias.

Not that he would notice her, she reminded herself. She wasn't glamorous or special—in the animal kingdom, she was the female who would be overlooked by the alpha male. While she teased Mathias about his love of bridesmaids, the truth was his type was more specific than simply anyone who was in a wedding. He gravitated toward the most beautiful, most feminine, most alluring of the single women in town to attend a wedding.

In a word or two—not her.

She and Pallas took seats across from each other, then glanced at the menu. On tournament nights there were special drinks in honor of the game du jour, along with easy-to-eat food. Carol generally stuck with herbal iced tea rather than one of the cocktails. She had to be up early to feed her animals.

Pallas was facing the door. When Carol saw her friend's face light up with happiness, she sighed. "Let me guess. Chris Pine just walked in?"

"Better." Pallas rose. "Nick's here."

The engaged couple embraced. Nick's kiss lingered a second more than was polite, then he grinned at Carol. "How's it going? Did you hear about Mathias?"

He seemed too happy for whatever it was to be bad, she told herself as she shook her head. "I've been out on the savanna all day. What happened?"

Pallas rolled her eyes. "Ignore him. He's being mean."

"I'm not," Nick protested as he sat next to her. "But I will admit, better him than me." Nick's grin returned. "Our mom stopped by with Sophie."

Carol tried to figure out what was funny. While she'd heard about Elaine Mitchell, she'd never met her and she had no idea who Sophie was. There was no sister, so a cousin maybe? A chill raced through her as she considered the possibility of an ex-girlfriend delivered to Mathias. For reasons she couldn't explain, the thought of that was incredibly unsettling.

Pallas put her hand over Nick's. "She has no idea who Sophie is, sweetie, so she's not going to get the joke."

"Sophie's a beagle. She's Mom's dog. My parents are going to be traveling for a month, so Mom brought Sophie to stay with Mathias." Nick snickered. "I'm in love, so I was spared."

A dog? Wasn't that nice? Carol liked dogs. "Why is this so funny?"

"You haven't met Sophie," Nick told her. "She's sweet and friendly as could be, but don't let those big eyes fool you. Sophie's also a terror. She's an escape artist, a food hound and all-around troublemaker. Mathias doesn't have a chance. The dog was in our studio for maybe ten minutes and she broke a dozen of his pieces. That was without trying. Imagine what she can do if she makes an effort."

Carol winced. "Is she okay? Did she get any glass in her paw?"

"She's fine. She's lucky that way. Nothing bad ever happens to her. Everyone else gets sucked into the vortex, but Sophie emerges unscathed."

"He's exaggerating," Pallas said. "I've only seen pictures, but she looks adorable. Mathias will be fine."

Nick snorted. "Tell him that," he said, jerking his head toward the door.

Carol turned and saw Mathias, a small beagle at his side and a fluffy dog bed under his arm. Sophie's eyes were bright, her tail wagging. She was every inch a happy dog.

"Oh, yeah, she's the devil," Carol murmured. "We should run while we can."

"You mock me but you'll see." Nick's tone was warning.

As Mathias and Sophie approached, Carol noticed the dog was wearing a red Service Animal vest. Her lips began to twitch.

Mathias reached the table and dropped the dog bed on the floor. "Don't say a word," he growled. "You have no idea what I've been through in the past few hours."

Carol glanced from him to Sophie and back. "Do you need her for emotional support?" she asked sweetly. "Does she help with flashbacks or is her job more to keep the sexy bridesmaids at bay?"

"Very funny." He collapsed in his chair. "I couldn't

leave her home alone. Everything is new to her. Mom told me she's a certified service dog, so I put her in her vest and brought her."

"That's so nice," Pallas told him. She turned to Nick. "See, it's going fine."

Nick chuckled. "Uh-huh. Tell her the rest."

Mathias's expression tightened. "It's been five hours. There's no way I can keep her for a month. She has more equipment than an NFL team. Leashes and collars, beds, toys, the service vest. My mom gave me a notebook of instructions. There are twenty-six pages. Twenty-six!" He cleared his throat, then lowered his voice. "She has canned food, dry food, treats, flea medicine."

"Poop bags?" Carol asked, trying not to laugh. "You know dogs poop, right? Usually on a walk. You're going to need the bags so you can pick it up and carry it with you until you get home and throw it in the trash. Oh, and make sure you tie the bag really tight when you're done because of, you know, the smell."

Mathias stared at her. "Stop it."

Nick shook his head. "Bro, she's not lying about the poop. We all do it."

"Thank you for sharing." Mathias flagged a server. "I'd like a beer, please, and if you could hurry, that would be great."

They all placed their drink orders, then Pallas smiled at Mathias. "It's going to be fine. I'm sure Sophie's a good little girl. You'll like having her around."

"You might learn something from her," Carol

added. "Dogs are loyal, committed companions. Of course, that might make you too uncomfortable."

"You think this is funny."

"I *know* this is funny," she told him. "Come on. She's a dog. People have had dogs as pets for tens of thousands of years. You can suck it up for a month."

Mathias didn't look convinced.

Their drinks were delivered and the game began. On tournament night, everyone played until there was a winner at each table, then those winners would play until only one was left standing.

As they rolled dice and moved from room to room, discarding suspects and weapons, eliminated players stopped by to say hello and sneak Sophie bits of bacon and burger. Sophie took each treat gently, offering a thank-you lick when she'd swallowed the bite.

Mathias was overreacting. Sophie was obviously well trained and used to being around people. He and Nick were making her into something that she wasn't, which was just like a man. A month with a lovely little dog was exactly what Mathias needed.

*Love it? Order your copy of*
*SECOND CHANCE GIRL today!*

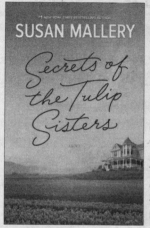

Turn your love of reading into
rewards you'll love with

# Harlequin My Rewards

**Join for FREE today at
www.HarlequinMyRewards.com**

Earn **FREE BOOKS** of your choice.

Experience **EXCLUSIVE OFFERS** and contests.

Enjoy **BOOK RECOMMENDATIONS**
selected just for you.

**PLUS!** Sign up now
and get **500** points
right away!

Earn
**FREE**
REWARDS
HarlequinMyRewards.com
Join
Today!

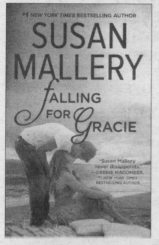

**Weddings are easy.
It's family that's complicated.**

**#1 New York Times bestselling author
and master storyteller**

# SUSAN MALLERY

**mixes her signature cocktail of love,
laughter and family drama in this must-read
novel of the summer.**

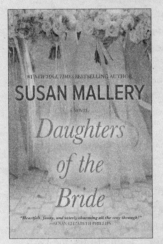

*With Joy, Love and
a Little Trepidation
Courtney, Sienna and Rachel
Invite You to the
Most Emotional
Wedding of the Year...
Their Mother's*

**Pick up your copy today!**

www.SusanMallery.com